Knights of the Roundish Table

by A. E. Chandler

aechandler.wixsite.com/author

To my brother, who's always got a spade.

Copyright © 2025 by A. E. Chandler.
All rights reserved.

No portion of this publication may be reproduced, stored in a retrieval system, or transmitted, in any form or by any means, electronic or mechanical, including photocopying, recording, or otherwise, without the prior written permission of A. E. Chandler. A. E. Chandler asserts the moral right to be identified as the author of this book. Although the author and publisher have made every effort to ensure the accuracy and completeness of information in this book, no responsibility is assumed for errors, inaccuracies, omissions, or any inconsistency herein. Any slights of people, places, or organizations are unintentional. Names, characters, places, and incidents are products of the author's imagination or are used fictitiously.

♣ *Knights of the Roundish Table*
ISBN 978-1-7772877-7-1 (paperback)
ISBN 978-1-7772877-8-8 (e-book)
ISBN 978-1-7772877-9-5 (Kindle)

Knights of the roundish table / A. E. Chandler.
p. cm.
ISBN 978-1-7772877-7-1
Issued in print and electronic formats.
BISAC: FICTION / Fantasy / Arthurian |
FICTION / Fantasy / Humorous |
FICTION / Fantasy / Historical |

This book is sold subject to the condition that it will not, by way of trade or otherwise, be lent, re-sold, hired out, or otherwise circulated without the publisher's prior consent in any form of binding or cover other than that in which it is published and without a similar condition including this condition being imposed on the subsequent purchaser. The sale of this book without its cover is unauthorized. If purchased without its cover, this book is stolen property, and neither the author nor the publisher have received any payment for this "stripped book."

Cover and Interior Design: A. E. Chandler in association with Canva, Mountain View Printing & Graphics Ltd.
Mountain View Printing & Graphics Ltd.
3656 – 60 Avenue SE
Calgary, Alberta T2C 2C7

Find your free copy of "Robin Hood and the Tinker" at:
aechandler.wixsite.com/author

CONTENTS

PRE-INTRODUCTION

Knights of the Roundish Table is a collection of seven connected short stories spoofing the King Arthur legend, plus another slightly-less-connected bonus story. Written over a span of about two decades, and not in order, the stories are here in order of how they occur for the characters. This will all be discussed in the introduction proper, which you can find at the end of this book. But don't look now; it'll be much more gratifying *after* you read the actual stories.

Trust me, I'm a medievalist.

- A. E. C.

The Knights of the Roundish Table

Once upon a time, on an island far, far away – but not that far away – there lived a man called King Xander. He had a dream, and that dream was to unite the fractured tribes of Britain to fight off the barbarians invading from Germania and Scandinavia. All the lesser Kings and knights across the land called this a very noble cause (because, if they had called it a bid for supreme power to satisfy a ravenous ambition, Xander would have had their tongues bitten off by similarly ravenous lampreys).

"The difficulty is," Xander was saying one morning as he sat enthroned in his great hall, "the Britons have softened under nearly four centuries of Roman rule. Once we were a great people, a battle-hungry people. When a dispute arose between tribes, the warriors of both sides would engage in such combat as would put ultimate fighting cage matches to shame. Now it's all staring contests, and thumb wrestling, and who can spit the farthest. Yesterday I spied two men disputing ownership of a goat resort to Rock, Paper, Scissors and, when the one man used rock, the other thought he was pulling a punch and broke into a sprint."

The King was speaking to his most trusted advisor, a magician of cunning power who, it was said, could gaze into the future. The old man paced the floor, his robes of deep blue swirling along the flagstones. "Yes, the Romans will take all of our best fighting men and ship them far abroad for their own army."

"Did," said the King. "The Romans did take our best men. The empire pulled out of Britain some hundred years ago."

Mervin sucked a sour face though, as his lips were always pursed, this was hardly a change of expression. "It's difficult for me to keep track, living backwards in time."

Xander sighed, slumping against his oaken throne, its armrests worn smooth by generations of the King's ancestors, all of whom had sweaty palms. Xander gazed at the gleaming wood, and his own warped reflection in it: eyebrows askew, beard greying, forehead wrinkles scrawling the words "screw up."

The King whisked his glance away, over the great hall: a massive room within a crumbling castle, with an ash-dry fireplace and dozens of mismatched chairs facing every direction.

"When a man lives for millennia," Mervin the Magician mumbled, robes swishing away, "you can't expect him to keep track of everything."

The King pointed to a dusty patch of floor. "You missed a spot."

"Oh." Mervin glanced about in subdued confusion.

A scream bounded through the hall, waving the faded tapestries as though they would spring from the whitewashed walls and flee for their lives.

In strode the Queen Mother. Her feet struck the floor so its stones groaned at the force. Amanita had never been one to tread lightly. She dripped scarlet satin, black lace flowing from its folds. Her greying hair was pulled back tight by gold pins set with pearls. None could guess her age, but they knew her health to be sturdy, for she looked no older than her son.

"Mother!" Xander shot to his feet. "How are you today?" He tapped down the dais towards her.

Queen Amanita waved him off. "Never mind pleasantries. Have you thought of a way to raise an army capable of bashing in the barbarians' skulls?"

The magician shuffled back from the corner. "We shall discuss it."

Amanita rolled her eyes. "You were discussing it. Were. Honestly, Mervin."

"Of course it's easy for you. You're not the one living your life backwards."

"What are you mumbling?"

Mervin jumped, his pointed hat popping atop his head. "Lunch. The kitchen is preparing tuna melt sandwiches for lunch."

"I hate tuna!" snapped the Queen.

"You mentioned you enjoyed tuna melts, so I had a chef brought from the seaside."

King, Queen, and magician glanced about for the source of the diminutive voice. A thin woman with slithering locks of shining blonde stood behind the Queen. Beneath the flowing silk of her white gown, she moved like the supple tip of a willow branch dipped in a stream. No one had noticed her slippered footsteps above those of the elder Queen. This young woman was yet in her twenties, though the lines on her brow spoke forty years.

"Jennivere." Xander beamed. "Why, I didn't see you there, my bushy-tailed squirrel."

She smiled back and dropped a dainty curtsy.

"I've always hated fish," said Amanita. "Save salmon. A determined salmon can outwrestle a wolf."

"Jenni, is it too late to change the tuna for salmon?" Xander asked.

His wife wobbled forth and back. "Salmon melts?"

"Salmon fillet," said Amanita. "A sandwich does not tally up to a proper meal. And be sure lunch is served a half hour early today; I ate a curtailed breakfast."

"That's no difficulty for my Jenni." Xander came forwards, pressing his wife's hand between his. "Is it, my cherub-cheeked chipmunk?"

Jennivere smiled to keep from heaving. "No, my love. I should be able to manage somehow."

"There's my sweet girl." The King kissed her pale, furrowed forehead.

She offered him a softer smile, then hurried off to overhaul the meal preparations.

The Queen shook her head. "Such a flighty girl. Imagining I'd like a tuna melt when everyone knows the only fish I eat is mackerel. Now, where stand your plans, my boy?"

"Well, we need an army. And we need to train them. So . . . Mervin?"

"Oh, uh, of course, of course." The magician stared at the Queen Mother's chin, for he could not meet her gaze. "I know what we've done."

"Will do."

"Will do." Mervin forced a chuckle. "You know, sometimes my memory isn't what it will be – "

"Once was."

" – and my so-called gift of prophecy dries up, but not in this case. Oh no, not in this case."

Amanita's eyes narrowed to arrow slits. "Quit stalling, you ridiculous little conjuror."

"Well, uh . . . . "

A series a chimes played out the first phrase of "Greensleeves." Mervin brightened. "The doorbell; I'll get it."

Amanita laid a hand on his shoulder, which action felt like being swatted by a grizzly bear. "As reigning Queen, it is Jennivere's duty to see to the efficient running of the household. As chief royal advisor, it is your duty to stand up straight, stop jabbering, and give my son your considered opinion before I have you devoured by diabetic geckos. Out with it!"

"Xander." Jennivere pattered into the hall. "Some men are at the door. They say – oh!"

Four large men entered the hall, each with rough, blackened hands the size of toilet seats. In these freakishly large hands they carried a freakishly large slab of wood.

The lead man grunted, though it could well have been a growl. "Where do we put this?"

"That depends," answered the King. "What is it?"

The man growled again – that was definitely what it was. "The table you ordered."

"I never ordered a table."

The four men looked about at the dozens of chairs and exchanged glances. Then, with one communal groan, they let their burden drop.

Xander raised a bushy brow. "Are you fellows certain that's a table?"

Jennivere squinted at it. "It's like when the school children play at waving a parachute."

"It's larger than a parachute," said Mervin, tiptoeing in for a closer look.

"The wood may have warped slightly during transport." The lead man extracted a tie-dyed hanky from his sleeve and set about dabbing his forehead.

"Warped?" Xander choked. "Warped? There isn't one square inch of this supposed table that's level. It has swells higher than I've seen at sea, dips lower than the four of you. And, moreover, I ordered no table!"

The lead man replaced his hanky, pulling a sheet of parchment from his other sleeve. "Says here the table was ordered by a Mr. Mervin the Magician, Esquire."

"You old fool!" bellowed the Queen Mother. "What on earth could you possibly want with so large a table?"

The magician's lip hung down, wriggling sporadically as he

perused his mind. "I must be going to send it to myself as a reminder."

"A reminder of what?" asked Xander. "A dinner party for fifty of your closest friends?"

Mervin snapped his fingers, spraining at least two of them. "Nay, majesty, but fifty of thy most loyal servants."

Amanita rolled her eyes. "Here comes a prophecy."

"I foresee fifty knights, the most skilled and chivalrous in all the land. They will accomplish great feats under thy leadership, oh mighty King. Peace will flow through the land like unto a wave of molten lava, burying all the old divisions among our people. Really, very, pretty deep. And thou, oh sage Xander, shall rule over all of Britain."

"Oh. Goody!" Jennivere smiled and squeezed her husband's hand.

Amanita sniffed. "So long as the money for this monstrosity doesn't come out of the royal treasury."

Mervin gave her a frown. "I've been saving up my allowance."

"Does that mean you have the money now, or you will have it?"

"If this is the present, then the future must . . . . " Mervin trailed off, counting on his fingers.

"Fifty knights, skilled and chivalrous." Xander passed his arm around his wife, pulling her close. "Mervin, where shall we find them?"

"Who? Oh, um, we hold a tournament. A no-holds-barred, freestyle battle until only fifty are left on horseback."

Jennivere laid her head on the King's shoulder. "We could sell tickets, using the money to pay for the table."

"Delectable idea, my delicious little lambchop."

"Speaking of which," said the Queen Mother, "is lunch ready yet?"

***

Sir Dwain sat atop his brilliant brown charger, its mane the same dusty colour as his own. His green eyes shone through the polished metal of his visor. He had ridden down from Eboracum in full battle array, his shield showing a green dragon on a yellow field, a white feather fluttering atop his helm, and a bouquet of lilies for the Queen lashed to his lance tip. Beneath his breastplate, next to his heart, was pressed his engraved invitation, written in the Queen's own hand:

Deer Sur Nite:

Yor king beeseecheth yu two cum at ons intwo hiss presents, that hee mite test yor sckil and find yu worthee uv a seet at hiss tabel. Cum with awl speeed two the jowsting grownds bi the royul palas.

Sinseerleee,

Kween Jennivere

As soon as a linguistics expert specializing in obscure and poorly spelled languages had deciphered the note and related its contents, Dwain had set out, eager for adventure and the chance to help save his country. Had he sprung for the services of the *foremost* linguistics expert specializing in obscure and poorly spelled languages, he might not have been the last to arrive.

A page led Sir Dwain to what looked like a giant outdoor hockey rink – boards below, chain-link above – and shut him inside with the rest. Rows of spectators had gathered 'round, placing bets, calling taunts, and spitting cherry pits at one another. They had come to Londinium from every nook in Britain to cheer for their favourite knights. The crowd was dressed in woolen tunics and mantles with multicoloured stripes, hearts, and polka dots. The aristocrats among them also sported twisted collars of precious metals, called torcs and, to show their good manners, dabbed their mouths with lace napkins after every spat cherry pit.

Dwain urged his horse to the far end of the jousting ground, where King Xander sat with the two Queens and Mervin the Magician.

The young knight removed his helm as he approached the dais, bowing before the royals on their thrones draped in red silk. "Greetings, your majesties. I am Sir Dwain of Eboracum."

"Greetings, Sir Dwain," returned the King.

"I was most flattered to receive the Queen's invitation to test my skill."

"Yes," said Amanita, "the invitations. If Jennivere had bothered to spellcheck, twice as many knights would have shown up."

"It's quality, Mother, not quantity," said Xander. "And my brazed dove does possess a beautiful cursive hand."

"Which would be useful. If the twit could spell."

"For you, your grace." Dwain maneuvered his lance over the chain-link so that Jennivere could reach the lilies.

The young Queen blushed as she took them, the petals dancing about the tip of her nose.

Dwain bowed again, replaced his helm, and rode out to do battle. Or at least mill about in the enclosure with the other knights whilst the heralds settled the last scraps of organization. His lusty steed halted beside a particularly ravishing mare and, whilst the stallion whinnied its best pickup line, Dwain sized up the knight astride: a man nearly seven feet in height, with a chest deep enough to marinade a side of beef in, and a back broad enough on which to grill it. Vert and white checked the man's shield, and a bushy pink feather swept back from his helm to flutter with his mount's tail.

12

"Hi there," called Dwain. "What's your name?"

The knight drew himself up in the saddle, casting a shadow over Dwain that was akin to the death of the sun. "My name," boomed a voice that made the Eboracum knight's armour reverberate, "has been handed down through generations of my family. My name has struck terror into the pagan souls of countless barbarians. My name, young man, is Sir Winifred IV of Huckleberry."

Dwain nodded, grateful his helm hid his expression.

A young knight, looking scarcely more than twenty, pranced up to them. "Greetings, fellow knight. I am Sir Tamarack of Broadbottom in Cheshire. You don't have any quests that you're currently too busy to finish, do you?"

"No, no, just waiting for the tournament to start."

"Because I could finish them."

Dwain squinted. "Recently knighted, are you?"

"Not recently – a whole fortnight ago. And since then, I've already completed a whole quest."

"What quest was that?"

"Why, there was this warning sign, set up by an evil, dictatorial warlord, striking fear into everyone, and only I proved brave enough to defy its oppressive order."

"Which was?"

"It said . . . stop."

"And when you didn't, what happened?"

"Why, that vindictive warlord sent a manure cart hurtling right into me."

"Uh-huh."

"It was very harrowing. And now, I'm off to inquire after a second quest. Good day, fellow knight."

"And to you." Turning to the knight on his left, Dwain murmured, "New Knight Syndrome. And what's your name?"

"Oh." The soft-featured man jumped at being addressed. Orange swans floated upon his white shield. "I'm Sir Keesh de Lattice . . . the first," he added, glancing past Dwain towards Sir Winifred.

"I'm Dwain of Eboracum."

"Nice to meet you." Sir Keesh attempted a sort of curtsy, forgetting he was ahorse. "Um, let's see, I can point out some of the others to you. There's Sir Smellias, Sir Dulfius, Sir Dodonas."

"Terrible name."

"The scuttlebutt is it was revealed to him when he flipped over a stone and discovered it written underneath."

"Oh. Well, if that's where it came from, then I suppose it isn't so bad."

"That fellow in the gold-painted armour is Sir Palomitus. The chap with the twig protruding from his visor is Sir Sycamore – "

"Is his armour made of wood?"

"Yes. More cost effective than metal."

Dwain nodded. "More flammable, too."

"I suppose. That's Sir Eepinogres. He's felled hole heaps of ogres."

"I gathered."

"The chap with the rose garland spun around his lance is Sir Kissram. The gossip is he's popular with ladies, which gained him a spot of trouble in Cornwall. And beside him is the seneschal, Sirs Day."

"You mean Sir Day."

"Actually, he pronounces it Sirs Day."

"Perhaps he has a lisp?"

"Fine. That burly fellow with the blue cross is Sir Gores."

Dwain regarded the knight's hog-sized battleaxe. "A bit obvious, isn't it?"

"What is?"

"Never mind. Who's the man on that magnificent white horse?" Dwain motioned to the only knight on the field whose armour bore not a single scratch and indeed, whose every inch glittered like a clear river at noon.

"Ah, you mean Sir Glancelot. I hear nothing but fine things concerning his skill and prowess."

"As do I." Another knight rode up to join them. Both Dwain and Keesh had to crane their necks downwards to see him, as his mount was quite short. Likely due to its being not so much a horse as a sheep.

Dwain pursed his lips. "What are you riding?"

The knight grinned. "Fine specimen, isn't he? Greetings, lads. I am Sir Robin of Bolderness, from the land of Estrangorre, but you may call me Sir Robin the Bold."

"Yes," said Dwain, "but why are you riding a sheep?"

"How dare you refer to my noble steed by such a name?! He is as *robust* a stallion as ever – "

"Grew a sweater?"

"I find it rather clever," said Keesh. "See how its mane is a mop and its tail a broom?"

"Wooly Bully is a horse, I decry you – a horse!"

"Yes," Dwain grinned, "and I am riding a nearsighted fluorescent badger."

A trumpet blast trumpeted through the air, trumpeting very trumpetly. "Attention," cried a paunchy old herald. "Give ear to me, good people. Here come the rules for yon tournament: anything goes. Let's get it on!"

The knights all charged each other, clattering in such a fantastic melee that it's almost a shame to call the thing a dogpile. They slashed and they hacked and they tickled one another, showing no mercy until an opponent fell to the ground crying, "Uncle." Such a gallant display of chivalry has hardly been equaled in the annals of history, or of Geoffrey of Monmouth.

When but fifty knights were left ahorse, the herald let out such a sneeze that it shattered the aristocrats' opera glasses, signaling an end to the tournament.

Many of the knights previously mentioned had kept the field. Sir Keesh de Lattice had kept his horse well – the animal, unused to battle, had pranced in circles, rendering it impossible for anyone to land a blow and sometimes even bowling over another horse. By the time Keesh had coaxed the beast into standing still, the tournament was ended, his sword remained sheathed, and he himself felt more than a little dizzy. Dwain had fought valiantly, using his precision with the lance to maneuver its point into the eye slots of helms, including that of Sir Winfred IV of Huckleberry. Robin the Bold was also still ahorse – though really that was debatable – none of the other knights having realized that the man astride a sheep had actually been participating.

The knights lined up facing the King, the two Queens, and the magician.

"Well done, well done," cried King Xander. "Herald, tell me, which of these worthies felled the most men, that he may sit by my side at the celebration feast."

The herald consulted the tally he had kept on his Etch A Sketch. "Sir Guy Longfellow, your majesty."

A bedraggled grey horse stepped forwards, the knight on its back a blonde lad whose well-cut face ran with sweat, and whose arms of a silver goblet dripping scarlet showed well nigh indecipherable, thanks to the many blows that contorted his shield. He beamed bright pride at the prospect of dining by the King, his innocent blue eyes alight with joy.

"Who felled the second most?" asked Queen Jennivere.

The herald squinted, bringing the Etch A Sketch nearer and farther from his eyes until it was in danger of erasing. "Sir Glancelot du Glac."

The albino horse stepped forth, displaying its rider, whose armour not only was still without so much as a smudge, but shone forth brighter than the glare of Mervin's balding head. So bright, in fact, as to render the knight's face invisible.

The young Queen grasped her husband's arm. "Sit next to him instead, darling, he's much better kempt."

Xander smiled and patted her hand. "As you wish, my melodic mosquito."

The sun passed for a moment behind a harmless-looking weather balloon. The glare vanished from Sir Glancelot's armour and those gathered could look upon his face. Men screamed, babies fainted, and senior citizens dove to hide behind goats.

Glancelot's face bore more misshapen lumps than a gargoyle's. His forehead slumped to the left and one eye drooped out – almost past his cheekbone – whilst his nose was smushed halfway to his ear, one nostril aimed straight up, the other wide enough to accommodate a walnut. Some of his teeth bit through lips more jagged than a jack o' lantern's, and his chin was cleft in three places.

"He's so *handsome*!" gasped the young Queen.

Keesh gave Dwain a questioning look, not opening his mouth for fear of screaming himself.

Dwain shrugged. "Perhaps his face is so ugly that it's looped back to handsome. And then ugly, and then handsome again."

King Xander bore the expression of a man watching a giant spider devour the corpse of a monkey that had been rotting inside out in the sun for a week. Speaking of the sun, it emerged now from behind the harmless-looking weather balloon, resuming its glare upon Glancelot's armour.

All stayed silent a moment, and then the King spoke: "I have never seen the like in all my born days. This is surely a sign from heaven. His face matches my table perfectly. Sir Glancelot du Glac, I invite you to sit beside me at dinner, and at the table where we shall plan our battles against the barbarian Saxon invaders."

Glancelot bowed. "I would be honoured, sire."

Dwain cocked an eyebrow. "Perhaps the King reasons that by sitting next to the man, he can talk to him without having to look at him directly."

Jennivere, meanwhile, looked incurably pleased, and Guy Longfellow incurably heartbroken.

***

The feast that night was marvelous to behold, and besmell, and especially to betaste. The chef served mashed turnips, boiled turnips, turnips with a side of baby turnips, turnips over easy, turnips *à la* turnips, turnips in turnip sauce, turnip stir-fry, and for dessert purple jellybeans nestled in the suction cups of a dead squid – stuffed with turnips. Most of the knights, rather than spoiling this sumptuous feast by eating it, proceeded to get drunk.

Whilst this celebration was slurring insults about mamas and confessing love to complete strangers, the harmless-looking weather balloon was engaged in communications of its own, for it was in fact not a harmless-looking weather balloon, but the barbarian chieftain's pet dragon Misty, cleverly disguised. When the chieftain learned that Britain's best defence against his invasion forces would be slobbering drunk that evening, he decided to send boats of warriors down the Thames to Londinium, in the hopes of at last capturing the capital.

By the time the lookout atop Londinium's outer wall gave the alarm, the knights' celebration feast had degenerated past the point of lampshades as fashionable headgear. Yet when those brave fighting men (and Sir Robin) heard that call to arms, they grabbed whatever they could find – spoons, chairs, leftover turnips – having forgotten where they had laid their weapons, and so rushed to the riverbank.

There, the barbarian Saxon warriors in their swanlike rowboats had begun to wade ashore, when they were confronted by half a hundred screaming, naked men, hair standing straight up with smeared jellybeans, squid ink coating their bare chests a shimmering blue in the moonlight.

The Saxons, startled and confused, splashed back to their boats under a hail of turnips and flatware, rowing like mad, praying their many deities that they would live to tell the tale.

***

"Frightfully magnificent job last night, men." Xander paced the great hall, his chest puffed like a stuffed mushroom.

The knights slumped about the roundish table, cringing at the volume of his voice.

"We scared those Saxons back without losing a man. Brilliant awe and shock strategy, but not one we can rely on indefinitely. Which is why we must now brainstorm strategies for our next encounter with the enemy. Any ideas?"

Dwain groaned. "In retrospect, the Jell-O shots weren't such a hot notion."

Keesh's cheeks looked as green as his eyes. "I recall doing those shots off a walrus, for some reason."

"That wasn't a walrus; that was Sir Gores." Dwain's neck went limp. "I'm so hungover this table looks like an amusement park ride for rats. Just rolling, and curling, and swerving, and – "

A disconcerting shade of grey flooded Sir Robin's cheeks.

" – swirling, and whirling, and jitterbugging, and doing the hustle – "

Robin belched, and with that belch came a flow of liquid the colour and consistency of wood stain. It flooded through the folds of the tabletop, washing down channels that branched right, left, and back in a loop. The fermented cocktail whisked into the laps of six different knights. Sir Smellias, who had been dozing with his head resting on the table, received the worst shock. Groans and exclamations whirled, drowning out Xander's musings.

"E-*NOUGH*!"

All noise ceased and everyone looked to the King.

"Now then, since you're all so distracted this morning, perhaps we'll leave strategy for tomorrow. I won't keep you from your garderobes, except long enough to impart some inspiration, with the story of how I came to rule."

The knights straightened out of respect, though some swayed as though aboard a ship. Only Sir Glancelot du Glac seemed unaffected by the voracious boozing of the night before.

Sir Guy Longfellow was striving to seem unaffected, but the thick scowl ribbing his brow betrayed him. "It would prove an honour to hear the tale from your mouth, majesty."

Glancelot nodded. "It would. Indeed."

The King beamed. "Thank you, Sir Glancelot. I appreciate your enthusiasm."

Guy shot a glare at du Glac that would have killed him, if the heaving table hadn't obscured it.

"I'm sure you've all heard how I pulled the thorn, El Caliburo, from the lion's paw and thereby gained rule of Londinium, but you may not have heard how I gained this sword." He drew the blade at his side with a clash of metal, holding it aloft so that all could observe its tempered blade, its jeweled crossbar, its turnip-shaped pommel. "This, my friends, is Ex Caliburo."

"It is magnificent, my liege," said Longfellow.

"Magnificent, indeed."

"Thank you, Sir Glancelot. I was riding through the woods one day with Mervin the Magician when we came upon a lake so blue the birds would have mistaken it for the sky and tried to fly underwater. Except they couldn't have at the time because it was the middle of winter and the whole lake was frozen solid. Yet, out of that water rose a woman's graceful arm, her flesh white as pig's milk, holding aloft this wondrous sword. And by that token I knew, knew with divine certainty, that I was not destined to be a King amongst many, but High King of all Britain, and with your help I shall beat back the invaders, establishing a kingdom of peace. My only regret is breaking off that woman's fingers when I pried the sword from her grasp."

"A necessary sacrifice, worthy King," said Longfellow.

"Necessary, indeed."

"Sir Glancelot, you are of great comfort to me. I go. Think on what I have said, my knights."

The men all stood as the King processed out, some of them tipping over as soon as he was through the doorway.

Sir Smellias and the six others wandered off to clean themselves.

Sir Guy plopped back in his seat. Beside him, Dwain lowered himself much more gingerly. Guy glared at Glancelot, who shook hands with the knights on either side of him before taking leave.

Dwain gulped, trying to swallow the lump of bile that pulsed at the back of his throat. "Keep staring at the man, and you'll do like Sir Robin."

"He stole my answers."

"And the King let him. So – go punch the blighter in the face. It might improve his looks."

"I hope you're referring to Glancelot, and not our sovereign lord and master."

Something gurgled deep within Dwain. "Oh, gosh."

"Besides," Longfellow stared at his fingers, "I couldn't punch a man."

"Why not? He's purposely cheating you, and you unhorsed enough men yesterday."

"The King ordered us to fight, so I did. But really, I abhor violence. It never solves anything, you know. That's what my mum says."

Dwain cocked his head and immediately regretted it. "How did you come to be a knight?"

"My father was a knight. He trained me. Then, one day, when we were in the woods on our estate watching a wrestling match between a wolf and a salmon, Saxon raiders arrived, killing my father, burning our crops, and turning our house into a Starbucks. Mother said we mustn't get upset about it, though. So we bussed tables and did the washing up, all for minimum wage. The barbarians made us wear hairnets – even when we weren't in the kitchen – that were too small and dug into our skulls until it felt like the elastic was grating on bone and we just wanted to scream and claw the things off and use them to strangle that bloody cur of a supervisor – and then Queen Jennivere's letter arrived and I came here." Longfellow grinned, his teeth grating in a rictus of repressed rage. "Excuse me. When I feel tense Mother says it's good for me to meditate."

Dwain smiled, eyes wide. "You know what might help – your name, Guy Longfellow, it's holding you back."

"It was my father's name."

"And it's great, but Dwain *of* Eboracum, Keesh *de* Lattice, Robin *the* Bold, Glancelot *du* Glac – you need a connector in there to fancy up your name so the King notices you. Sir Guy *of* Longfellow – now that's a name to remember."

"Hm. Guy Longfellow. Guy *of* Longfellow. Guy Longfellow. Guy . . . . " He left the hall mumbling to himself.

Dwain watched him go, sighing, "Sometimes it's too easy."

Sir Tamarak of Broadbottom squelched by, soaked from top to toe.

"What happened to you?"

"Ah, fellow knight. A tyrannical roadworks peasant told me I couldn't cross a stream because the bridge was out. Let me tell you, his challenge did not go unanswered."

"Okey-dokey. Carry on." Dwain turned his attention across the table to a group of knights gathered about Sir Robin.

The ringleader was a greasy little fellow with thick eyebrows and stringy black hair that could well have turned red if properly washed. "I saw you were riding a sheep yesterday. Do you ever *ride* sheep?"

Robin frowned up at the ringleader. "Is that some sort of riddle?"

"I just want to know if you ride sheep, as in *ride* them."

"I don't catch your meaning. Are you insinuating something?"

"Can someone explain to this idiot?" The ringleader looked 'round at the knights still present. "Dwain, you're Scottish, aren't you?"

"Not really, no."

"Fine!" the ringleader shouted, storming out of the hall as the other knights grasped their heads in pain.

Dwain turned to Sir Keesh, who sat on his other side. "Who was that thug?"

"Sir Sordid," Keesh whispered back. "He claims to be King Xander's third cousin's wife's therapist's nephew, but can't prove it, thanks to doctor-patient confidentiality. Still, he wants to lead

Britain's army. There's a rumour," Keesh lowered his voice even further, "he has aspirations for the throne."

"Speaking of which," Dwain reclined, gesturing about the great hall, "do you think he'll be able to find it amongst all these?"

***

"You weren't at the assembly." Xander strode into the lower solar.

Mervin looked up from the wand he was whittling, three fingers bloody. "Who wasn't where?"

"You. Missed the first meeting of my Knights of the Roundish Table."

"Oh dear," mumbled the magician.

"It doesn't inspire confidence in your prophecies when you can't make it to meetings."

"You should have reminded me."

"I did."

"Not before, after." Mervin flourished his whittling knife. "I'm living backwards, you know."

"I'm reminding you after now. You still weren't there."

"If I forget something, then I can't know it will happen until it happens, you see."

"No I don't see. We have got to get you a day planner."

Jennivere's head popped up from behind a wooden chest. "I'd be happy to have the servants fetch you one."

"No, no, no!" cried the magician. "If you give me a day planner it will go forwards in time whilst I go backwards. By writing future events in it, I would be recording my own past, and the book won't help me to remember to be anywhere."

The King frowned, his brows weighed down like wet wool. "If I understood that, I'd argue with it. Forget the day planner! But thank you for offering your help, my curvaceous weasel."

"You're welcome," beamed the magician.

"*Not* you!"

A scream shook the wall tapestries. Queen Amanita marched in, pinching the ear of a girl with limewash bleached hair, who wore a navy sweater, white blouse, plaid skirt, knee-high socks, and Mary Janes with nails punched through their soles, converting them to cleats.

"Gene." Xander's face fell blank with surprise. "What are you doing here?"

"She's been kicked out of another boarding school." Amanita pinched harder.

Gene cringed, clawing at the grip and not managing any good. "Helen and her friends called me a sissy. Honour was at stake – I had to wail on them with a two-by-four."

"Is it *honourable* to be expelled from thirty-seven private schools for fighting? At this rate, we'll have to found over a dozen schools each year to keep up with you."

"Let me fight in Xander's army – I'm as good as any knight."

Amanita scoffed, tightening her grip until Gene's face shifted into a silent scream. "Not yet you're not. Being a knight isn't just about fighting – you also need to know how to play chess, write poetry, manage an estate. Mervin, she's your niece, if she gets kicked out of *one* more school, you're taking her out into the wilderness and completing her training yourself. I won't have another purely *decorative* young woman hanging about."

Jennivere blushed to the tips of her ears, pressing her lips together so they turned ghostly white.

Gene rolled her eyes. "Managing an estate is just bossing people around. I can do that."

Amanita gave the girl's ear a good yank. "This is exactly why you need to attend school. If you don't, and can't govern with discernment, the people are bound to grow restless and demand credentials. If enough landowners thought your way, there would be rebellion, and in the ensuing anarchy the barbarians would take advantage and conquer our homeland. Is that what you want, Gene?"

"*No.*"

"Then go to your room and think about what you've done." Amanita let go of the ear, which was by now an interesting shade of blue.

Gene snorted, coddling her ear and trooping off. Just outside the doorway, she smacked into Guy of Longfellow, spinning him one hundred eighty degrees. He watched her barge away, shoulders hunched, thighs pumping, plaid skirt twitching side to side.

"Who is that?" he breathed.

Amanita came to the doorway. A scream sounded, though it could have been a dog howling. "That," she answered, "is one very naughty girl."

∗∗∗

Meanwhile, Sir Sordid was hatching an evil plan, guaranteed to bring him power beyond his wildest dreams. That, or fail utterly, leaving him one of those lonely never-beens who live in their mothers' basements gluing grain wagon and chicken coop models to their fingers and catcalling women in parks.

Blissfully unaware, Queen Jennivere had retreated to her private solar, to continue weaving a tapestry of a Greek symposium with Bacchus leading the conga line. And as she wove, she wept.

When Jennivere looked up, it was into the concerned face of Sir Glancelot. At least, she supposed concern to be the emotion expressed by the muddle of features before her.

"Please, forgive the intrusion, your grace. When I see a woman's

26

tears they are as stains upon my peace of mind. Prey, is there some task I may perform to relieve somewhat the suffering of thine heart?"

Jennivere blinked, her eyelashes sticking together with damp. "Oh, no. Thank you, I'm fine."

"Is there some trouble with the tapestry thou weavest? Yet, surely not, for it is as beauteous as though 'twere strung together by the magic of fairies."

The young Queen blushed, bending lower over her work. "It is a poor tatter, I know. That is what my husband's mother will say. She prefers scenes of battle to those of more harmonious pastimes."

"Perhaps she would not mind an harmonious one were it produced by means of a gun."

A sly smile pursed Jennivere's lips. "A very Dalinian suggestion, sir knight. How do you propose to carry it through?"

Glancelot reached into a pouch he always carried on his belt, pulling out a bedazzling gun. "Come, your majesty – if thou wilt permit me – let us to work."

***

"Your majesty." Whilst the above encounter was taking place, so was a second. Sir Sordid bowed before King Xander. "Gracious King, I hoped we could speak in private?" He eyed Mervin, who had accidentally whittled a flute instead of a wand and, to prevent it whistling when he waved a spell, was now plugging the holes with chewing gum.

"Of course. Mervin, would you mind continuing your infernal mischief somewhere else?"

The old man looked up, wand dangling from his beard, hairs mashed into the gum mashed into the holes. "I should have done what?"

"You should have gone away a minute ago."

"And I thought *I* was the one with foresight," mumbled the magician, wandering from the room.

"And now, sir knight, what matter merits discussion? Have you a suggestion on how we might ward off future barbarian invasions?"

Sordid straightened, but kept his head lowered in a farce of obeisance that cast a purple shadow across his eyes. "Alas, my words carry only ill tidings. Your majesty, Sir Glancelot dropped this." Sordid thrust a soiled handkerchief at the King.

Xander swooped back in his chair, harnessing his expression. "If Sir Glancelot dropped it, shouldn't you give it back to him?"

"Examine it more closely, my liege." Sordid took a step forwards.

"No, no thank you. I can view it fine from here."

"Don't you see, your grace? This handkerchief is your wife's."

"How do you know?"

"Just here, sire – "

"You'll wash your hands momentarily, yes?"

" – she has embroidered her initial: *J.*"

Xander shrugged away an itch on his neck. "Sordid, I'm certain more than one person has a name beginning with *J.*"

"No, this handkerchief is your wife's. It proves she's having an affair with Glancelot. You should kill them both. And if, after that, your majesty is too traumatized to rule, I would be delighted to step in and assume command."

The King frowned. "I think you've assumed enough already. Ahh, here's my Jenni now."

Queen Jennivere entered the room, her face as pink as though her cheeks were filled with ketchup. She approached the King and kissed his furrowed brow, soothing it with her cool lips.

He, in turn, pressed her hand and gazed on her with the impassioned love of a nerdly teenaged boy. "You seem in good spirits, my jubileed cherry ladybug. What have you been up to?"

The Queen smiled and kissed him again. "I have been with Sir Glancelot du Glac."

"Have you?" The King's serene expression faltered an instant. "Discussing cankerous sores whilst sitting on opposite ends of the room facing the walls?"

"No, silly dear. I talked about my feelings, and he listened quite attentively."

"Really? And, by feelings, do you mean those emo-whatsits everyone in my family prefers to imagine don't exist?"

The young Queen tapped his nose with her fingertip. "Those are the ones. But I'm interrupting your conversation. I should leave."

"Don't be silly, my observant little meercat. Interrupting! Sir Sordid found this handkerchief and wanted to know where the lost and found was. You don't by chance recognize it, do you?"

"No."

"It bears the initial *J*, my love. Might it not be yours?"

The Queen shook her head. "My handkerchief is here." She whisked it from her sleeve. "Sir Glancelot just bedazzled it for me."

Xander relaxed, even smiled. "That was nice of him, wasn't it, Sir Sordid?"

The outside corner of the knight's left eye trembled. "Yes. Quite nice."

"That will be all, Sir Sordid."

The knight cringed as he bowed. "My lord. My lady."

As he walked from the solar, Sordid swore an oath within his mind. He would topple Xander's reign, or else be unrecognizably disfigured in the process. But first, he had to pull the embroidery out of his handkerchief.

✳✳✳

That afternoon, the Saxons made a surprise raid on a

farming community two miles outside the walls of Londinium. With them came the chieftain's dragon Misty, whose muscles slithered beneath her pale blue-green scales. The farmers and their families were so poor and superstitious and lowly they could do nothing but run around in pointless circles panicking when the barbarian warriors arrived. If only they had been modern enough to run in straight lines! Misty coughed flames, hacking a path through the settlement. Smoke from the burning homes alerted Xander and his knights. They donned their armour, took to their mounts, and galloped to the farmers' aid.

Fortunately for the knights their hangovers had worn off for the most part, as battle is a noisy business and the shouts and clangs of this one could be heard even within Xander's dungeons.

The Saxons were indeed fearsome foes, and the fearsomerest of all was Misty. That day she was giving out third degree burns and grilled cheese sandwiches – and she was all out of cheese.

Sir Glancelot charged the fiery beast, lowering his lance at Misty's chest. When he came within two yards of striking, the dragon wheeled about, causing the knight to gallop past without landing a blow.

Sir Guy had begun his charge seconds before Sir Glancelot, though from farther away. When the dragon turned, Guy shifted to wound the beast's flank.

Misty cried out in rage. The whites of her eyes flashed red. Her scales seemed to flutter like the flap on a tractor's exhaust pipe. Tail, claws, and fire, she lashed out at anything that moved, whether it was a knight, a barbarian, or a family of fuzzy baby chicks.

Dwain's horse was swept from underneath him, Keesh's steed disintegrated so he sat astride a stack of ashes, and Sir Sycamore's wooden armour was cut to kindling.

Sir Sordid threw himself flat to avoid a kick that would have dented his breastplate to squash his heart still against his spine. Doing so, he observed a barbarian unwrap a Tootsie Roll and toss it at the dragon. The sugary log bopped Misty's nose and plopped down between her talons. She hesitated, then only roared, rather than spurting fire.

The Saxon repeated his performance.

This time, Misty curved her neck, lapping up both Tootsie Rolls and a tongueful of dirt. The barbarian shouted, and Misty joined in an assault that left the Knights of the Roundish Table hanging from wall pegs by their pantaloons, stuck with their bums in barrels, or buried up to their necks in manure. Sir Sordid for one did not mind the smell, for he was preoccupied with another plot to position himself on the throne.

About that time, Sir Robin arrived on the scene. He would have been sooner, but his mount's short legs – combined with its tendency to pause and chew wildflowers whilst proceeding blissfully unaware of what direction the reins were urging it towards – had made the journey rather longer. Looking around the settlement at his humiliated colleagues, Robin stood, allowing his mount to meander out from between his legs. "Well," he said, "evidently it's up to me to rescue you chaps from this mess."

The knights arrived back in the great hall feeling bedraggled, belittled, and bedazzled – for, on the walk back, Glancelot had sought to raise their spirits by sprucing up their now mangled armour.

King Xander paced behind his seat at the roundish table, awaiting them. "Men, I fear my confidence in you was misplaced. You outnumbered the barbarians and yet – I watched the entire travesty through a wand with glass lenses Mervin bought in the future – what's it called again, a telescope?"

The magician looked up, hunched by the fireplace, heating popcorn. "A telephone, your grace."

"Right, right, a heliphone. At any rate, I'm gravely disappointed in you all. Except you, Sir Glancelot. That was very brave, charging the dragon like that."

"Thank you, your majesty." Glancelot bowed.

"And you only missed her by a few feet!" The King thumped his back, blushing with pride.

At the same moment, Guy of Longfellow's face was turning red with quite another emotion. He felt the familiar ooze boil within him, and forced it down deep in the pit of his stomach, where he had been caching all his anger since the day he was three and his mother informed him – after he had stomped his foot in a pout and thus inadvertently crippled a butterfly – that a true knight was a gentleman, and it was the charge of every gentleman to control himself at all times, so that he might protect beauty rather than destroying it.

"Go, clean your armour, bind your wounds," said the King. "Sir Glancelot, you will sit by me at supper again tonight."

Longfellow watched as they all left, including Mervin, who had finished inflating his popcorn and was now sprinkling camel dandruff on the kernels to lend them spice. When all were gone, and he was certain he was alone, Longfellow reached out, nudging a chair with his first two fingers. It wobbled, but didn't quite tip over.

"Shove it harder," said a voice. "Better yet, smash it across the room."

Longfellow whirled, thoroughly embarrassed at having been caught in a fit of temper.

Leaning in a nook by the fireplace, Gene stood in her school uniform, as Queen Amanita had thrown out all of her decent armour, leaving only ballgowns and crenellated dresses. The spikes on the bottoms of her Mary Janes clinked as she crossed the stone floor, aiming towards him.

"Forgive my behaviour, my lady. I did not notice – "

"Yeah, yeah, nobody cares. I, too, was watching the battle today. I nicked Mervin's brineovulars." Her thighs batted the pleats of her plaid skirt. "I saw you draw blood from the dragon. Why did you not tell the King?"

"His majesty wouldn't – "

"I heard you felled the most knights in the tournament, then let Glancelot upstage you." She took the last step up to him.

"It was not my place to – "

"Every time you let someone treat you second best you disgrace yourself. Britain is dead if her most worthy knight is also her most cowardly."

"Beg pardon, but I am no – "

Gene slapped him, hard enough to turn his head. "You should react to every slight as though someone had struck you."

"I don't – "

She socked him across the other cheek.

"This is not – "

Gene balled her fist, cracking Guy under the chin so that for a moment his vision bleached black and he stumbled backwards.

"Stop doing – "

"Swear!"

"My lady – "

"Curse! *Threaten*! *SCREAM*!" Her voice scraped dust from the walls, splitting into a yell and a howl.

Longfellow's hands flew to his ears. "Blast it, woman. Are you mad?"

Gene swung for him again. When he dodged she nearly tripped. "I hate you!"

Longfellow turned to the nearest chair, shoving it over. "I hate *you*! And I hate Glancelot – he can rot on his own lance point! I hate that the Queen favours him. I hate that the King praises him. I hate that the others look at him like adoring fawns. And I *hate* my MOTHER!"

Gene screamed again. The two of them tore through the hall, hurling and smashing chairs until there was nothing left to sit on but splinters. Sweat dribbled from their pores, mixing with dead skin cells into a greyish mush all over their hot, heaving, athletic bodies. They stood panting by the table, blood streaming – nay – shooting through their throbbing veins.

Longfellow's gaze traveled up Gene's knee socks, her skirt, the white blouse now soaked with perspiration and clinging to her torso.

"Do you really hate your mother?" she asked.

"More than anything else in this world." Longfellow grabbed her head in both hands. Their lips scraped together like two rival sets of claws. Whether they were showing affection or killing one another was anyone's guess.

Guy and Gene tumbled onto the roundish table, floundering in its depths, thrown by its hills, crashing into the wood and one another. Thus preoccupied, they failed to notice the inhuman cry that announced Queen Amanita's entrance.

The old dowager squinted at the pair, recognizing the school uniform rather than the girl. "Caesar's paunch, are you fighting *again*?"

Gene broke half away from Longfellow, their legs still entangled. Too breathless to speak, she shook her head.

Amanita reexamined the scene. "Ah. Well, as long as you're not fighting. You're the lad from the tournament, aren't you? Pity my harebrained daughter-in-law invited that ogre fellow to dine. It's only right for men to get dirty when doing a dirty job. Well, carry on."

There was a scream the next room over as the Queen Mother walked out.

"Perhaps we shouldn't," said Longfellow. "I may have discovered a pool from Sir Robin's bout with nausea this morning."

Gene ran her hand up his chest to grasp his throat. "And doesn't that make you want to rip out his intestines through his toes?"

Guy lunged for her. They rolled into a fissure, ignoring the splash, legs flailing, lips gouging, straining to keep their hands from choking too hard.

***

Sir Sordid wasted no time putting his newest diabolical plot into action. Collecting every Tootsie Roll he could find, he ascended to the castle roof, knowing the barbarian chieftain sent Misty several times a day to monitor the number of lookouts on duty, any bolstering of Londinium's defences, and the knights' toilet habits. He had not long to wait. A shape like a paunchy snake with wings soared through the lacelike fog above the castle. Sordid grinned, watching the dragon wheel lower and lower. Then higher, then lower, then too low, then onto the roof to gorge on the pile of Tootsie Rolls beside him. The knight clicked his purpling fingernails together. "Perfection."

He laid a trail of Tootsie Rolls, leading Misty down a turret, along a passageway so narrow it nearly suffocated the beast whilst doing nothing to her appetite, and down another set of spiraling stairs to the door of Glancelot's private chamber.

Sordid chuckled, fancying he was being interviewed for the feature article in next month's *Most Villainous Plots* magazine. "Once the King's best and favourite knight has been consumed by this ugly beast – " Misty was chewing too loudly to overhear this " – I shall insert myself into his good graces, gaining his trust until the next battle, when poor Xander will meet his doom and the land will turn to its most able knight to be his successor: me. Bwa ha ha ha!"

Misty sniffed about his clothes for more Tootsie Rolls.

"Down. Down, you infernal beast! No more until you perform a trick for me."

The dragon whimpered, her glassy eyes opening so wide that their balls nearly spun out.

"None of that now. You must charge into this chamber and incinerate its occupant. Once you've done that, I'll give you the rest of the Tootsie Rolls and you can be on your way. Understand?"

Misty's tongue lolled out and her wings gave a flap, skidding the ceiling. She rammed into the oak door, busting it to toothpicks.

Sordid ducked back as a red glow lit the doorway, radiating livid heat. He grinned to himself. "So much for that."

***

Word spread through the castle like . . . permafrost. The barbarians' dragon had invaded Londinium and left only a pile of ashes in Sir Glancelot's room. As they heard, the knights gathered outside in the passageway.

Sir Dwain had been practicing his juggling with a turnip, a balled-up sock, and two more turnips when Sirs Day had popped in to share the news. Keesh was in the crowd outside du Glac's room. Dwain shoved a path through to join him.

"Keesh, is Glancelot really dead?"

De Lattice dabbed his eyes. "I'm afraid so. It happened quite suddenly."

"It usually does when a person is incinerated by a dragon. At least he couldn't have felt much pain."

"But we shall." Keesh lapsed into blubbering.

Dwain shifted from foot to foot and patted him on the shoulder.

Sir Robin approached. "Splendid day, isn't it, lads? What's this about, then?"

Dwain glared. "Glancelot du Glac's been killed."

"Oh my." Sir Robin gave a little jump. "This day keeps becoming splendider and splendider."

"*Excuse* me?"

"My minstrel can sing at his funeral."

"Your horse is a sheep. Is your minstrel a cockatoo?"

"I'm not certain. Bernard, are you French?"

A black-haired boy stepped from behind Robin. "Maybe a little, on my mother's side."

"Lads, I'd like you to meet Bernard. Isn't this smashing? No more snipes about ol' Robin. My minstrel will sing epic songs of my bold deeds and soon all the world will respect me. Sir Glancelot's funeral should be perfect for Bernard's debut."

Keesh shook the boy's hand, sobbing too vehemently to speak.

Dwain shook as well. "So, you're a troubadour."

"I am now, sir. Until a half hour ago, I was a portcullis to portcullis peddler."

"And what did you sell?"

"Rocks."

Dwain nodded. "I'm sorry, my grief must be affecting my hearing. You sold rocks?"

"Yes, sir."

"What kind?"

"Just rocks."

"I see. And you also play the lute."

"Of course." Bernard grinned at Sir Dwain, cocking his head and winking.

"Out of my way! Out of – move or I'll boot you out a window."

Xander barreled through the gathered knights. He halted in the doorway, taking the crown from his head and laying it over his heart. "Poor bastard. He was the best knight I've ever seen. Lads, please, let's have a moment of silence for Glancelot du Glac."

Everyone clasped their hands and angled their chins to their chests. The only noises heard then were rustling clothing, short coughs, and the occasional flush of a garderobe.

A voice whispered in the King's ear. "Excuse the interruption, majesty, but what goes on here?"

"We're having a moment of silence to honour Sir Glancelot."

"That's very nice of you."

"It's the least we can do, now that he's dead."

"But, your grace, I am not dead."

Xander looked up. "Praise God!" He grabbed Sir Glancelot by the shoulders and shook him. "May weasels chew through my ankles if I didn't think we'd lost you, dear boy."

The knights gathered 'round, slapping du Glac on the back and the front and the backside, grunting compliments and endearments.

Dwain smacked Sir Glancelot between the shoulder blades. "Good to see you, you big ogre."

"Ogre?" Sir Eepinogres tensed.

"But, Glancelot, if you're here, who's the pile of ashes in your room?"

"I couldn't say. I was taking a constitutional in the courtyard before my late tea with – " Horror liquefied Sir Glancelot's eyes. He broke free of his comrades and rushed into his chamber. Kneeling by the ashes, he pinched a charred fabric fragment in their midst, drawing out what had been a bedazzled handkerchief.

Xander stared, his mighty shoulders frozen. "My perky little frog?" he breathed.

***

The knights had gathered at the roundish table, sitting on overturned laundry baskets, fraying ottomans, and stacks of old newspapers.

"With the King indisposed," Sir Sordid announced, "I shall step in to lead you. Just because the Queen is dead doesn't mean the country will stop being disunited, or the barbarians will stay at home with their crisps and beer."

Longfellow was crouching on a tree stump, pinching where his nose met his brow. "The funeral this morning was appalling."

Sir Robin shrugged. "I thought my minstrel performed well."

"He sang 'For She's a Jolly Good Fellow,'" said Dwain. "To the tune of 'Greensleeves'!"

"He's still expanding his repertoire. Besides, he came off better than that priest."

"The one who kept referring to Queen Jennivere as *his* majesty, or the one picking his nose during the eulogy?"

"Erm – the first one."

"Thank you, sir."

Robin glanced down at the lad on his hands and knees. "Not at all, Bernard. But keep still and silent; proper chairs don't talk."

"I thought the eulogy very heartfelt." Keesh flicked a residual tear from the corner of his eye.

"And uncomfortable." Dwain shifted atop his sack of turnips. "All the King said was, 'My slender little silkworm,' and then we watched him bawl for twenty-six minutes. I'll never get that sound out of my head."

"We're all sad over the Queen," said Sir Sordid. "However, now's the time – "

"The caterers were good, though," said Keesh.

Longfellow pinched harder, frowning at the pain. "They got our menu confused with someone else's."

"Yes, but the food was delicious."

"Barbecue? Bloody barbecue after what happened?!"

"Sir knights – " began Sordid.

Sir Sycamore interrupted. "Burying her ashes beneath that oak tree was lovely."

"Yes," said Keesh. "Sir Glancelot, you did a beautiful job bedazzling the urn."

Glancelot's face was contorted with grief – probably – as he moaned, "My only hope is that dear Queen Jennivere would have shared thy sentiment."

There came a flurry of assurances.

"Shut *up*!"

Everyone looked at Sir Sordid.

"As I was saying, whilst the King is unfit, I shall assume the command of you."

"Where is the King?" asked Sir Robin.

"In his private chamber." Longfellow's brow blanched nearly as white as his knuckles. "He refuses to rise from bed."

"Perhaps we should send him a sympathy card," Keesh suggested.

"I said I am your leader now!" Sordid was turning as pink as Sir Guy was white.

"If only I had been earlier to meet the Queen," murmured Glancelot.

Dwain stood. "I'll go find Mervin. He knows the King better than anyone; perhaps he'll know how to cheer him."

"Come back!" shouted Sordid. "All of you stop moving about. I lead you now. *I* am King!"

Robin followed Dwain. Bernard arose and swatted sawdust from his knees. "Now I'm a minstrel, I can see I'll have to start visiting a chiropractor."

✳✳✳

At the sound of the scream, Xander tunneled headfirst into his pillow.

"My boy, you've got to stop this nonsense." Queen Amanita charged into the room, flinging aside the bedcurtains. "Sulking won't bring back your wife."

"Please, Mother, not now."

"We'll all miss the little mouse to some degree, but now is neither the time nor place. The barbarians will attack again soon, and you must stand ready."

"Have Gene lead the men; I'm not up to it."

"I sent Gene to another boarding school late last night. This one will stick or I swear by St. Cyril's sausages I'll send her into the hills somewhere she can't pick a fight, and have Mervin tutor her."

"You sent her away? After what just happened?"

"Exactly, Xander, your wife is dead – the last thing you need is to be surrounded by friends and family. A victory on the battlefield – that's the ticket."

"Poor Jenni. I loved her better than going to the circus, better than turnips, better than horseback riding in the nude, better than plunging my sword into a foe and feeling warm blood spurt across my face."

"Bite your tongue, boy! Better than blood – or turnips, or the circus – enough foolishness. Get out of bed, into your armour, and go kill something!"

"Yes, Mother."

Queen Amanita hurtled out of Xander's chamber, nearly screaming into Sir Guy.

"Your majesty." The knight bowed. "Excuse me. I was looking for the blonde girl in the school uniform. Do you know where she is?"

"Din Guyardi. And there she'll stay."

Longfellow jolted and stammered, "Did she leave me a note, her name, or word of any kind that she was leaving?"

"No. You're better off. She's the most callous girl you could imagine."

"Yes." The corners of Sir Guy's mouth began to curl. "She is that. Thank you, majesty."

Amanita did not wait for him to finish his bow, but continued on her way. She was looking for Mervin, who happened to be in the solar, bent over a steaming cauldron.

Dwain found him first, however.

As the young knight entered the room, Mervin swatted him on the head with a large wooden spoon.

"Ow! What was that for?"

"Oh." Mervin wiped the spoon with his beard before slipping it back into the cauldron. "I thought you were somebody else."

Robin came in. "Sir Dwain, your gait is certainly wide and – OW!" Mervin had whammed him across the face with a frying pan. "What was that for?"

The magician shrugged. "I mistook you for the first fellow."

Dwain cast a glance at Robin. "In any case, we've come to see if you know a way of cheering up the King."

Bernard came in. Mervin hurled a hotplate at his head as he ducked. "What was that for?"

"Sorry. I thought you were this fellow here." The magician pointed to Robin, who was swaying side to side with a grin splitting his otherwise vacant face. "I must be remembering in the wrong order. What is it you want, now?"

"To cheer up the King." Dwain enunciated, hoping that would help.

"What do you think I'm doing?" snapped the magician.

Robin tipped, leaning into Dwain. "I've never seen so many badgers."

Dwain shoved Robin away and Bernard caught him. "Are you mixing a potion to banish his grief?"

Mervin scuttled about the room, checking behind books, up the chimney, and under his hat in case of spies. "I am mixing," he whispered, "the elixir of life."

"Isn't that only possible with the Philosopher's Stone?"

Mervin withdrew a dirty grey lump from his robes.

Dwain smiled and nodded, his eyes shooting to the doorway. "And where did you get that?"

"Get what?"

"That there. That rock you're holding."

"I don't have a rock."

"Yes you do; I can see it. Where's it from?"

"Oh, this?"

"Yes, that rock in your hand."

"This is no rock."

"Then what is it? A paperweight? Cricket ball? Venus de Milo's fist? What's left of your mind?"

"No; it's a stone."

"If it's a stone, then where did you get it?"

"A peddler stopped by not long ago. Come to think of it, he looked like this chappie here."

Bernard pawed his bangs into his face. "Wow! The real Philosopher's Stone, you say?" He fell into a crouch, shielding his ears from the mighty scream as Queen Amanita entered the solar.

"Knights," she snapped, "into your armour. Boy, up off the floor. Mervin, tell Xander where the barbarian camp is so he can attack. MOVE!" She stormed out.

Dwain yanked Bernard to his feet. "Don't worry, lad, it's happened to the best of us. You never quite get used to it."

***

When Xander rode at the head of his knights onto the field of battle, he experienced a shock. Wooden stands of stadium seating had been built up. People from all over Britain had come to enjoy the spectacle, not to mention a good chilidog. Upon the knights entering the makeshift arena, the people cheered, though some of these cheers were muffled and resulted in soggy bits of bun arcing through the air.

The King raised an arm to shield himself from the barrage. "What on God's earth is going on here?"

Out of a private box, covered from the sun by the finest plaid linen, strode King Bark of Cornwall. At the sight of him, Sir Kissram slid from his saddle and hid under his horse. Cornwall's King opened his mouth, speaking with such volume and harshness it pained the ears worse than if they had been bitten. "King Xander, how lovely to see you up and about. Our deepest sympathies after the loss of your wife."

Xander winced, gleaning both physical and mental pain from his fellow sovereign's words. "Yes, thank you, but what are the lot of you doing here?"

"Why, we've come to root for you, of course. This will prove a great victory, if you can manage it."

"I can manage fine." Something of Xander's old tone seeped in.

King Bark nodded. "No doubt, no doubt. This will be the real test of your band of elite knights. I and the other rulers were discussing it and, if you win today, we shall proclaim you
High King of Britain and follow your leadership in the defence of our mighty isle."

"Dreadfully decent of you."

"I realize. However, if you shame our people here today, the barbarians will surely take Londinium and from there spread like syphilis to the rest of Britain, thereby dooming us all."

"Why don't you and the other Kings add your forces to ours? Or call on the people to take up whatever arms they can find, and come down from the stands to assist us?"

"That wouldn't be very sporting, now, would it?" King Bark thumped Xander on the back, his rings clanging the latter's armour. "Fortune's favour." He returned to sit upon his cushioned throne and sip margaritas.

Sir Kissram peeped out from under his horse. "Has he gone?"

"Not far," said Longfellow, whose mount stood beside.

"I can't let him catch me. Quick, Sir Guy, let us trade heraldic shields."

"Back on your horse, coward."

"Coward, am I? Give me your shield!" Kissram lunged, grasping it and yanking for all he was worth.

"Having a tug of war, are we?" Dwain called from a few yards away, where he waited with Sir Keesh.

Longfellow kicked Sir Kissram in the neck, causing the latter to fall to his bottom and let go. "Save your energy for the enemy, you fool."

"Just trade with him, Longfellow," Dwain droned.

Sir Guy recomposed himself, rolling his muscles until they returned to a dignified position. "No. I want the King and everyone else to see that it is I myself performing feats of skill in this battle. Glancelot won't steal credit this time, nor any man else."

"Would you like to switch with me?" Keesh asked Sir Kissram.

The latter shook his head, staring up at Longfellow. "Sir Guy has the right idea. We are fighting for King and country and ought to comport ourselves with the pride that deserves." He swung himself back into the saddle. "To the honour of Britain and her noble children!"

"Is the battle over then? Have we won?" Sir Robin came riding up on his sheep, Bernard panting along behind, lugging a lute of solid gold.

Dwain sighed. "What are you doing bringing your minstrel into battle?"

"Do you *see* all these people? Here is where I need him most. Bernard will sing of my prowess, frightening the enemy and impressing the bystanders."

"Master," stammered the minstrel, "isn't the golden lute a bit much? It sounds horrible and – "

"It sounds like angels' song."

"Tone-deaf," Dwain whispered to Keesh.

"I am not! Now Bernard, mind you stay close so I can protect you. And sing loudly; battle can make quite the ruckus, but you can't let it drown you out."

The minstrel nodded, his knees rattling like maracas.

Longfellow snorted. "If you or your minstrel live to this battle's end it will be a miracle on par with Daniel and the lions."

Robin puffed out his chest, though no one could tell beneath his armour. "You flatter me, Sir Guy."

Dwain scoffed. "And may I compliment you on your masterful posture and superior fashion sense."

A great noise arose down the field – horns sounding every note in the scale – bending and looping in a cacophony fit to split heads from shoulders. The knights' armour vibrated so it appeared as though they trembled. A horde of barbarians faded into sight, starting as a purplish haze at the field's far end, and condensing into warriors with wild manes, bright clothes, and battleaxes the size of

46

wombats.

A twitter flew up Sir Robin's throat. "Those aren't the men we're meant to fight, are they?"

"*No.*" Dwain rolled his eyes. "Those are their cheerleaders. See the pompoms?"

Keesh squinted. "Not from this distance. Perhaps it's time to invest in a set of spectacles."

At two hundred yards' distance, the Saxons broke into a run, screaming and cursing and blaring their horns.

"Charge!" cried Xander, unsheathing the mighty El Caliburo.

The Knights of the Roundish Table shouted and, almost as one, spurred their horses into battle. Except for Sir Robin, who had Bernard nudge his sheep in the general direction of combat.

"How droll," remarked King Bark to the monarch beside him. "Xander's men have let their company mascot tag along for sport."

The two sides met in a clash so epic, so historic, so fearsome, that one word only can describe the sound: BAM. Followed quickly by numerous "ow"s from the wounded, and "argh"s from the dying.

The spectators huddled to the edges of the bleachers, eyes round as properly transported tables, lips pressed white shut, except for the occasional call to one of the salted turnip vendors meandering the stands.

Xander looked into the faces of the enemy surrounding him, half hoping one would cut him down. But the man to his right was too scrawny to have the honour of killing a King in battle, the man to the left too short, the man straight ahead too sunburnt. Xander moaned as he dispatched them all. "Jennivere."

Longfellow cut through the throngs of Saxons until his horse was soaked red with blood. The poor animal absorbed so much gore that at last it could hardly walk for what dripped from its coat. Longfellow dismounted, barreling ahead on foot, sword in one hand, axe in the other.

A shadow circled overhead. Sir Sordid had been awaiting it, and was the first to notice.

Xander's horse was hewed down under him. The King disappeared beneath a flood of mangy red manes and hairy, hacking arms.

Then he was up, fighting as bravely as ever, identifiable by the golden circlet embracing his helm.

Sir Sordid wasted no time, but moved towards the King, slipping his secret weapons from a pouch at his waist. He maneuvered to strike.

In the press of battle, Xander never noticed the Tootsie Pops inserted through the two armpit openings in his armour, nor did he notice the devious chuckle Sir Sordid gave as he made his retreat. The exertion of combat had Xander sweating like a pineapple at a luau. (Pigs are also served at luaus, but have no sweat glands.) When he sweated through the candy coating surrounding the chewy Tootsie centre of the Pops, Misty would swoop down, gobbling the King and making room on the throne for Sir Sordid, the untainted and innocent. In the depths of the King's armpits, the candies were already dissolving into sticky globs. Xander made a mental note to switch deodorants, if he survived the battle.

Sir Robin, on the other hand, experienced few problems avoiding death. None of the barbarians attacked him, as none of them saw a man riding an aimless sheep as a particular threat to their cause.

Bernard, however, was encountering problems aplenty, as Saxon warriors lashed out at the twangs of the solid gold lute.

"Louder, Bernard – play louder! You've got the barbarians so afraid of me that none of them dares strike." Sir Robin chortled in high glee.

Bernard ducked and danced and sidestepped behind the sheep, striving to avoid blows. A warrior charged him with a spear. Bernard yipped, circling ahead of Wooly Bully.

"What is it?" Robin asked as the warrior went screaming by.

"The barbarians, master. They keep attacking me and – "

"Good gravy! What's happened to your lute? The head's bent back at a right angle. Those Germanic blighters!"

"That's how a lute is, sir."

"Really? What a ridiculous instrument."

The warrior circled back with his spear, driving for Bernard's chest. The minstrel used the lute to bat aside the spear tip.

Dwain and Keesh, mounted and swirling in the midst of a crowd of hacking Saxons, passed by, Dwain calling, "Robin, do *something*. Even your minstrel is more useful than you are."

"Hardly." Sir Robin sniffed at the beam that ricocheted into young Bernard's expression. "All he's done is batter a perfectly expensive musical apparatus."

Bernard's face slouched back to its former expression.

Longfellow kept one eye on the dragon circling overhead. Misty could not attack with fire, lest her own side suffer loses as great as the Britons', but she seemed to be waiting for something, some signal before swooping down with her razor claws and serrated teeth. Longfellow's other eye was trained on Sir Glancelot who, after Guy had sliced a barbarian beyond medical recuperation, would nudge each foeman to fall on the blood-slicked earth.

Meanwhile, the King's sweat glands – intending only to cool their sovereign in the heat of battle – had unwittingly (as sweat glands don't have wits) leaked the last drops to dissolve the Tootsie Pops in his armpits, and unleash the sweet scent of chewy brown sugar into the air.

Misty's neck snapped, pointing her scaly head towards the King.

Sordid saw and, unable to resist watching his plan come to fruition, edged back nearer Xander.

The dragon's circles turned lower, tighter, as she zeroed in on the King.

Longfellow noted the change in Misty's movements, scanning the field of men and corpses for her motivation. Upon locating it, his eyes gaped, and he began shoving his way across the battlefield.

Xander fought on, oblivious to the shadow of doom winding around him. He lashed out at every movement, not knowing if any of his blows struck home, his eyes blurred – with sweat and tears.

Misty coiled in midair. Her wings froze, and for a moment she hung suspended. Then she folded her wings, dropping towards the King like a sack of wet turnips.

Sir Sordid lurked beside the King. When the dragon barreled the last few feet he realized that, as things stood, he would be killed – or at least grievously wounded as collateral damage. He squealed.

Xander turned, following Sordid's gaze skyward.

Guy lunged, tackling the King to the ground. Glancelot followed after, knocking into Sordid. Misty came next, closing her snaggletoothed jaws around the first body that came to tongue, which happened to be Sir Glancelot's.

Longfellow rolled off the King, both of them joining Sordid in staring up at knight and monster.

Glancelot, his top half engulfed in Misty's mouth, was kicking fit to make the Olympic swimming team.

"God have mercy," Longfellow breathed.

Misty tossed her head back, trying to slurp the legs. Once, twice, thrice, fource. Only Glancelot's feet were visible now, paddling fiercely as ever.

As Misty made to jerk her neck a final time, the point of a sword broke out through her snout, halfway between her nostrils and her eyes.

The dragon yowled, spitting flames across the sky. She spun away from Londinium, wings galloping for the barbarians' encampment.

At the burst of sound and heat the combatants had stilled to stare overhead. Now, upon seeing their leader's formidable pet flee the field, the Saxons followed suit.

Xander climbed to his feet and walked a few paces. He picked up Sir Glancelot's bejeweled and saliva-soaked boot, which had toppled from Misty's mouth the instant before the rest of him was swallowed by flames.

He looked around at his remaining knights, blood dribbling down their armour. The field was drizzled with it, but the corpses were gone. The Saxons had taken them back to camp as per custom, to sever the heads and bring these out as dinner guests on special occasions, such as the anniversary of a great victory, or a deity's feast day, or a particularly lonely Friday night.

King Bark of Cornwall, swallowing the last mouthful of his salted turnip, stood up and cried, "Britons, behold: Xander, your High King."

To which Xander brandished aloft all that remained of the brave and loyal Sir Glancelot and cried, "Britons, behold: The Council of the Boot, your last line of defence."

Dwain glanced at Robin, who in the confusion of battle had come to be seated backwards on his sheep, murmuring to Keesh, "God help us all," before being drowned out by the cheering crowd.

✳✳✳

During the ride back to the castle, the Knights of the Roundish Table – now also known as the Council of the Boot – tallied those missing from their ranks.

"Sir Sycamore is dead," said Dwain. "I saw a barbarian plant an axe in his back. The man went stiff as a log and fell forwards full-length."

"Sirs Day is passed," said Longfellow.

Keesh jolted. "Surely not. I watched him face a great, heaping fellow, saying, 'This is the instant thou diest, thou stupid, scummy rapscallion.' Filled the man's eyes so full of spit he couldn't see to defend himself. Very cunning indeed."

"In any case, he's dead."

"Should have hired a minstrel. Best move I ever made." Robin slapped Bernard's back. The boy was trotting alongside his master's sheep, carrying the golden lute over one shoulder. The instrument had been battered almost beyond recognition which, consequently, had improved its sound.

"I don't see Sir Tamarack of Broadbottom anywhere," said Dwain.

"Oh, he died two days ago." Keesh shook his head. "Completely ignored everyone trying to warn him. Rode under a cliff used by professional anvil droppers to practice their craft."

"A shame. He seemed rather put out at being lured over by cries of distress to open pickle jars, but it was quite convenient to feign helplessness or repugnance and have him do dirty laundry."

Robin sighed. "Kind lad clipped my toenails once, after Bernard put up such a fuss."

"'Perilous fumes' certainly seemed to seal it," said the minstrel.

Dwain hemmed. "New Knight Syndrome."

The council arrived at the castle, handed their reins to the ostler, and followed their King inside. Sir Sordid followed closest of all, half-mad after his scheme's failure. One hand clutching his sheathed dagger, he kept a fantasizing eye on the King's back, closing to within arm's reach. So close, so close – so close that when Xander halted at the entrance to the great hall Sordid smacked into him, bashing his nose into the King's armoured shoulder so it bled.

"MERVIN – what in God's holy name – "

Dwain, Keesh, and the others moved to peer around the King into the hall.

"What's that sparkly thing caked in dirt?" Bernard whispered, then, "Oh no, oh no."

Dwain's eyelids stretched practically to his eyebrows. "Mervin was mixing the Elixir of Life to cheer up the King."

The magician stood at the hearth, stirring a cauldron that hissed and spewed blue fumes. By him on the roundish table was the Queen's unearthed urn. Dirt stained the hem of Mervin's robe and accented the wrinkles in his hands. With his nonstirring hand, he lobbed the supposed Philosopher's Stone into the cauldron. "Hello, majesty. Don't worry, it's nearly done."

"What's nearly done, you minger? What are you doing with my Jenni?" Xander stormed the room, followed by his knights.

"Bringing her back to life, of course. Do you have any eye of newt? Though I suppose I can substitute it with three hairs from an untainted virgin." Mervin yanked a handful of red strands from Sir Robin's beard.

"YOW! You silly old man! I suppose you're confused again and thought I was Dwain or Bernard or somebody."

Mervin shook his head. "Oh no, I'm perfectly lucid at the moment."

Dwain snorted. "He's right. You are the only one of us untainted by intelligence."

Mervin scuffled back to his cauldron, sprinkling in the last ingredient. The mixture sizzled, and the smoke gurgling from it flickered to purple. "There we are. Soup's on."

Xander flew to the table, snatching his wife's urn and pressing it to his chest. "Stay back! No one touches her."

A low laugh echoed through the great hall. It crawled up the knights' bodies, swelling to the ceiling. Everyone turned to look at Sir Sordid, who seemed finally to have lost his mind.

"You fools," he chuckled, "you fools! This is how I shall achieve my great victory – not by killing your precious King, but by outliving him – I shall have all the time this world offers to achieve my goal!" He bolted to the cauldron, slapping the ladle from Mervin's hand, and dunking his head to slurp his fill as the knights looked on in horror.

Sordid's shoulders heaved at each gulp. He raised his head, wiped a strand of purple fluid from the corner of his mouth, and promptly fell to the floor – stone dead.

The shocked knights were holding their breaths.

"Elixir of Life?" Dwain burst out. "The Elixir of Life? Correct me if I'm wrong, but shouldn't it have the opposite effect?"

"Is there an antidote?" asked Keesh, staring at the limp body.

Mervin blew between his lips, flapping them as horses were wont to do. "The antidote to the Elixir of Life is simple enough: all we have to do is kill the lad, and he should be fine." The magician set about kicking Sir Sordid in the head. "Wakey, wakey. Up and at 'em, George McFadden."

Longfellow took hold of Mervin and yanked him back. "Stop that, you old hack. Respect the dead, or you'll soon be one of them."

"Everybody out!" shouted the King.

The knights, with Mervin and Bernard, filed from the great hall, closing the massive wooden door behind them.

Xander sighed, setting his wife's remains on the table and passing a hand over his face. "We won today, Jenni. We won, and the Kings elected me to lead them. We united Britain, Jenni. You would have loved to see it." He circled the table, taking care to step over Sordid's corpse. "I miss you, my shiny-shelled turtle. In my arms, in my bed, in my heart. But then, you'll always be in my heart, won't you, Jenni?" A smile creased the King's lips as he came back around to his wife's urn. "Heaven has a palatial room for you, no doubt and – one day – I shall come to share it." Xander sat down. "So long, my angel." He leaned forwards to kiss her.

The sack he sat on burst a seam. Turnips tumbled out, lowering the King until his tailbone bumped the floor.

"Mervin!" he cried. "What's happened to all the bloody chairs?"

The Council of the Boot

Once, an *extremely* long time ago, there lived a knight named Sir Dwain. But he wasn't just any old knight – he was any young knight – ready humor his trait, and shining green eyes his asset. He and his friend Sir Keesh were retained by King Xander, a ruler with a heavy brow and exacting presence, ever deep in thought devising ways to repel the invading Saxon barbarians.

Also with the King was auburn-bearded Sir Robin the Bold of Estrangorre – about whom many a ballad had been sung (and not all of them favourable) by that knight's dark-haired young minstrel, Bernard – and Sir Guy of Longfellow, a handsome, blond knight with hard eyes that grew cheeky in battle. These six made up the renowned Council of the Boot: Britain's last defence.

"This time we have the ultimate weapon, my lads," King Xander was saying.

They were sat about a table in the dim hall of a rundown castle. When first made the table had been circular, yet its wood had warped, rendering it not quite round and not quite anything else.

"Our bravest knight, Sir Glancelot, along with many other stout fellows, has been laid to rest by the barbarian chieftain's vile dragon. Now, thanks to this ultimate weapon, we shall avenge our comrades."

"And what weapon is that, majesty?" asked Sir Keesh, his hands fidgeting in his lap.

"'Tis called a long-range cowapult. Instead of a catapult that throws cats, the cowapult can throw aurochs – aurochses? – which are the largest animals we have in Britain, and more likely to cause damage. The cats have outgrown their usefulness – keep landing on their feet instead of on the enemy. The cowapult can hurl an aurochs over a hundred Brythonic metres, utterly collapsing anything in its wake."

"I thought the aurochs was extinct," said Robin.

"Nearly. We're fortunate to have rounded up the last few for this operation."

"Why not throw rocks and be done with it?" Guy of Longfellow sulked.

"Because this is more a*moo*sing. Get it?" Bernard the minstrel chuckled.

"It'll never work," Sir Dwain interrupted, staring abstractedly at the ceiling.

"And why is that?" huffed the King.

"Well," Dwain straightened up, "you see, Saxon metres are much shorter than Brythonic ones. So, if it can only throw one hundred metres in Britain, 'twill be completely useless in the territory the Saxons have claimed as New Saxonia."

"By Jove, he's right!" exclaimed Sir Robin. He had taken part in many great battles, or at least he was supposed to have done. The knight, it turned out, was rather skittish around swords, blood, barbarians, yelling, liverwurst, fighting, soldiers, and common household plants.

Keesh shrugged. "Perhaps we should just call off the whole thing, then."

"Never!" cried Sir Guy, outraged. "Just hand them Britain on a silver platter?! No, say I! We shall fight to the pungent death, never giving over, even if they pry off all our fingernails, our toenails, and our eyeballs. Even if they pour superglue up our noses, and into our ears – never shall we admit defeat! Though they feed us English cooking, and tap us upon the left shoulder when actually standing to our right. We shall prevail! Are you *balde mine beornes?*"

Sir Robin raised an index finger. "Um . . . are we what?"

"Don't you bloody know old English?"

Dwain leaned back in his chair, closing his eyes meditatively. "Oh, come on, Longfellow. It's the five hundreds; no one talks like that anymore."

"Actually, old English will be in use until around eleven hundred," Keesh pointed out. "And, on a related topic, I thought we were Celtic."

Dwain sighed. "Oh, you know how it goes. The longer a legend's around the more distorted from its origins it becomes. Just look at us. We call ourselves 'knights' when a more culturally appropriate term would be 'warrior aristocrats.'"

"Order, I say!" called King Xander. "We must think of a new plan to defeat the barbarians."

"That's easy," Dwain scoffed, "just get Robin to fight on their side."

Sir Robin crossed his arms. "Look, it's not my fault your foot almost got cut off that one time. It's hard hanging onto a sword."

"Like you'd know."

"Hey!"

"All you care about is whether you're wearing enough armour. We all remember the time you were so eager to crawl into your brand new suit that you ordered yourself dressed whilst the metal was yet hot from the forge."

Robin pouted. "I do, too. I burnt my bottom."

King Xander was turning maroon. "Men, please! This is a war council! Now, what can we throw at the Saxons?"

"Our knees? Our praises? Our country?" Dwain rattled off. "I think they'd appreciate the latter most."

"Alas! it may not be."

Everyone turned to look at Sir Keesh.

"I just took up the lease of this quaint little summer cottage – it's right on the shore, where you can go swimming and hunting and the like – and I am not giving Britain to anyone until after mongoose season."

"Fair enough," said the King. "So, what can we do?"

In the end they decided to vote on their course of action, as each had his own proposal.

"Hear ye," called Xander, "each man may vote but once – so you'd better make it good." He glared at them. "Who is for Sir Keesh's suggestion of having a jousting tournament to decide the winner?"

Only Keesh raised his hand.

"Sir Guy's idea of going to the Saxons' homeland in Germania and killing every living thing in our path?"

Guy of Longfellow's hand was the only one to rise to the occasion.

"Alright, how about Bernard's motion to build a big wall around Britain, and not let anybody in?"

Again only the suggester voted.

"What of Sir Robin's proposal to hide in the keep until it's safe to come out?"

The same.

"*My* plan to build a brace of cowapults?" Despite his tone, the King still had no response save his own. "Fine. Sir Dwain's suggestion to move to Hawaii?"

At this everyone's limb roused to attention.

Dwain kicked up his feet onto the table circular. "Gotta love these people."

"You can only vote once!" Xander shouted.

"Look." Dwain took down his feet, assuming a more businesslike posture. "Reality check. Keesh's plan won't work because Glancelot was our best jouster and, let's face facts here, he's dead. As for Guy Longfellow's idea, we'd have to go to Germania and we still haven't gotten our passports in order."

Bernard interrupted. "See, I told you – better safe than sorry."

"Besides," Dwain continued, "hiding and throwing cows won't do any good. What we need is . . . "

Everyone leaned forwards, tensing fiercely.

" . . . a miracle," Dwain concluded, tilting back again.

"Is that all?" Sir Robin scoffed, waving his hand at the trifle. "*I* know where to get one of *those*."

***

So the Council of the Boot adjourned to Mervin the Magician's house, led by the renowned Sir Robin the Bold.

As they rode through the gentle hills and swaying grasses, Bernard favoured them with a song of his master's valor:

"Oh, Sir Robin the Bold is a wondrous man,
He does great deeds like no one can.
He's slain a baby dragon,
And fixed a Saxon's wagon.

"Oh, Sir Robin the Bold is a valiant man.
He rescues men like no one can.
He's loosed a fox's snare,
But the dead beast hardly ca-ared.

"Oh, Sir Robin the Bold, Sir Robin the Bold,
He'll be a legend before he's old.
Sir Robin, Sir Robin, thou art the tops –
For 'hoo could cle-ean thy messes op!"

60

"Thank goodness we're here," sighed Robin, who was quite sick of hearing himself "praised."

They dismounted before a thatched hut nestling between two low hills. Entering, the war council beheld an old man with pursed lips and long, tangled, silver hair waddling about in the smoky interior. He wore a deep blue robe, and upon his head sat a cone emblazoned with the word "dunce." This was Mervin the Magician, the King's own mentor. The renowned tutelage had begun long ago, upon Xander pulling the thorn El Caliburo from a lion's paw when no one else would dare face the rabid beast. Xander had succeeded in first crushing the lion beneath a pile of month-old turnips before performing this noble service.

"What d'ya want now?" complained the old man. "Can't you see I'm busy?!" He waddled to a chemistry set in the corner and set about mixing ingredients.

"We don't mean to bother you," said the King. "What are you doing, anyway?"

"Baking a cake. If I knew you were coming, I'd have made it sooner. But then my insight is failing. I don't know where you come from, and I don't know where you been."

"But it really doesn't matter. What matters is that we stand in desperate need of a miracle. We're going up against the Saxon barbarians in a horrific, cinematic battle destined to be remembered until the end of time itself, and we need a secret weapon."

"Weapon . . . weapon . . . now let me see."

"I say," Dwain was peering past the magician, "is that a pineapple upon that shelf?"

"No, of course not." Mervin looked away.

"Oh yes it is; it's a pineapple. Where did you get a pineapple from?"

"I don't have a pineapple."

"Yes you do, I can see it. Pineapples only grow in tropical zones."

"How d'you know Britain isn't tropical?"

"Because it's always bloody cold out."

"Maybe it's tropical, but it's just got an amazing windchill factor."

"Fine," said Dwain. "All I want to know is where you got that pineapple."

"I told you – I don't *have* a pineapple."

"But I can see it."

"Maybe it's an upside-down rat with a grass skirt on."

Guy Longfellow murmured, "How does he know it isn't a right-side-up rat, and the grass skirt is on its head?"

"Now why would a rat be wearing a grass skirt?" Dwain continued.

Mervin shrugged. "Because it's cold out."

"Well it should be wearing a bloody parka then, shouldn't it? Or at least some trousers. Besides, if it's so cold out where did you get a pineapple?"

"A peddler stopped by not long ago."

King Xander deemed it prudent to intervene. "Now that's settled, what about giving us a new secret weapon?"

"Ahh, yes." The magician stroked his beard. "How about a cannon?"

"But that won't be invented for another eight hundred years," Dwain countered. "How could you possibly be in possession of a cannon?"

"Heatseeking missile?"

"Still no good," Dwain said. "Their dragon's coldblooded."

"I've got it! What about a singing sword?"

"Nah – that'll just give away our position."

"Well, the only other secret weapon I have in stock is the Ultimate Warrior."

King Xander perked up. "You mean a gladiator?"

"Nope, better. Gentlemen – and I use the term loosely – I give you my niece: Gene of Arc!"

A brunette of about eight or nineteen entered the room and began sizing up the knights.

Guy of Longfellow's eyebrows raised. "Umm . . . what can she do?"

"Why," said Mervin, "she can kick those barbarians' butts back to the days of the Roman Empire! Did I mention that I trained her myself? I can't give you a miracle, but Gene is pretty close."

"As long as she isn't a cow." Bernard approached. "Give ye good den, my lady." He bowed accordingly.

Gene pushed past him. "Yeah, yeah, when do we fight?"

Dwain leaned closer to Longfellow. "I think she's your type."

***

Gene was superb at planning battles, and soon came the time for attack. Girded in plate armour gusseted with mail and flaunting their heraldic shields, the Council of the Boot mounted their horses. They marched on the barbarian chieftain's wooden castle, hastily erected out of prefabricated pieces to the south of Xander's capital of Londinium. With them they brought a band of farmers who had pledged their King absolute loyalty in exchange for two sacks of turnip seeds and, if they won the battle, an extra helping of dessert that night at dinner.

A broad field surrounded the barbarian fortifications. All the nearby trees and shrubs had been burnt away by dragon's breath. The castle's vast outer walls were spray-painted with insults, mostly regarding the Saxons' barbarian mothers. The Saxon army, though, being illiterate, didn't seem to mind. The courtyard was said to be where they dwelt in tents and lean-tos, alongside Misty the bloodthirsty dragon, who also happened to be adept at roasting kebabs and opening soda cans.

Now Sir Robin the Bold and Bernard advanced to the castle gate. Bernard readied his ever-handy lute, and Sir Robin dismounted. Then, with the strumming of a chord, both began to sing, as Robin flailed about in an effort to dance.

"Can can, can you do the can-can?
Can you do the can-can?
Can you do the la la la la la la la . . . .
Can can, can you do the can-can?
Can you do the can-can?
Can you do the la la la la la!"

Barbarian troops burst from the castle but stopped cold. What began as a sputter and progressed to a guffaw soon gushed into such roaring laughter that Sir Guy of Longfellow was able to outflank the Saxons, sneaking unnoticed into their castle. Drawing his sword, Longfellow entered the keep, creeping along the various passageways to seek out the chieftain.

✳✳✳

Once the adversary's army had gotten hold of itself, their dragon Misty was loosed among Britain's forces. Most of the farmers fled in panic, yet it did them no good. The dragon, fleet of wing, burnt them to crisps all the same.

The King and what remained of his council convened.

Sir Keesh shuddered. "What do we do?!"

"Call it a war and sail for better lands?" Dwain suggested.

"I second the motion," Robin chattered. "Carried – let's get the heck outta here." He made to leave.

"Wait." Xander's voice stayed him. "Gene, you're our secret weapon, even if you aren't airborne cattle. Why don't you slay the dragon?"

"I'll have a go." Gene slowly drew her sword, to great dramatic effect.

Approaching the pale blue-green beast, she of the Arc called out, "Hey – down here, coward! Cook me if you ca-an," this last part in a sing-song voice.

Dodging the dragon's fireballs, Gene strove to sprint close enough to strike. The dragon was crafty enough to realize its opponent's plan, warding her off. It seemed that all – lives, freedom, Britain – was udderly . . . utterly lost.

∗∗∗

At that very moment, Sir Guy of Longfellow had come upon the castle's throne room. Sheathing his sword, he strode gallantly into the Saxon chieftain's presence.

The chieftain rose, swathed stereotypically in furs to make him appear more animal than man. "Who ist thou, British bulldog?!"

"Question asked and answered." Longfellow bowed impertinently.

"You schall die!" cried the chieftain, motioning to his warriors.

"Hold there, faceless stock characters. I've come to challenge your brave chieftain to a climactic fight to the death, in which one of us shall rise victorious, whilst the other finds his body hacked apart and his skull used as a tacky aquarium accessory. So how about it?" Longfellow turned to the chieftain. "Or art thou such a coward that thou wouldst ignore my challenge and set all of thy men upon one . . . single . . . knight?"

Shuffling forwards with his gaze locked upon this intruder, the chieftain called for a sword. Longfellow drew his. The duel commenced.

Circling one another, their two styles were soon shown to be quite distinct. Sir Guy had been taught to first make quick, testing strokes to find his opponent's weak points. The chieftain drove in hard and fast, slicing vehemently, striving to rush the combat to its end.

Longfellow moved with grace whilst skewering the chieftain in the eye. The Saxon squinted with his remaining eye, running at the knight. This eye was also dispatched. Losing his eyes meant the chieftain also lost his status. Saxons chose the best warrior for their leader. Seeing their best defeated would dishearten the barbarians more than having to listen to any number of their favourite pop songs ruined by roving groups of child minstrels.

Longfellow smirked at this victory. "You are indeed a brave fellow, and one so determined need not lose his life." He turned to go.

"Dat's okey-dokey, you can keel me. I just a bad people."

"I say, are you sure, old chap?"

"Yeep, I shoore. Gotta leev oop to historee books."

"Well, if that's what they all say, I suppose there's no arguing."

The chieftain was dead before he hit the blood-stained floor. And definitely before he bounced and then hit it again.

✳✳✳

Meanwhile, Gene of Arc was having rather a hard time of it disposing of Misty. The armies had long since lost interest in fighting amongst themselves and stood wholly absorbed in her match.

Gene dodged fireballs with the athleticism of a well-trained mongoose. The frustrated dragon torched anything that moved.

66

Fortunately for Sir Robin the Bold, he was scared stiff.

Then came a blood curdling scream, and Sir Keesh blanched white as a sheet.

Everyone spun. Charging straight for them was – Xander's mother, Queen Amanita. She had been vacationing nearby, as evidenced by the flip-flops beneath the hem of her swishing royal robes. Everyone stood frozen in her presence, including Misty.

Marching over to her son, Queen Amanita spoke thusly: "What in heaven's name do you think you're doing, young man?"

"Well . . . um . . . ."

"You're disgracing Britain, that's what you're doing. You can't even kill a lizard!"

"See . . . ."

"Your majesties." Longfellow approached the royal pair, bowing.

"Here comes my favourite knight in the whole world," the Queen crooned, embracing Sir Guy. "Now this is a fighter. How many hast thou slain, sir knight?"

"Alas, majesty! but one so far. If it matters, 'twas the chieftain of this tribe I slew," Longfellow replied matter-of-factly.

"Then only the dragon need be killed if thou art to win, my boy!" The Queen thumped Xander's back.

"We've been trying, Mother, but . . . . "

"No excuses. Hand me that sword."

Gene obeyed the Queen's command.

"Dragon, come hither."

Misty shambled over accordingly.

"Now, lower thy head."

Misty looked around for another option before obeying, cringing with reluctance.

The Queen punched Gene's sword full-length into the dragon's eye. "And that's how you kill a lizard," Amanita concluded as Misty went limp.

At this awesome sight the Saxon forces turned towards the coast and ran in fright, with no chieftain to bid them stay.

"A sword in the eye is worth two in the hand," Dwain observed as the Britons cheered.

Bernard strummed a victory song on his lute.

"Bernard's Masterpiece"
Oh, sir Ro-bin the Bold is a won-drous man, He does great
deeds like no one can. He's slain a ba-by dra-gon, And
fixed a Sax-on's wa-gon. Oh, Sir Ro-bin the Bold is a
val-iant man. He re-scues men like no one can. He's

loosed a fo-x's share, But the dead beast hard-ly cared.
Oh, Sir Ro-bin the Bold, Sir Ro-bin the Bold, He'll be
a le-gend be-fore he's old. Sir Ro-bin, Sir Ro-bin, thou
art the tops — For 'hoo could clean thy me-sses op!

The Knights with the Goat

Sir Dwain, his armour glinting in the dawn, was mounted atop his gallant steed, bent over its neck, snoring gently. Beside him, Sir Keesh de Lattice sat bolt upright as his horse grazed, his hands gripping its reins, his eyelids softly fluttering beneath his raised visor.

"Sir knights!"

Both bolted awake at King Xander's call.

With a yelp, Sir Robin the Bold sprang up into a sitting position amidst the long grass next to his horse.

Xander frowned. "*What* is Sir Robin doing on the ground?"

"I must have fallen asleep, sire." Robin looked around. "Where is Bernard? Why didn't he catch me?"

Dwain had already drifted back to sleep.

Sir Guy of Longfellow, who was stretching after having been leaned against Gene of Arc whilst they both dozed in their saddles, said, "He wandered off calling for that goat you're making him ride."

"He should tether himself to it properly."

"You don't find it humiliating to have your minstrel prance about on the back of a goat?"

"Well he's not a knight – he can't be seen on a horse."

"What do you expect," Dwain murmured, eyes still closed, "from a man who used to ride around on a sheep?"

"They're quite comfortable," said Robin, "well-padded. Peasants don't need padding. They're gratifyingly adaptable."

"Yes," said Longfellow, "I can't wait to see your minstrel adapt to being skewered by an irate goat's horns."

"Knights!" Xander glanced askance. "And Gene. We must have

decorum on our progress."

"Is that why we're up this early?" Dwain asked. "Progress?"

"Indeed. We have won back our country from the barbarian hoard. Now we shall progress through the land, showing ourselves to the people and dispensing justice where it is needed."

Keesh's eyes popped open. "Um . . . this sounds like more than a daytrip, and we haven't packed any luggage to speak of."

"Nor do we have reservations, I'm guessing," said Dwain.

"Perhaps if we brought along some tents." Keesh brightened.

Xander's face clouded. "*Camping*? A King hunched in the wilderness over a tiny fire?"

"Not tents," said Dwain, "pavilions. Great palaces of brightly-coloured silks, trunks with money for our journey. Changes of clothes. Perhaps Robin's mouthguard to stop him grinding his teeth."

"Nonsense. We shall stay at whatever castle we near come nightfall. Subjects cannot be denied the privilege of showing gratitude to their King for his leadership and protection."

Bernard staggered out from some trees, his goat in a headlock. "I found it in a ditch eating thistles. Where are we going?"

"West." King Xander reared his horse and struck off.

Robin hauled himself up into his saddle. "I don't suppose we're getting breakfast first?"

***

The west country grew rocky, then hilly, then positively mountainous (except that it wasn't covered in real mountains so much as rocky hills, often mistaken by Britons for actual mountains). The party travelled by the coast of a river winding along the bottom of a narrow valley through the slopes. Their path lay wide enough to ride barely three abreast, and the level ground dropped into the river just inches below it with no real coastline to speak of. The blue-green water surging past them frothed white like milk along the shore.

It was well past midday when the river turned away, the valley opened up, and they saw the first sign of a settlement.

"Thank the Lord," said Keesh, "at last a chance to obtain provisions."

Dwain's stomach rumbled, echoing inside his armour. "See, this is why most people pack before a journey."

The huts ahead sat in only a corner of the large valley they had entered, their walls almost touching.

"I don't understand why people would build their houses so close together where there's nothing but space."

"I've been thinking," said Robin.

"Uh-oh."

"This excursion seems a good chance to try out different names."

"Like what? Hobb the Horrible?"

"It's just that the name Sir Robin the Bold hasn't necessarily bestowed the aura I had hoped it would. Perhaps Sir Robin the Courageous might."

"Too long."

"Sir Robin the Daring?"

"You've never dared to do anything."

"Sir Robin the Intrepid?"

"Too many syllables – it doesn't flow."

"Hm. This may take further thought, then."

Dwain popped out a breath through formerly set lips. "The peasants who live here can't possibly have a view of anything through their windows except the inside of each other's huts."

"It's the land," Xander said. "They only have permission to

build on that small piece so their houses don't take up space that could be used to grow crops for the kingdom."

"What if one of the peasants snored? He'd keep awake the entire village."

"Or they would simply kill him," said Longfellow.

"That would be homicide."

"Justifiable homicide."

"What if it were a baby crying?"

"Oh, I love babies," said Keesh. "I hope to have quite a brood one day. Don't you agree, Lady Gene?"

Gene, who had hardly been listening, snapped into focus. "*Excuse* me? Because of my gender I'm automatically supposed to want lots of babies crawling about me? Is that it?"

"Oh, I – "

"Because I've spent my life in training to become the ultimate warrior – that has been my goal – and you don't ask Dwain or Robin or even Bernard to agree with you – you only ask me. I don't want a massive brood, no, what I want is to find a village that needs us to fight something for them."

"There will be no need for fighting," Xander said. "We've repelled the barbarians from our shores. This is not a mission of war, but of peace, to show ourselves to the people, and renew their relationship with their native monarchy."

"And they get to put us up and feed us," Dwain said.

Robin grinned. "Like a free vacation. For Sir Robin the Gallant and his merry companions."

"Too fairy tale."

"Sir Robin the Valiant?"

"Still in that fairy tale vein."

"Oh bother."

"Surely," Gene said, "there will be something for us to fight.

Some strongman seeking to fill the power vacuum, or an ogre or something forced out of isolation by the upheaval of the invasion."

The King shook his head. "No, peace has been restored. Everything is perfectly peaceful now."

"I could spar with you," Longfellow offered, "when we stop for the night."

Gene sighed. "Yes, but I can't cut off your head or run you through."

"You can try."

She gave a small smile.

As they rode nearer, the villagers gathered to stare. Six riders in gleaming armour – and one dark-haired lad on a goat – was a sight none of them had expected. Not just today, but in their lifetimes.

"Greetings, Britons," Xander boomed. "It is I, your King, come to assure you of lasting peace now that I and my warriors have repelled the threat of the barbarian hoard."

The villagers frowned, murmuring to one another. One man with greyish tufts starting to show over his ears, and in them, took a step forwards. "Thank you for coming, your majesty. It is a great honour, and you are most welcome. We know, however, that it was not your warriors who defeated the barbarians, but the talking head."

Xander's brow furrowed. "The what now?"

The man turned and pointed. "The talking severed head buried in the midst of those three yew trees. As long as it remains buried there it repels all attempts at invasion of our shores."

"No, that would be the work of I, your King."

"The head used to belong to our King."

"I've never owned any severed heads."

"No, it was your father's."

"He didn't own any severed heads, either. He collected hatchets and buttons."

Gene spoke up. "King Uber is buried in Glastonbury, before the great abbey's high altar."

"His body may be but his head, which is still alive, lies amongst the yews."

Xander tsked. "Preposterous."

"We must exhume the head."

He looked back at Gene. "You're serious?"

"We ought to know why we're executing this man: for lying to a King or mutilating the corpse of one."

"You can't dig up the head!" the man pleaded. "If you do, there will be nothing to stop the barbarians from invading again and this time succeeding."

Xander glanced back at Gene. "Go on and exhume the head."

The crowd of villagers lurched forwards.

"Knights, prevent their interfering."

The four knights steered their horses in between the villagers and the yews as Gene dismounted, striding for the trees, picking up a shovel leaning against a hut as she advanced.

"Stay back, all of you, for I am the renowned Sir Robin the Confident!"

Dwain scoffed.

Bernard tried to steer his goat in between, too, but it shook him off. He had barely gained his feet when the goat reared up, placing its two front hooves on his chest and gobbling at his hair. Bernard swatted at the goat's face and backed up. Undeterred, the goat followed after on its hindlegs, continuing to graze along the minstrel's scalp.

"I have it." Gene pulled the head free of the earth by the hair, and brushed the dirt from its face.

Xander came over. "And is it – "

"No. I have no idea who this is."

The head opened its eyes. "I am the defender of this isle."

"You are not." Xander squinted one eye. "I don't recognize him, either."

"I am the guardian of Britain."

"Although he does slightly resemble Great Aunt Organza."

"I am the protector of the people. I repel all invaders."

"You do not. My kingly might does that. Yet you act as though you had some mystical power."

"It *is* a talking severed head," said Dwain.

Gene clenched the hair tighter in her fist. "Have you been impersonating King Uber?"

"It's not a person, really, just a head."

"A head can still be a person," said Keesh.

"So he could impersonate the old King, but not embody him."

"Shut up!" Sir Guy growled. "You're making jokes about treason."

"Exactly," said Gene. "And treason deserves execution."

"Erm . . . " Robin hesitated, "how does one hang, draw, and quarter a severed head?"

"We'll burn it."

"*No!*" The villagers pressed forwards, clawing and wailing.

The knights had to draw swords to keep them back, swinging at the air in front of their faces. Bernard tripped and fell over, but the goat still stayed firmly fastened to his hair.

"Yes, do burn the head," Xander told Gene, then turned to the villagers. "This will show you that it is my might, and not some jabbering buried head that protects you."

The villagers moaned in despair as Gene jammed the head on the end of a shovel, and entered the nearest hut. Lighting the head in the cooking fire, she re-emerged with the flaming head as though she carried a torch.

"Beware! Beware!" shouted the head. "Now Britain will fall."

"Fear not, good people, the head lies," said Xander.

"Indeed. As surely as my name is Sir Robin the Brash."

The anguish on the villagers' faces deepened. "You said your name was Sir Robin the Confident before."

"Oh. Well, I have many names."

"I have only one," Xander told them. "You can trust it. You will be safe in the future as you have been in the past."

∗

As they continued their progress, Longfellow kept his horse abreast of Gene's. Meanwhile, she slowed her mount until the two of them were riding a short distance behind the others. Red flowers spilled like blood across the sward.

"You created quite the spectacle, my lady," Guy murmured, "brandishing that burning head impaled on that shovel."

"Thank you. The village seemed to need reminding of their true King."

"Your actions were indeed memorable."

Gene smiled to herself. Her horse walked through a puddle, splashing muddy water onto the toe of her sabaton. "It would seem, Sir Guy, that you are minded to be less bold towards me than a water droplet."

"Not at all, my lady." He glanced over. "Where do you wish me to touch you?"

Gene grinned, keeping her eyes strictly forwards. "Underneath my armour, I should think."

"It seems unlikely I shall have the opportunity to take it off of you, as during this journey we shall be always in the company of his majesty and four nincompoops."

"Still, you might search out some chink in my armour, if you can find one."

Longfellow steered his horse nearer, so their legs nearly touched. "That would give me deep pleasure, my lady."

"Hm." Her cheeks beamed.

A swallow swooped over their heads, landing on a tree branch with a nest nuzzled next to its trunk. Four gaping heads popped out cheeping, but the swallow's beak was empty and it flew away again.

"Poor baby birds," said Keesh.

Dwain nodded. "Maybe we should eat them and put them out of their misery."

"I'd prefer an enormous omelette myself."

"No breakfast, no lunch – "

"Those villagers certainly neglected their hospitality after that head incident."

" – and nowhere else to eat for miles. At this rate, we'll have to roast Bernard's goat if we want any supper."

The goat cut across their path, dragging Bernard along behind it as he clung to its tail.

"Fine by me," he shouted, skidding into a patch of thorns.

"If you eat that goat," Robin called, "I'm not buying you another one."

"If you don't let us eat that goat," said Dwain, "we'll consider eating your horse."

"No one is eating any horses," Xander snapped over his shoulder. "Knights should be able to fast for a day without all this whining."

"Couldn't we stop to hunt, sire?"

"We are making our progress, Sir Dwain. We are not hunting nor camping nor sightseeing. If you're so restless, have Bernard sing some travelling music."

Bernard, atop his goat and with his legs wrapped around its

middle, came speeding up from behind, passing between Guy and Gene, then Dwain and Keesh. Reaching out, he clung to Keesh's stirrup for dear life, his knees still clamped onto the goat as it sought to drag him and now Keesh's horse.

"Bernard," said Robin, "the King has granted you permission to grace us with a song, and you're dithering."

"Well, one song comes to mind that I learned from a barbarian." Bernard started to slip and stiffened, his knuckles turning white.

> "Būtan beorhtnes
> Hit is lǣssa bealo.
> Hēr wē sind nū
> Gefeormaþ ūs.
> Ic frēde witlēas
> And ādlsēoc.
> Hēr wē sind nū
> Gefeormaþ ūs.
> Cornwēalas,
> Norđwēalas,
> Mustflēote,
> Mīn heortean –
> Gea."

"That's catchy," said Robin. "What does it mean?"

"I believe it's a commentary on what happens when people come together to praise a cause and get caught up rather than thinking for themselves."

"Oh. Well that's not very fun, then."

Either side of the road was now curtained by leaves and needles stacked up one atop the other in a rippling, solid wall separating the highway and the forest. Through this seemingly impenetrable barrier now popped a man with rolled shoulders and long limbs, the knobs of bone at his elbows, wrists, and knees standing out against his drab garb like knots in wood. He said nothing, but matched the pace of the knights' horses.

Robin's eyes had grown wide and remained so. "Erm . . . your majesty . . . someone has joined us."

Xander glanced back over his shoulder. "Who dares to join our company without first asking royal permission?"

"Erm . . . . " Robin squinted down at the man effortlessly matching the horses' pace.

The man looked back up at him, blinking slowly.

"I have no idea. Would someone else like to talk to him?"

"At least introduce yourself," Dwain called.

"Right. Presumptive peasant, I am Sir Robin . . . the Self-Assured. What are you called?"

Bits of moss flaked off the man's short cloak as he ran. "I am the Green Man. I heard your minstrel singing in the tongue of our great enemy."

"Oh, yes, he is rather versatile."

"It was a traitorous song."

"You understood the words?"

"No, but it is a barbarian song. It is treason to sing it."

Xander frowned. "I am the King. I shall decide what is treasonous."

"Everything to do with the barbarians is treasonous."

"If the barbarians clipped their toenails," said Dwain, "would clipping your toenails be treason?"

"They don't clip their toenails," said the Green Man, "they're barbarians."

"If he sang the same song in Brythonic, would that be treason?" Keesh asked.

"If it was written by a barbarian."

"I think it's originally a Latin song," Bernard said.

"Still bad. The Romans took over our island."

"And integrated with us," said Dwain, "forming the Romano-British culture we still enjoy the benefits of today."

"The Romans invaded us."

"Who's 'us'? We are Romano and British now."

"Your minstrel shouldn't be allowed to sing anymore."

"A non-singing minstrel?" Robin asked. "That doesn't sound very useful."

"His singing is offensive."

Bernard's mouth hung open as he desperately gripped Keesh's saddle. "One song! And it isn't meant to be offensive. It's about – "

"It offended *me*."

Xander stopped and turned his horse around. "Enough. Bernard is free to sing. We are not at war with Saxon culture or language. The barbarians tried to invade us, we repelled them, and the matter is dealt with. You have no authority to dictate what others are allowed to say or listen to simply because you interpret a thing to mean something you don't like."

"The minstrel seeks to corrupt the court!"

Xander roared, "We can have a territorial war without hating every aspect of another culture!"

The Green Man dashed at Bernard, swinging his arm and slapping him in the throat. "Down with barbarian oppression! My voice will not be silenced! Down with intolerance!"

Bernard made a choking sound, letting go of Keesh's stirrup and falling flat on his back in the middle of the road. His goat hustled far ahead of them as the Green Man skittered back into the leaves, and was lost to sight.

Dwain dismounted with a sigh, pulling Bernard back up to his feet. "This trip keeps getting better and better. Robin, the boy will have to ride with you.”

"Me? Why not you?”

“Because he’s your minstrel.”

“Sir Robin,” said the King, “we shall not slow our pace. We must reach accommodation by nightfall. The boy rides with you.”

Late in the afternoon they entered a long mountain valley. At its far end arose an enormous stone house. As they neared, however, it became apparent that the house was in fact made of wood and merely painted to look constructed from stone blocks. Balconies, vines, and flowers were painted on as well as great, wide windows flanked by blue shutters and showing scenes of the inhabitants feasting.

Guy scoffed. “Pretending their house is a castle, and painting on windows one could drive a pair of sheep through. What fool would have windows wider than an arrowhead in his castle?”

Gene pointed. “Let alone balconies one steps onto through an exposed door?”

“But they have food,” Dwain said.

Guy hmphed. “Their food may well be as real as their castle.”

“Before the hut where you found us,” Gene said, “Mervin and I used to live in a glass house. This is at least better than that. Here you couldn’t look up to find your uncle standing on the floor above you, not having bothered to don trousers under his wizard’s robe.”

Dwain’s eyebrows rose. “Did the house also have a glass garderobe?”

Keesh said, “You must have had to get dressed every morning underneath your blankets.”

“Why did Mervin have you living in a glass house?” Longfellow asked.

“It was better than where we were living before,” Gene said.

“Which was?”

"A blooming whitethorn bush."

"That sounds horrendously uncomfortable," said Robin.

"And before that we lived in a puff of smoke."

Dwain's jaw dropped. "Who is your realtor?"

Xander wheeled his horse around. "Mervin had you living on a puff of smoke? There's no shelter in that."

"No, and it was rather hard to breathe, but quite cheap."

"Are you sure you weren't just camping?" Dwain asked.

"Mervin didn't want to worry about housekeeping. We were concentrating on my training."

"The thorn bush, the smoke . . . . "

"When we get back," Xander said, "I shall be summoning Mervin to court to live under a proper roof, and giving him a piece of my mind. Having a young girl living in a puff of smoke. Goodness knows how it's inhibited your lung capacity."

"My lung capacity is fine."

"An ultimate warrior needs excellent lung capacity."

"What did you do when it rained?" Keesh asked.

Dwain grinned. "Or did you also live in a mud puddle?"

"Keep moving." Xander directed his horse forwards again. "We don't want to spend the night in a mud puddle ourselves."

As they approached, it became apparent that the tree to the left of the door was painted on the wall, whilst the tree to the right was real.

"Maa-ah!"

Dwain peered up into the branches. "There's your goat, Bernard."

Robin beamed. "You thought I cheaped out, but it made excellent time."

"And now it's in a tree."

"Bernard, get it down."

"I'd rather not."

The door opened. "Greetings," said a man wearing a torc and rings made of rolled up tin foil. "I am the master of this castle and very pleased of your company."

"Greetings," said Xander, "I am your King."

"And I am Sir Robin the Audacious."

Xander cleared his throat. "This is my Council of the Boot. Your hospitality is most welcome."

"Of course, of course. I do apologize for that dreadful goat roosting in the tree. It got up there somehow, and no one can seem to get it down."

"How annoying." The King eyed Sir Robin.

"I do hope the spectacle won't stymie your visit. Come, allow me to show you the wonders housed in my castle whilst the servants prepare a great feast."

"Very well." Xander dismounted.

"A man will come to bring your horses to the stable." Their host ushered them inside.

"Oh my." Dwain looked around as they crowded into the barely lighted foyer. He whispered to Keesh, "All of these walls are made of plywood."

Keesh bumped into one avoiding Robin's elbow. "They wobble."

"There isn't even any furniture. It's all just painted on the walls."

Robin managed to wrench off his helmet. "There we are. Much better that."

Their hose let out a cry, pointing at Sir Robin. "A fairy!"

"Excuse me?"

"You're a fairy!"

"I doubt that very much."

"You have red hair. Fairies have red hair!"

"Don't they also have wings?" asked Bernard. "And stand very small?"

"I don't want any fairy tricks played upon my castle."

"You mean like turning it from stone to cheap plywood?" Dwain asked.

"Yes, something like that would be awful." Their host shivered and stepped over to a blazing fireplace painted on the wall, holding out his hands to the static red flames.

"I can assure you that all of my men are men," said Xander. "Except for Gene, but that's only because she's a woman."

"A King's assurance is worth much." Their host sent Robin a doubtful glance. "Come, I shall reveal this castle's wonders to you. Please, leave your helmets on that bench."

The bench like everything else being painted on the wall, they left their upturned helmets on the dirt floor underneath.

Their host led them through a series of rooms, all small and dimly lit, all empty except for their murals and wall-mounted candles.

"You seem to have no windows," Dwain said.

"Yes, well, it's a castle, isn't it? You can't have your enemies just climbing in through a window when you've gone to all the trouble of making your walls eleven feet thick."

"Can't afford glass," Guy muttered to Gene.

"Or manage an imitation of it," she murmured back.

"Here we are," said their host, "the first wonder." He swept his hand towards a sack hanging from a hook in the middle of the low ceiling. "This is the Bottomless Bag. It can never be full, excepting that a wealthy man stamp down its bounty with both feet. Then he can be tied up inside and kicked about."

Keesh beamed. "Like a game of Badger in the Bag."

"Precisely. If you wish, we could play after supper."

"Do you have any wealthy men lying about?" Dwain asked.

"Not myself." The host leered at them, smiling.

"It will hardly prove a satisfying game, then," said the King. "What is your next wonder?"

They passed through another series of rooms.

"Here," their host gestured to another ceiling hook, "is the Veil of Illusion."

"It looks exactly like the Bottomless Bag," said Guy.

"Not so, sir knight. For the Bottomless Bag is a bag and suspended with its opening uppermost, whilst the Veil of Illusion is a veil, and is therefore displayed with its opening at the bottom."

"It must prove a strain not to accidentally switch them."

"Switching them would indeed be unfortunate, for the Veil of Illusion, when thrown over a person's head, has the power to deceive them according to the thrower's will."

"Deceive them how?" Robin asked.

"By having them think that you have suddenly turned invisible. Or that day has suddenly turned to night. Or that they have – suddenly – lost their power of sight."

Dwain raised his eyebrows. "Can it deceive a person into thinking that they're eating soup?"

"Well, we could always give it a try."

Xander marched out. "Next wonder."

Their host hurried to resume the lead. "This next wonder is in quite a distant room. Stay close, please." Forth they went.

After awhile, Dwain matched paces with Longfellow. "Do you get the sense that we keep doubling back on ourselves?"

"Hm. Evidently we're supposed to believe this a sprawling estate, rather than the pile of matchsticks we saw from outside."

"We haven't seen one staircase," Gene put in. "The outer walls must have been built up to look like another two storeys, when really there's only the ground floor."

Keesh whispered over his shoulder, "His servants probably just need more time to prepare our meal, so he's having us tramp back and forth."

"As long as the meal isn't our own butchered horses," said Dwain.

Longfellow nodded. "Served in our helmets."

"Then we'll all have to take turns at riding Bernard's goat."

Their host cleared his throat. "This," he announced, "is the Golden Bowl."

"More painted wood," Dwain murmured.

Longfellow cocked his head. "Undoubtedly."

Their host gazed fondly at the bowl sat on a narrow, waist-high pillar in the middle of the room.

"All of the royal plate is silver," said Xander. "Gold may not tarnish, but silver doesn't tolerate odours, and you can always have servants polish away any tarnish."

"Ah, but the Gold Bowl is not merely a golden bowl, for anyone who dares touch it becomes frozen in place. Would anyone care to try it?"

"If anyone freezes who touches it," said Dwain, "who managed to put it on the pillar?"

"We used tongs."

"So the power to freeze isn't transitive."

"Very long, enchanted tongs."

"Of course."

"Come now, we have more wonders to behold."

Dwain mumbled, "None of this bodes well for supper."

They walked on and on, throughout the house.

"We've been *through* this room already," Robin whined in

exhaustion.

"No we haven't," replied their host, never breaking pace.

"We have. I recognize that tapestry of a boar hunt painted on the wall."

"Tapestry on the wall, you mean. We have so many tapestries, you can be forgiven for not being able to distinguish between them."

"The hunters in the scene are beating the boar to death with spatulas," said Bernard. "It's quite unique."

Robin threw back his head. "My *feet* hurt."

"Mine host," said the King, "surely we must be at the end of our trek."

Their host hunched slightly. "Of course, your majesty. The final wonder is just here."

They turned aside into a room with a cauldron sitting in the middle of its floor.

"Is this a larger bowl that freezes people in place?" Dwain asked.

"How ridiculous. No, this is the Resurrection Cauldron."

"Used to make our Lord the first Easter breakfast, I suppose?"

"When a corpse is placed inside the Resurrection Cauldron, the person comes back to life, though as a mute."

"The cauldron brings people back to life?" Xander's expression slackened.

"I have witnessed it myself, majesty."

"The Queen . . . my sweet Jennivere . . . she died, you know."

"Yes, majesty, my condolences."

"The cauldron resurrects corpses . . . does it work on ashes as well?"

"It is worth a try, majesty."

"But she would not be able to speak, you say."

"Wives are full of nagging." Robin shrugged. "A mute one might be preferable."

Gene smacked him in the nose so he tipped over backwards.

"That's more effective than nagging," Dwain observed.

"We could ride back to Londinium and return with her ashes." Xander's face had gone pale with excitement.

"Perhaps," said Longfellow, "a test would prove prudent before investing such effort."

"Right," said Dwain. "We'll split Robin's skull, toss his corpse in the cauldron, if he comes back to life mute then alright, if he stays dead then it's still an improvement."

Robin withdrew an inch. "Wouldn't it be better to test using Bernard?"

"What would you do with a mute minstrel?"

"I think Sir Guy meant that we should test the cauldron using an animal."

"Perhaps our entree from supper could be repurposed," suggested Keesh.

"As long as we can kill it and cook it again," Dwain said. "It's been a *long* day."

"The cauldron doesn't work on animals in any case," said their host, "only people."

"So we're back to splitting Robin's skull."

"But he's a fairy."

"I'm not a fairy! Red hair really isn't as out of the ordinary as you're making it out to be."

"No one's died here recently who we could chuck in?" Dwain asked.

"No one," said their host. "Come, let's go in to supper."

Dwain whispered to Keesh, "Ten shillings says we all can't fit around the table."

The dining hall, as nearly as any of them could figure, was situated in the centre of the house and, unlike any of the other rooms, stretched to nearly full-size for a country manor's hall. It was more long than wide, though, so that everyone had to sit along the one side of only one long table running down the room, rather than the usual setup of having everyone around the outside of a three-sided rectangle with servants running up and down within.

"My King," said their host, "you, of course, must sit in the centre, nearest the fireplace, and array your knights upon either side of you in order of precedence. I should be most honoured to sit beside you and hold your feet in my lap."

"That, will not prove necessary."

"But some high officer must hold your majesty's feet in his lap whilst you are at meat. It is a most ancient custom. Do you deem me less than worthy?"

Xander glanced about at his knights, who were all avoiding his gaze with arched eyebrows. "You may hold my feet, good host, and sit upon my left. Gene's rank entitles her to sit upon my right, and Sir Guy of Longfellow must sit upon hers, as my best knight. Then . . . well, Bernard must be last upon the left."

"Absolutely," said Dwain, "with Keesh and myself, and Robin should sit next to Longfellow."

"Surely," spake Sir Guy, "Robin ought to sit beside you."

"I'm fairly certain he should sit with you."

"No, his place is rightfully at your side."

"So then you want Keesh?"

Longfellow cringed. "Not really."

"You have to take one of them."

"I could take you."

"Yes, but I plan on doing my Attila the Hun impression all evening, including his entire lack of table manners, so food will be a-flying."

"I really don't see why the three of you can't fit in together beside Bernard. Surely there's enough room."

"Sir Keesh," said Xander, "sit next to Longfellow." The King stepped over the bench and seated himself at table. The next moment their host had scooped Xander's feet up into his lap so the King sat almost sideways.

"I don't know why you don't wish to sit by me," Robin told Dwain. "I'm a delightful dining companion."

"Good. You sit next to our host, I'll be beside Bernard."

Their host cast Robin a momentary glare as he alighted. "Bring out the feast!"

The King tucked the edge of the white tablecloth over his lap.

Out popped two servants, struggling to balance a large platter loaded with meat between them. They swayed a couple steps left and right, slowly homing in on the table.

"Here, here," hissed their host.

The servants teetered towards the King, knocking the platter into the table edge, heaving it higher, and at last dumping it so the mound of steaming flesh lurched almost into Xander's lap.

Gene scoffed. "Are we to eat without trenchers or utensils?"

"I thought, you all being accomplished warriors, you would be carrying knives you infinitely prefer to mine."

"A thoughtful assumption," said Xander, casting Gene a look. "What manner of beast is this?" He reached to cut himself a piece.

"Goat, your majesty."

They all froze a moment.

"Surely you don't mean," Robin ventured, "the goat from the tree."

"The very same. My servants at last managed to knock him out of it by a coordinated throwing of quite a lot of gardening implements: two shovels, a spade, a rake, and at least half a dozen scythes."

"But, I *paid* for this goat, and now you kill it, and I have to haul my minstrel about on the back of my horse like some sort of peasant?"

"To be fair," said Dwain, "the goat wasn't exactly working out well as a form of transportation."

"You are *not* a delightful dining companion."

"Sir Robin, this is unseemly before our host." Xander unsheathed his knife. "I shall reimburse you, now be quiet and eat your goat."

Robin attempted a disdainful glance at their host, but found he was already being glowered at from that quarter.

Goat turned out to be the only course for supper and so, once they had eaten their fill, there seemed little else to do. Their host became almost flustered. "We have many entertainments for ourselves at such feasts, but I dared not to think that any might measure up to that of a minstrel from the royal court. Surely, his singing must be the only amusement worthy for this gathering."

"Such unflagging thoughtfulness," said Xander, knocking Gene's elbow as she rolled her eyes behind him.

"Indeed," said Robin. "I might have hosted this feast on my own estate, where I could feel at home, with all this thoughtfulness being shown me. Sing, Bernard. Show my hospitality here and everywhere."

Bernard hoisted himself up, having consumed more than a healthy portion of goat. Rounding the table to stand before them, he said, "This song has been sung since ages past, of love and sweet contentment." Filling his lungs, Bernard stuck all his fingers in his mouth and spluttered, "Blerwm, blerwm, blerwm."

Keesh frowned. "I don't think I've heard this one."

Bernard's mouth hung open. "My sincerest apologies, your majesty. I don't know what – I'll begin again." He composed himself, then put his fingers in his mouth. "Blerwm, blerwm, blerwm."

"Maybe if you tried it without the fingers," Dwain suggested.

Bernard had turned white. "I don't seem to be able to help it."

"Put them behind your back or something," said Robin.

Bernard clasped his hands behind his back, and took a deep breath. His fingers wrenched apart and flew into his mouth. "Blerwm, blerwm, blerwm. I'm so sorry, I – " He looked close to tears.

"I must apologize as well," Xander told their host. "This is no way for a court minstrel to behave."

Gene groaned. "There's no need to apologize. He's been enchanted."

"Enchanted? How can you be sure?"

"I was trained by a magician. It was probably that Green Man who struck him because he didn't like what the boy was singing."

Robin leaned forwards, looking down the table at Gene. "Then how do we fix it?"

"How should I know?"

"But what's the use of a minstrel who can't sing? He hasn't even got a goat now – what am I having to drag him around on my horse for?"

Bernard's eyes were bright red as he struggled not to cry.

"It seems like a fairy enchantment to me," said their host, turning his gaze upon Robin.

"I am *not* a fairy!"

"Though you have red hair, a goat trickster, and a minstrel marred by a curse."

"It is high time we went to bed," said the King. "Perhaps Bernard will be better in the morning."

"As you wish, my King. Sir Robin and his minstrel will be

shown to their room. Everyone else, of course, will have their own."

Gene felt Longfellow give a light pinch at the back of her knee, where there was a gap in her armour between the greave and the cuisse, and the poleyn didn't wrap all the way around. She looked over at him, and he slowly shifted his eyes to hers.

***

By the time Gene had removed her armour and arming doublet, standing in only a chemise in the candlelight, it had grown quite late. A knock sounded on her door.

She opened it. "Sir knight."

Longfellow nodded. "My lady." He wore a loose shirt, open at the neck, and leather breeks. "Do you find your accommodation suitable?" His blue eyes travelled down her bare legs.

"The bed seems to be made from three wooden crates pushed together."

"How irksome."

Gene half shrugged. "I like a firm bed."

Longfellow's hand slipped around her neck as he slipped inside the bedroom. He pressed her to the wall beside the door as it shut.

Gene smiled. "Kiss me, sir knight."

The kiss quickly became rough as she pulled him closer. They bit and clutched at one another, breathing as though they fought.

At last Longfellow whirled her over to the bed of crates, pushing her down onto it.

Gene reached up, covering his mouth with her clawed fingers before he could descend upon her. Through panting she said, "I am yet a maid, Sir Guy, and shall remain so until my wedding night."

He looked more animal than man, his back arched, eyes dilated, teeth bared. "Of course, my lady." He fingered the top of her left breast through her chemise, where he had bitten her particularly hard earlier, whereupon she had thrown back her head against the wall and gasped, digging her nails into his shoulders. "I hope at least to have left a mark upon your heart."

Gene grinned. "I daresay that hope is well-founded."

Longfellow leaned down, tearing another kiss from her. "Goodnight, my lady."

"Sleep well, Sir Guy."

Longfellow eyed her bare legs again as he turned to leave. "I doubt I shall sleep at all."

***

Sir Robin awoke the next morning to find his face feeling sticky. Swiping at it still half asleep, the wet stickiness smudged off on his hands. Upon hoisting open his eyelids, he found himself covered in blood.

"Oh!" Scrambling up to stand upon his crate bed, Robin first conked his head on the ceiling, and then surveyed the floor strewn with bits of bone all splattered red.

Their host burst in. "Ah, you have awakened, treacherous fairy knight."

"I am *not* – what is all this?"

"It is a vile tale to tell! Last night, in a fit of unconscious madness, you killed your minstrel and devoured his flesh. My servants heard the commotion and rushed in, but you fought them off, and they could not wake you."

"Are you saying that I *ate* Bernard?"

"Perhaps under an enchantment from that Green Man who made your minstrel so discourteous to my hospitality last night."

"You can't be serious."

"I have sworn my servants to secrecy, and we shall conceal the shame of your blood-drenched cannibalism, *if* you inform the King that you intend to remain here as my castle porter, and use your fairy magic to help the good fortune of mine estate."

Robin stared, horrified, his red-rimmed mouth hanging open. "Are you absolutely loony? How stupid do you think I am? Ate my minstrel."

"You see the proof all around you."

"Ate my minstrel in my sleep. That's really the best blackmail chit you could come up with?"

Keesh popped his head in at the door. "Sir Robin, are you awake? Oh my. Is this where they slaughtered Bernard's goat for supper?"

"He's trying to convince me that I ate Bernard in my sleep."

"Well, I suppose that would explain the mess."

"Whilst fighting off all of his servants."

"Ah. Yes, obviously that didn't happen."

Dwain came in. "Good morning, fellows. How – oh, wow. What happened here?"

"Our host told Robin that he ate Bernard in his sleep whilst fighting off a host of servants."

"Our host did all this?"

"No, Robin."

Dwain burst out laughing.

Robin turned to their host. "In all seriousness, now: where is my minstrel?"

Dwain gasped. "All this time – that's what we've been doing wrong – having him fight when he's awake!"

Xander came in, followed by Gene and Longfellow. "What is all this hullaballoo?"

"Your majesty – " said Robin.

Their host cut him off. "Your majesty, this fairy has eaten his minstrel in his sleep, and must make reparations for disgracing my castle with so infamous a deed."

Xander sighed, rolling his eyes. "Where have you put the boy?"

"Nowhere, sire. He churns in shreds in the bowels of this fiend!"

"Either you return the boy immediately, or I shall send Sir Guy of Longfellow to search him out and, I warn you, Sir Guy is not one to be careful of what he may break when charged with a mission." Xander rapped a plywood wall with his knuckles.

Their host turned his gaze to Longfellow's glare, but could not keep it there long. "My servants may know where he's got to."

"How convenient. Send them immediately. By way of reparation for this incident, it would seem seemly for you to offer us a gift as a show of your friendship. The Resurrection Cauldron would fit the bill."

"Unfortunately, your majesty, the cauldron was shattered into four pieces last night in the chaos. I fear its magic has departed. I shall see to your minstrel now." He stepped out.

"It was a fraud anyway," Gene said.

"Of course." Upon the second attempt Xander was able to set his expression. "Let us collect Bernard and continue our progress."

As they filed out, leaving Robin to wipe off the blood covering him with his bedclothes, Longfellow fell into step beside Gene, murmuring, "My lady. I trust you are well this morning."

Gene grinned. "Very. Except just here." She pointed to the top of her left breast. "It feels rather more tender than it did yesterday."

"Indeed." Longfellow matched her gaze, and very nearly smiled himself.

Dwain, walking behind them with Keesh, made kissy sounds.

Longfellow whirled, jamming his finger in Dwain's face and stopping him dead. "Any more of *that*, and I tear the lips from your face and feed them to him." Guy's finger moved to Keesh, but his glare did not.

"Okay." Dwain's lips shrank back between his teeth. Once Guy and Gene were out of earshot, he asked, "Which one of them do you think will kill the other?"

"Oh," Keesh puffed, "it's hard to say, really."

"We'll have to start a pool when we get back to Londinium."

* * *

Continuing on their way, munching goat meat sandwiches, the King and his council rode through the morning mist, as though the mountains had risen them up to a new plain and they now ventured through the clouds. Cresting a hill, they saw before them only a wall of cloud with a single opening, like a portal to another world. Beyond, a rocky mountain sloped up to the heavens.

The mist swirled even about their horses' feet, and did not thin until noonday, when they reached the flower strewn shore of a river and stopped to let their horses drink, gazing around them at the new trees and old mountains.

"There seems to be a settlement across the river." Keesh squinted, his mouth gaping and his lip drawn up so he looked like a beaver.

"Only a small one," said Robin.

"Yes, but look at the houses. They're not farmers' huts. It's as though some giant had picked up two blocks of Londinium's finest houses and dropped them here, in the middle of this wilderness."

"They're very swank houses," Dwain agreed, "and yet still built practically on top of one another in all of this space."

"Hello."

Robin screeched, jumping so high he fell out of his saddle and nearly took Bernard with him.

"You look important." A boy, about Bernard's age, had popped out of a bush and now stood gawping at them.

"That is King Xander," Keesh nodded, "and we are his Council of the Boot."

"Even him?" The boy pointed at Robin, who was scrambling to his feet.

"Unaccountably, yes," Dwain said.

"I am Sir Robin the Nervy. Bernard, come down here and give me a boost."

"Oh, you fought off the barbarians."

"Some of us more than others," Gene said.

"What are you fighting now?"

"With any luck we'll find *something*."

"Okay, I'll join you."

"The Council of the Boot is Britain's most elite fighting force," explained Xander. "A person can't simply decide to join."

"You should see me use my sling, though. I can kill anything."

"Yes, I'm sure you've killed your share of squirrels and birds, but it is a very different thing to kill a man."

"But I use brain balls. They kill anything."

"'Brain balls'?" Keesh asked.

"Of course. You take some brains – from whatever's handy – and you mix with lime to harden them, and there you have the perfect ammunition."

"Actual brains?"

"How . . . creative," said the King, "but that is artillery, and we are a cavalry unit and we must continue our journey now."

"Oh! I can be cavalry! I've got a cow I can ride."

Guy pinched the top of his nose where his brows were bunching. "Sheep, goats, cows – maybe our next recruit will be mounted on a chicken."

"But being a warrior isn't just about riding around fighting," said Dwain. "Warriors must be quite well-rounded in their accomplishments, versed in at least twelve books of poetry, able to read and write."

"And to braid hair," put in Keesh.

Longfellow looked at him as though he'd gone mad.

"Yes . . . " said Dwain. "A warrior must be able to braid his hair and be chased through a forest without being overtaken or having his hairdo disturbed, and never a stick cracking under his feet."

The boy grimaced. "But your hair is so short. How do you braid it?"

"Such is my skill. A warrior must also be able to pull a thorn from his foot whilst running and not slow his pace a jot."

"And leap over a staff held at his brow level," said Keesh, "and run at full speed under a staff held at his knee."

"Exactly. And defend himself from nine other warriors casting spears at him without being wounded – with only a hazel stick and a shield – whilst buried up to his waist in the ground."

"And take a wife with no dowry," added Keesh.

"Sure," said Dwain, Longfellow looking as though he'd have an aneurysm, "and a bunch of other criteria, but you get the idea: it's a very, very difficult field to break into."

"Yes." The boy rubbed his chin. "Who would want a wife if she didn't come with a dowry?"

Robin was frowning. "And, all of that is mandatory?"

Bernard slipped down and approached the boy. "Tell you what, you've got a cow you have no reason to ride about on, you not being a warrior, so I'll trade you for it." He reached into his purse. "These are three magic beans given to me by Mervin the Magician, of great renown."

"Really?" The boy's eyes grew wide. "Deal!" He grabbed the beans. "The cow's just over there behind those rose bushes."

Bernard went to fetch it, and off they rode.

Once they'd gone a ways, Dwain asked, "Did Mervin really give you those beans?"

"When we went to find Lady Gene, I mentioned I was hungry and Mervin gave me those three beans. Then he told me not to eat them all at once, because they were magic."

"And, knowing Mervin, you didn't want to eat them and start hiccupping badgers or something."

"I was beginning to think I'd never be able to unload them."

"Let's just hope he didn't trade you an enchanted cow."

The beam went out of Bernard's face. "I'm fed up with enchantments."

"Don't worry, maybe Mervin will be able to undo the Green Man's curse."

"Or maybe he'll fuse my lips together."

"And make you live in a thorn bush."

"Airier than the crate I was shut up in all night."

As they rode on, the council passed a mountain with the hollow of an eyeball seemingly bored into its side as though it stared them down. Just beyond this glare, as the sun reached its highest point, they reached a community of hovels rotting back into the earth.

"Looks like no lunch again today," Dwain said.

Bernard's eyes roved. "I see people moving about."

"There are actually people living here?" Robin tensed.

"I might have to live here, if the Green Man's curse can't be broken."

"Nonsense, Bernard. You have other opportunities open to you besides minstrelsing."

"And they include?"

"Well . . . ."

"Pottering," Keesh suggested.

"If I could find a supply of clay, and knew how to pot or glaze."

"Or braiding hair."

Dwain raised an eyebrow. "What did you do before becoming a

minstrel?"

"Erstwhile door-to-door salesman."

"Right. You could try that again."

"I wasn't getting repeat business."

Xander rode to the hovels crying, "Britons, come forth and see your King, who has delivered you from the blades of the barbarian hoard."

People began to emerge.

"Greetings to you all."

"Greetings," some called back.

"My knights are hungry. A hearty meal would show your gratefulness to them for your continued freedom."

A man with a red cloak stepped forwards. "Gladly, my King, though we have little to spare."

"Do you not expect a bountiful harvest soon?"

"We did, sire. Our crops are now all but ruined."

Xander frowned. "Was there some storm or pestilence?"

"No, your majesty. In fact, it was maliciously done."

"Did some band of barbarians burn your fields?"

"No, your majesty. The criminal is a most horrid mouse."

"A mouse?"

"Yes, she ate her way through most of our crops within a fortnight before we were able to capture her."

"Was she a particularly large mouse?"

"No, your majesty. In fact, she is just here." The man turned, taking a clay jar from his wife, its opening covered with a cloth tied on by a leather thong.

Robin whispered to Bernard, "See, you could learn to make jars just like that."

"It has been most difficult preventing her escape."

"I see," Xander said. "And you didn't wish to simply kill it?"

"That would have amounted to mob justice, sire, and we are a law-abiding people. Now that you are here, will you at last grant us permission to execute the criminal?"

"By all means. Once we return to Londinium, I shall see to it that you are sent sufficient provisions for the winter."

"Your majesty is most gracious." The man held out the jar.

"Go ahead and kill the mouse yourself."

"Very well. The gallows stand just at the next crossroads. Would your majesty care to watch his justice being carried out?"

"Gallows?"

"Thieves on such a scale are hanged, after all."

"And you wouldn't want to just drown the thing, or stomp on it, or feed it to a cat?"

"Hanging is what the law requires. Will your majesty not preside over the execution?"

"Of course. Let us go to the gallows. With the mouse."

Past the hovels, they saw fields with only a few stalks of grain still here and there. At the crossroads stood a platform ten feet high. The beam supported over it was long enough to host almost a dozen nooses.

The King and his council dismounted, climbing the scaffold steps with the man in the red cloak, whilst the other villagers stayed below to watch.

The man dug about in his purse. "Rope is too wide, and wouldn't fit properly around the mouse's neck. My wife has fashioned a noose from yarn."

"Excellent planning." Xander forced a smile.

"I'm sorry, sire, would you mind terribly?" The man passed over the clay jar, and set about pawing through his purse with both hands.

As he was thus rummaging, a group of half a dozen travellers happened by, pausing at the scaffold.

104

"Greetings," the lead man called to the King, who was holding the clay jar at arm's length. "Who is to be hanged?"

"A, erm, mouse, who has brought these good people to the brink of desperation by devouring their crops."

"I shall pay you forty pounds," said the man, "if you give the mouse to me."

"*Forty pounds?*" Robin echoed.

Dwain scoffed. "Are mice really so rare where you come from?"

Xander frowned. "The King's justice cannot be bought."

The travellers rode on.

The man in the red cloak pulled the yarn noose from his purse. "Here it is. Thank you, sire, I'll just fetch out the mouse . . . slip the noose around her neck . . . . "

Another group of travellers rode up, pausing before the scaffold. "Are you really going to hang that mouse? See how frightened it looks. We shall pay sixty pounds if you spare it and give it to us."

Dwain's eyebrows rose. "People travelling through here seem to be really into animal welfare."

"The King does not accept bribes!" Longfellow barked. "Away with you, before you join your precious mouse for such insinuation!"

The travellers continued along the road.

The man in the red cloak was trying to toss the end of the yarn noose up over the scaffold bar. "Rope is much easier. Doesn't blow about in a breeze. We'll be ready in a trice, just as soon – "

"Weight it with a stone." Gene rolled her eyes.

A third group of travellers approached, pausing their journey. "Look at that poor mouse, whose only crime was hunger. We shall pay a hundred pounds if – "

"Stop!" said Xander. "What is going on? Why is everyone so interested in this mouse, offering higher and higher sums than those who passed along before? Who are you people?"

"Got it." The man in the red cloak smiled at Gene. "Excellent suggestion, my lady."

"Please." The head of the travelling party dismounted. "I am an enchanter, and that mouse is my wife."

"You married a mouse?" Keesh asked.

"No, I turned my wife into a mouse."

"That's not any less odd," Dwain said.

"She was ravenous, and I thought turning her into a mouse would diminish her appetite, but the transformation only caused it to grow, and she has gorged herself on this village's crops. Please," he fixed his gaze upon Xander, "she is only so very hungry because she is with child."

"A pregnant woman cannot be executed," Xander said. "Whatever her crime, her child is innocent of it."

"Actually, in this case," said the man in the red cloak, "her crime is stealing our food, and it has gone to feed both her and her child, so —"

"And did the child within her also conspire in the plot with malice aforethought? We do not execute pregnant women!"

"Yes, sire. The gestation period of a mouse cannot be so very long."

"Then I'll turn her into an elephant!" cried the enchanter.

"Wouldn't a ravenous elephant strip the whole mountain forest?" Bernard asked.

"Being a mouse increased her appetite," Keesh said, "perhaps being an elephant would decrease it."

"That's ludicrous." Dwain squinted at the enchanter. "Did you go to magician university with a man named Mervin?"

The enchanter shrugged. "It was more of a community college."

"That explains it."

106

"Enough," said Xander. "I shall pardon your wife if you agree to repair the damage done to this village's crops, and leave them in peace from now on."

"Of course I agree, your majesty."

"And if she steals again, both of you will be held responsible."

"Yes, your majesty."

"Give him back his wife."

The man in the red cloak pursed his lips, but loosened the noose and handed the mouse to her husband.

"Oh, darling, I was worried so." The enchanter kissed her whiskered face.

Dwain winced. "So we're leaving?"

Longfellow motioned for Gene to go ahead, and they bustled down the scaffold steps.

The council continued on, stopping for badger burgers and turnip fries before reaching a dangerous pass along the mountain slopes with a sheer drop on their left. The narrow path was enclosed by a tunnel made of square wooden posts. As thick as the posts were the slats of light they let through, with a fractured view all the way down the cliffside. Red graffiti stalked them along the greying, splintering posts, foretelling doom for those who refused to turn back.

Following a bend, they spotted daylight ahead. Yet, as they neared, the glare came to silhouette a figure clad in thick furs, the sword in its hand propped upon its right shoulder.

"Finally." Gene spurred her horse ahead, stopping just inside the tunnel. "Warrior, do you dare bar our path?"

"The land beyond is wild." The warrior's voice vibrated off the wooden boards. "It is no place for young girls or old men." He nodded to Xander.

"You will respect your King!" Longfellow roared.

"This side of the Mountain Passageway there is no King but Gruffudd."

"I am the King of all Britain," said Xander.

"Britain ended on the other side of the passageway."

"No it didn't. Britain is an island. I rule the entire island. You would have to cross a sea to leave my realm."

"The passageway crosses a sea."

"No it doesn't," said Dwain.

"How would you know? You were inside it the whole time."

"Because a tunnel cannot cross a sea!" yelled Xander. "Only ships can do that."

"And birds," said Dwain.

"And gusts of wind," said Keesh.

"And butterflies!" cried Robin.

"*No*," Xander said, "butterflies cannot cross seas, and we are still in Britain. I know my own kingdom."

"If you deny Gruffudd, I am obliged to do battle with you." The warrior swung his sword out before him.

"Excellent!" Gene's sword flashed in her hand the next instant.

"Half a dozen men, and you cower behind a girl rather than fight me?"

"That's *exactly* it," Dwain said. "Cremation or burial?"

The warrior grinned. "She cannot kill me."

"Then stop prattling and face me!" Gene shouted.

"I've no wish to kill a girl."

Gene levelled her sword at his throat. "Then you will die by the hand of the King's best warrior."

He slashed.

Gene circled her blade around the arc of his and charged, plunging her sword through his neck, up to the forte. Blood burbled out, slicking her sword and caking the furs wrapped around him.

The corners of her mouth turned down in disappointment. "All that boasting, and you can't even put up a fight."

"Mercy . . . " the warrior hissed, sinking to his knees. "Finish me."

Scoffing, Gene drew her sword from his neck, raised it above her head, and swept it down to sever his head from his body. The blade sliced clean through.

Then the warrior rose to his feet, slashing at Gene again, his neck completely healed.

She leapt back, else she might have been gutted.

The King and his Council of the Boot choked back shouts of surprise. Keesh gasped. Bernard yipped. Robin shrieked.

Gene squinted at the warrior's neck as she dodged another two blows. It showed no mark, neither from the first cut, nor the second.

Blinking sharply, she bared her teeth, crying out and beating down the warrior's sword with a profusion of quick blows.

He looked for an opening to strike her, but never found one.

She hacked into his shoulder, snapping the collarbone and burying her blade deep in his chest so he gasped. "*There.*" She waggled her sword to work it out of his flesh.

The warrior gurgled, lips foaming with blood. "Finish me – " The last word had no breath behind it, and was mouthed but not heard.

Gene raised her sword above her head in both hands, pausing a moment before swinging down dead centre to cleave the man's skull. She felt the crunch and then the easy squelch, and eased the blade back up.

To leap back as the warrior nearly swung his own sword through her middle. She stumbled, throwing herself back but still feeling his blade's tip scrape her armour.

Gene toppled, rolling on the ground, kicking the warrior's shins as he lunged, to keep him back as he tried to run her through.

Longfellow dropped from his horse, but managed to plant his feet and stop himself from interfering.

Gene flailed, clawing the dirt beside her before grasping a large stone. The stone halted the warrior's blade, loosing a horrible screech. Her other hand drove her sword up into his bowels.

The warrior staggered.

Gene slid out her sword and rolled aside, back onto her feet.

The warrior stumbled, trying to catch himself using his sword as a staff, but toppling onto both knees. He shuddered in pain. "Finish me."

She lurched at him, pointing her blade at his heart.

Longfellow caught her wrist in both hands, leaning his weight in to stop the blow.

"You would interfere?" she spat.

"He is beaten. Leave him, my lady."

"I shall finish him before he pulls any more tricks."

"Yet it is always upon being dealt a second blow that he heals."

Gene froze, her gaze locked on the warrior.

"Have mercy," he choked, "the pain is such that I can hardly breathe."

"Then it should not prove long now."

"Please – "

Gene waited as his blood burbled onto the ground. "You seem to be right, Sir Guy. He cannot play his trick this time."

Longfellow's hands relaxed on her wrist. "I am pleased."

"I'm not," said Robin. "Are we supposed to stand about for the next ten minutes watching this fellow bleed out?"

"Quite right," said Xander. "Much to do yet. Gene, Sir Guy, catch us up when he's finished, would you?"

Bernard, who was trying not to see anything through his fingers splayed over his eyes, felt his cow move along with the others' horses without urging.

Dwain swallowed hard. "There's a magical ability that backfires quite badly."

Keesh nodded, a shade whiter than usual.

Robin nodded, too. "I should much prefer being able to die instantly of a single blow."

"Not to worry," Dwain said. "I'm sure you already possess that talent."

Leaving the tunnel behind, they entered a field where a lone eagle stood amidst the thorns and weeds. Beyond the field stretched a patch of uneven ground strewn with broken stones, amongst them a carved griffin, hobbled and standing a sad watch in the tangled ruins of a rose bush. An enormous wooden beam lay beyond, returning into the earth. As the knights rode past, a snake bearing a long, yellow stripe slipped out of sight beneath it.

Gene and Guy rejoined them.

"This looks recent," Dwain murmured.

"The rest of such a grand place can't have decayed so quickly," said Gene.

Longfellow eyed the remains. "Yet it's hardly overgrown. The destruction must have been thorough, as well as quick."

As they crested another ridge, the sea came into view.

"There," said Xander. "*That* is the edge of my realm. *That* is the end of Britain."

Down the beach they could hear a seagull cracking shells. Rocks like castles surged up through the sand. Whenever they stared, the tidepools stirred to life. Riding down the slope to weave amongst these stone mounds, they spied populations of barnacles with tongues that licked out rhythmically, purple-tentacled green anemones, and miniscule crabs spurting water jets many times their size. The sand path was littered with a crab's arm, a congealing jellyfish, and conical shells with vertical stripes that looked like miniature fair tents.

A youth, all arms and legs and stringy blonde hair, bounded into view atop one of the tidepool mounds. Long ribbons of every hue dangled from his neck to his thighs. "Hold there! Travellers, this is great Gruffudd's land, and you have not his permission to venture farther."

"This is Britain," said Xander, "of which I am King. If this Gruffudd claims otherwise, let him face me." He urged his horse forwards.

The youth jammed his finger at them. "*Halt!* I place you under gaysh, that you cannot invade unless you first stand on one foot and make a wreath from an oak sapling using a single hand, keeping one eye closed."

"We are *not* invading. I've told you I'm King. This is my land."

"I have placed you under a gaysh!"

"Is that like a spell?" Keesh asked. "Are you a sorcerer?"

"A man does not need to be a sorcerer to lay a gaysh."

"I've had enough of spells," Bernard murmured.

"So then what's a gaysh exactly?" Dwain asked.

The youth rolled his eyes. "A gaysh is a rule that you make up for another person and, if they break it, misfortune and death will befall them."

"But it's not a spell."

"*No.*"

"So what power causes death for the disobedient?"

"Nothing. It just happens."

"And you make up whatever rule you want, whenever you want to, and people follow it?"

"They have to. I myself am under a gaysh. I cannot eat a dog. If

I do, it will mean my death."

"If its owner catches you."

"Is this something you were doing often?" Keesh asked. "Eating dogs?"

"I've got it," cried Robin, "teamwork!"

"What?" Guy squinted.

"That's how we solve the riddle. You didn't count on Sir Robin the Forward, did you, my lad? Why, if we each only use one hand to make the wreath, we'll still have seven hands. It'll be easy if we work together."

Guy gritted his teeth. "We're not making a bloody wreath."

"But the misfortune and death – "

"The boy is a lunatic, you ninny."

"Enough of this," said Xander. "Boy, where is Gruffudd?"

"He resides father up the shore, but he cannot be killed by the likes of you."

"We shall see about that."

The youth threw back his head and choked out a laugh. "Gruffudd can kill with an angry look from his dreadful eyes. Long has he used this power to rule his land. There is only one way he can be killed, and you will never discover it."

"Really?" said Dwain. "Then we place you under gaysh to tell us what it is."

The youth's jaw dropped. "Curse you! Forced into betraying my lord." He pressed the heels of his hands to his forehead. "Gruffudd can only be killed by a spear one year in the making, and formed only during the Sacrifice of the Host on Sundays."

"Is there a spear like that already available?" Keesh asked.

"I'm sure they're a dime a dozen in this part of the country," Dwain said.

"Even armed with such a spear," the youth continued, "Gruffudd cannot be slain in or out of a house, on horse or on foot."

Bernard looked heavenward. "What about on cow?"

"Or laying down?" Robin suggested.

"But, neither in nor out of a house," said Keesh, "does that mean in the doorway of one?"

"Is being in a barn considered being in a house?" Dwain asked. "Or out of one, technically?"

"Wait, does Gruffudd have to be neither in or out, or his slayer, or both?"

The youth shook his head. "Gruffudd can only be killed if he has one foot on a dead buck, the other foot in a cauldron used as a bath and with a thatched roof – and then only if the strike of the spear is a good one."

Dwain squinted. "But the cauldron would still technically be out of a house, though."

"It doesn't matter!" Longfellow spat. "Who stands with one foot on a dead buck, and the other in a cauldron, especially when they know that is the only position in which they can be killed?!"

"No one," said Gene. "Gruffudd just wants people to believe that he can do as he likes, and cannot be killed."

"*Exactly.*"

"But anyone can be killed, and I should quite like to have a go at this man."

"Really?" said Dwain. "You've already battled a man this morning."

"And now I'm going to fight another." Gene spurred her horse.

Xander did the same. "Come, men."

"I've decided who I'm betting on," Dwain murmured to Keesh. "She's definitely going to kill Longfellow."

The youth stuck out his tongue as they rode past.

Sir Guy's hands shot out, grabbing him by the back of the neck, severing the tongue's tip, and dumping the youth onto the sand almost all in one motion.

Keesh hemmed. "I'll take that bet."

"Excellent. Maybe we can get them to take out Robin whilst they're at it. That way, everybody wins."

***

The waves that reached the shore were bubbling with foam. Paths rippled through the water, and the council felt warm wind pressing them all over, even through their armour, now they rode close to the sea. The rocky castle vanished behind them, and they passed a single tidepool in the wet sand, containing only dead seaweed and the stink of it.

After nearly a mile they came upon a sandcastle the size of a castle, out of reach of the tides. On its side in letters made from hundreds of sea shells was spelled "GRUFFUDD."

Dwain raised his eyebrows. "Looks like we've arrived."

"We can just charge through the wall," Longfellow said.

"I wonder what they do when it rains."

"Let's ask them." Longfellow slung his shield around from his back.

"Indeed," Xander said. "Charge!"

The charge that took place was rather less dignified than those involved would have generally preferred. The wall of sand crumbled slowly, sliding down into their armour and engulfing their horses' hooves in more of a drawn-out process of wading than a spectacular bursting through. In the end, the horses slogged over the slowly collapsing wall as much as they pressed through it.

This breech of the curtain wall triggered no response. The knights looked about. In the courtyard's centre loomed a squat *papier-mâché* volcano the size of a keep, with red madder dye spilled down its sides to imitate lava. Around the inside of the curtain wall crouched lean-tos and tents, as well as a deep-bellied ship with pairs of animal statues lining its gangplank.

"Dwain, you and Keesh go see if anyone is inside that replica of Noah's Ark," said Xander. "The rest of you, keep your eyes open as we advance on that volcano."

Dwain turned his horse, murmuring, "There are some weird people living on this island."

Passing a tent, Longfellow used his sword tip to lift the flap and peer in.

"Any signs of men-at-arms?" Gene half whispered.

Longfellow let the flap fall closed. "No, it's full of frogs."

Robin cocked his head. "They're being awfully quiet."

"Frog figurines."

Xander paused at the opening of another tent. "Apparently this Gruffudd has quite a liking for frog figurines."

"We ought to smash them," Gene said, ducking to spy inside a lean-to with its door ajar.

"Why?"

"Because no one should be subjected to the sight of thousands of ceramic frogs wearing overalls and straw hats, smoking pipes, and nuzzling bunches of flowers."

Bernard was leaning as far left as possible without toppling to the ground. "This barrel is entirely full of broken or blunted quill pens."

Robin sniffed. "All just plain goose quills. Not even nice ones like peacock or golden eagle."

Bernard kept leaning. "This one is full of used napkins. This has a few dozen identical plungers. And . . . this one is overflowing with butter packets."

"Perhaps all the men-at-arms have dropped dead of botulism, then," Longfellow grumbled.

"Oh look," Robin pointed, "a tiny frog with a lute. He looks just like you, Bernard."

Dwain and Keesh rejoined them.

"Was anyone aboard the ark?" Xander asked.

"There was a banqueting table inside that spanned the length of the ship," Dwain said. "Hundreds of dolls were sitting along it, and it was set up for a tea party."

"We also saw a tree," Keesh said, "decorated with forty-seven bells. A sign said that each bell represented an historic day in Gruffudd's life."

"Such as?" Xander asked.

"The sign didn't elaborate, sire."

Dwain twitched. "Probably the number of victims lured to a doll tea party, and then murdered in the bowels of that ship."

"Have you noticed the frogs?" Bernard asked.

They reached the volcano's base, a ledge winding up its side to a doorway.

"Another sign," said Keesh. "'Vesuvius.'"

Xander spurred his mount up the ramp, the Council of the Boot following after. At the door he reared his horse to kick, and they found themselves in an enormous banqueting hall decorated with Grecian pillars, Roman mosaics, and thousands of sea shells plastered to the walls, floor, ceiling, and furniture.

A squat man in sandals and a toga came scampering up to them. "May I know the name your reservation is under?"

"I am Xander, King of Britain."

"I'm sorry, sir, but I don't believe we have a reservation under that name. Perhaps you used a different one when you booked?"

"People book banquets here?" Keesh asked.

"Oh yes. For weddings, anniversaries, graduations. Gruffudd has created a wonderful fantasy world here for people."

"You do realize," said Dwain, "that when the real Vesuvius erupted it killed thousands upon thousands of terrified people, including children, wiping out entire cities."

"Well, yes, but I didn't know any of them personally."

"At these banquets," Bernard persisted, "do you serve people the butter packets sitting in that barrel outside?"

The man gasped. "Of course not! Those are part of Gruffudd's collection. It has taken him years to amass such an array. Care has gone into the acquisition of every last one."

"Of the broken goose quills?"

"Where is Gruffudd?" Xander interrupted. "Take us to him."

"Oh he's far too busy for guests, sir. You can sort out your reservation with me."

"This isn't about any reservation! I demand to know where he is."

"I do apologize, sir, but he really is far too busy."

"Doing what?"

"Napping."

"Napping?"

"Yes, sir. Gruffudd has ruled this country since time immemorial. He's quite old, needs his rest."

"This country is Britain, and he hasn't ruled anything, certainly not since time immemorial. He is an ordinary man – a very strange man, if his frog figurines are anything to judge by – but a mortal man nonetheless."

"A giant of a man."

"Figuratively?" Dwain asked. "Or physically?"

"Both, surely. He is easily twice the size of other men, and not ordinary at all – have you heard how he can kill with an angry look? Old age has not diminished this ability, though his eyelids droop now, so that men using ropes and pulleys must lift them."

Gene groaned. "He can't even open his *eyes?*"

"Once they are opened, he's as lethal as ever. All hail Gruffudd."

"Where *is* he?" said Xander.

"He really cannot be disturbed." The man's eyes flicked upwards.

"Where is the turret?"

"This is a volcano. There are no turrets."

"The floor slopes up as it goes farther back," Longfellow said.

"Oh – "

They set off, reaching the rear of the banqueting hall elevated a good twelve feet higher. Turning back the way they came, they saw two concealed ramps folding back along the walls, leading even farther up. The man had vanished. Xander led them single file, with no room to ride abreast. The volcano's curves played with their vision, so it was not apparent they had passed into the second level until they again reached the volcano's front, the ramp met its mate, and turning back they observed a chamber drenched in mosaic tiles that, though cavernous, held only half the area of the one below. Light poured in from the volcano mouth storeys above, tinted the otherworldly pink of the sky before a storm. At the far end sat a throne and an old man sleeping upon it. There was no way of telling how much a giant he was until half a dozen other men popped out, seemingly from nowhere, scrambling about pulling ropes rigged to the throne's canopy.

"That unseasonably dressed fellow was right before," said Keesh, "Gruffudd does appear roughly twice the size of an ordinary man, if those are ordinary-sized men, though his head appears rather, erm – "

"Bulbous." Dwain cocked his own. "At least twice as big as it should be, whilst already being twice as big."

Robin eased his horse a couple steps back down the ramp.

"Ought we to be at all concerned that those potentially ordinary-sized men seem to be lifting Gruffudd's eyelids so he can glare us to death?"

Gene slammed her sword pommel into the wall so this shed a handful of mosaic tiles. Sheathing her sword again, she wrenched off one of the now loose tiles. "Let's see how deadly his eyes are, then."

The creak of pulleys jagged through the chamber. The potentially ordinary-sized men contorted their backs hauling ropes attached to enormous, rust-crusted hooks snagged under Gruffudd's upper eyelids.

"There are so many of us, perhaps we ought to try flanking him." Robin backed his horse farther down the ramp.

Keesh lowered his visor.

Xander removed his helmet. "I am Xander, King of the Britons, and of this land. Gruffudd, you will kneel and pay homage."

They could see the eyelids parting, and all that bulged behind them was a greyish white haze.

Robin flinched, trying to hunch behind his horse's head.

Gruffudd's eyes opened fully, empty orbs. Then the pupils rolled down into view.

"Eeep!"

Gene let fly the razor-sharp tile.

It lodged in Gruffudd's left eye and seemed to slowly lose its hue. It was sinking, deeper until it reached and penetrated his brain.

Gene wiped the mosaic dust off her hand on her horse's neck. "So much for that."

The potentially ordinary-sized men were crying out in dismay and scattering.

"Cleanly done," spake Longfellow. He sounded almost disappointed.

120

Gene did sound disappointed when she replied, "Yes, very clean."

"Nevertheless," Longfellow lowered his voice, "my heart is at your mercy, Lady Gene."

She smiled quietly.

"We've made as much progress as we can," Xander said. "It's time we turn back for Londinium."

***

They camped the night in the tunnel, listening to the rain that started the process of dissolving Gruffudd's castle on the beach now no one was left to defend it, even from the elements. The morning brought a cream yellow sunrise that yielded to a robin's egg sky, tinging pink and orange over the darkened forest. The trees greened and then faded in the daylight. As the mist was clearing, they reached the river amidst the mountains again, where Bernard had obtained his cow.

Whilst the horses – and cow – were drinking their fill, Sir Robin craned his neck upwards and asked, "Was that beanstalk here before? I don't remember it."

Bernard's jaw dropped open. The beanstalk stood as wide around as the Roundish Table, stretching up into the clouds.

"Looks like that boy planted those beans you traded him," Dwain said. "Good thing you didn't eat them."

Gene humphed. "They must have been leftovers from Mervin's attempts at a spell to solve world hunger."

Xander nodded. "A noble goal."

"This beanstalk may have grown ten thousand feet high," Longfellow said, "yet it hasn't any actual *beans*."

Gene frowned. "It has leaves. People can eat salad, can't they?"

The boy who had traded his cow for Bernard's beans came scampering up. "Good, you're here. I want to switch back. My mother was very upset about the beans. She threw them out the window."

"No refunds," Bernard said.

"Everyone's upset with me. They say the beanstalk is ruining the village. It's unsightly, the roots are cracking people's foundations, and the giant keeps threatening to eat everyone."

"Giant? What giant?"

"The one that lives at the top of the beanstalk."

Dwain craned his neck. "How did he build a treehouse all the way up there?"

"Not a treehouse. He lives in the clouds."

"Wouldn't a giant fall through a cloud?" Robin asked.

Dwain stared. "Wouldn't anyone?"

Gene shrugged. "It wouldn't be so different from living in a puff of smoke."

"But the cloud is hovering ten thousand feet up. There's nothing to stand on. And it would rain itself out eventually."

"I've climbed up there," said the boy. "It's quite nice."

"See?" Gene said.

"Like a fluffy castle."

"Much better than a blooming whitethorn bush."

"Except the giant keeps threatening to eat everyone."

"Why?" Longfellow asked. "Britons can't be his natural food if he lives up in a cloud."

"It gets pretty foggy." Dwain pulled a face. "Perhaps his cloud drifts down periodically."

"Well," said the boy, "the giant only started threatening to eat people after I stole his goose that lays golden eggs."

"Have you considered, oh I don't know, giving it back?"

"Of course not."

"Ah."

"Are there baby geese inside the golden eggs?" Keesh asked. "Or are the eggs solid gold?"

The boy started. "I *hope* they're solid."

Xander cleared his throat. "What does your mother say about returning the goose?"

"Oh, the giant already ate her. But you're here now. With all the wonderful things you knights can do, running and jumping and braiding hair, you must be able to kill the giant."

"*Where* is this giant now?" Robin seemed to shrink as his eyes darted about.

"Up in his cloud castle."

"So," said Dwain, "why don't you just chop down the beanstalk?"

"He has a lot of nice stuff up there. On my second trip I snagged a singing harp."

"More stealing. Well, that seems worth the lives of innocent people."

"The giant is responsible for his own actions."

"So let's kill him," Gene said.

"Young man," Robin sidled up to the boy, "you mentioned a singing harp. Tell me, Sir Robin the Forthright, the very truth: is it better or worse than a minstrel, would you say?"

Bernard looked stricken.

Dwain joined his thumb and index finger in a loop. "Classy."

"Right," said Xander, "here's what's going to happen. That goose is now the property of the whole village. Its golden eggs are to be distributed to all residents as compensation for the loss of their crops, property, and loved ones. This beanstalk is coming down. We are not killing the giant in retribution – he doesn't live in Britain so he isn't subject to our justice. As long as he refrains from invading again, further violence is unnecessary. Knights – and Gene – chop down the beanstalk."

Robin eyed the thick stem. "Couldn't we just set fire to it?"

"And have burning hunks and leaves falling through the fields and forest?" Dwain asked.

"At least the smoke might asphyxiate the giant," Gene murmured.

"To be perfectly clear," said Xander, "be sure the beanstalk topples *away* from the village. Get chopping."

They leapt down, drawing their swords.

The boy stood beside Bernard, twiddling back and forth on his toes. "You're a minstrel?"

"I suppose."

"So you could teach me to play the singing harp."

"As long as it's not fundamentally different from a non-singing harp, and for a fee."

"Golden egg?"

"Done. Fetch the harp."

The boy scampered off and returned with a harp no bigger than the belly of a lute. Even its strings were of gold. And attached by her back like a maiden to a ship stood a golden woman, her head slightly bowed and her hands clasped down in front of her. Bernard stroked the strings and the harp sang:

"Oh my darlin',
Kiss me, kiss me,
Black-haired boy, I –
Am talking to you.
You need to kiss me.
Just pucker and kiss me.
Black-haired boy, I am
Talking to you."

Bernard blinked. "Does it always sing those words?"

"It sings whatever words it wants generally. How did you play that tune?"

Bernard stared at the harp. "I – erm – " He ducked, kissing the golden tresses of the golden head. "Let's try a simple tune first. Watch my fingers now.

"Maistres Heldris de Cornuälle
Escrist ces viers trestolt a talle.
A çals quis unt conmande et rueve
El commencier dé suns qu'il trouve
Que cil quis avra ains les arge
Que il a tels gens les esparge
Que quant il oënt un bon conte
Ne sevent preu a quoi il monte."

Bernard grinned. "Did you hear that? I sang along."

"Yes, but I don't want to duet. I just want to play."

"I didn't spout nonsense words or stick my fingers in my mouth or anything."

"It sounded like nonsense words."

"It was French."

"It sounded like nonsense words."

"This harp has cured me of the Green Man's curse!"

"If my harp's cured you, I don't think I owe you a golden egg."

Bernard opened his mouth to argue.

"Whoopsie!" Sir Robin's sword went sailing through the air. "Lost my grip."

Dwain straightened from ducking. "Yet another 'shining armour' moment."

"Find a blasted axe," Longfellow shouted, "if you can't hang onto a sword!"

"One with double-sided tape on the grip."

"We're nearly there, aren't we?" Keesh asked.

"Very nearly." Gene hacked one last blow.

A crack reverberated up through the beanstalk. It towered shaking for nearly a minute before starting to lean.

The beanstalk toppled, not into the village or the crop fields, but into the road, flattening Bernard's cow with a rumble that threatened to shake down the mountains themselves.

Xander raised his eyebrows. "Now we'll need a tunnel through the stem for traffic to pass. Let's get to it. There's no rest for Britain's heroes. And someone lash Sir Robin the Bold's sword to his wrist this time. Bernard, do play us a tune."

"My pleasure, sire." Bernard took a deep breath.

The Quest for the Slowly Mail

There are men who get married in tuxedos, and men who get married in suits. Guy Longfellow belonged in the latter category. He was married in a full twenty-four-piece suit of armour. It might have looked rather ridiculous, except for the fact that the bride was dressed almost identically. And there was no more touching moment in the ceremony than at the end when the two raised their visors and kissed.

The grand but dilapidated hall at King Xander's castle in Londinium hosted the reception. Present were Gene's uncle, Mervin the Magician; the Queen Mother, Amanita; and the other three Knights of the Roundish Table. Said table was at present employed as a stage for Bernard the minstrel, who had taken it upon himself to provide music for the occasion. His performance was cut short when the newlyweds began throwing things at him, including goblets, bits of turnip, and a live wombat.

Sir Dwain sat beside his King, watching Guy and Gene engaged in a beautifully choreographed swordfight. The long, pointed toes of their sabatons had been swapped out for short, rounded ones, as their footwork took them all over the dancefloor.

"They'll just tire themselves out doing that."

Xander's mind had been focused on quite a different matter. "Hardly anyone attended the ceremony."

"It's not surprising, sire. Mervin is the only family either of them has. They're both so callous neither have any friends. The only reason I'm here is because there's a betting pool to see how long it takes for one of them to behead the other."

"They must have mailed out invitations. People just didn't get them in time. The post office is to blame for this."

Dwain sensed danger. "Sire, you're not going to get carried away, are you?"

"Monarchs never get carried away."

Dwain raised an eyebrow in disagreement, but kept his peace. Perhaps monarchs only got carried away because no one dared to say outright that their plans were outlandish.

✳✳✳

Guy and Gene's wedding night was magical. They left the hall, hurrying to their chamber. The massive bed was hung around with heavy scarlet brocade. They stayed awake until dawn, trying in vain to unlace and unbuckle all their bits of armour by candlelight.

The only person to actually experience the magicalness of the night was King Xander. At four thirty in the morning, the King sat bolt upright in bed. He summoned a servant, and demanded in no uncertain terms that the Council of the Boot assemble at the Roundish Table. He also garbled something about a grand journey and a glass of milk, but Xander was yet half asleep, and prone to muttering about some glorious deed or knickknack.

The King arrived at the Roundish Table clothed in elegant silken moccasins, and a purple robe with tiny crowns embroidered in gold thread. The others fell short of such sleekness.

Guy and Gene were still sporting scraps of metal over their arming doublets, not having managed to entirely undress yet. Sir Robin the Bold was wearing footsie pajamas with cheerful yellow duckies on them, so that Dwain, Keesh, and even his minstrel Bernard could not forebear chuckling. Then laughing loudly. And then nearly falling out of their chairs with mirth. All this silenced when the King entered the room.

"Men, I have called you here for a very important reason."

"Um, sire."

"Yes, Sir Keesh, what is it *you* have to say. Heaven knows we're all up at this hour to listen to *you*."

"Sorry. I only thought it right to point out that Gene is an honourary member of your illustrious council, and she isn't a man."

"She might be," Dwain mused, "even Longfellow can't say for sure yet."

Sir Guy lurched forwards, nearly sailing over the table at Dwain. "Another remark like that, and I'll rip open the veins of your scrawny neck with my bare hands!"

"Not here, I hope." Xander frowned. "It's difficult to get blood stains out of a wooden table, or so the servants keep telling me. Maybe if they put a bit more effort into the job . . . . "

"I don't mind being called a man," Gene interrupted. "Someone wake Sir Robin, and let's hear the news."

Bernard elbowed his patron, whose only response was to gurgle. A second attempt brought the same result.

"Oh, let me." Sir Guy pushed back his chair, strode over to slumbering Robin, and slapped the back of the latter's head with all his might.

"*Aaah!*"

"Now then," Xander puffed out his chest as Guy returned to his seat, "I have a most exciting announcement to make: I have had a vision."

"You mean a dream?" Dwain asked.

"No, a vision."

"I was having a vision about tanning on a beach when I was summoned."

"Mine had a singing carrot," said Keesh.

"Shut up! Lowly knights may dream dreams, but Kings have visions."

"I got seasick in mine," Robin twittered drowsily.

"Why haven't I had all of your tongues cut out? – In my vision I was charged to take on a quest, and you are all going to accompany me."

"To the ends of the earth, sire," called Longfellow.

"Suck up," Dwain mumbled.

"Our task shall be known henceforth as the Quest for the Slowly Mail."

Dwain sighed. "Majesty, dreams are only accumulations of what has happened during the day, bits of stuff knocking about in your brain. When you mentioned mail to me earlier – "

"Precisely, I was onto something. We shall sally forth and do battle with the postal system."

"Speaking of postal – "

"I think it's a wonderful idea, your majesty." Robin had perked up a bit now. "My latest sweepstakes letter is taking forever to get here."

"I'd like to check my bank statement," Bernard agreed.

"I always wait an age for my monthly issues of *Stone Cottage Digest* to arrive," said Keesh.

Dwain shook his head in dismay. "Not you, too."

"We shall set out as soon as sufficient supplies are gathered. Prepare yourselves, men."

They all bowed as King Xander effected his exit.

Dwain glanced at Longfellow. "How strange for a knight to care so much when one calls his wife a man, and so little when a second repeats it."

"Look to yourself on this journey. You won't have me there to save you, and I doubt Sir Robin or de Lattice will be of much help."

Keesh squinted, unaccustomed to being lumped into an insult meant for Robin, or a threat meant for Dwain.

The newlyweds, quite fed up with plate armour, went off to

change into leather and mail.

"I don't know which is worse," Dwain confided to Keesh as they made their way back to their rooms, "being forced to risk our lives on some goofy, pointless quest, or being present on Guy Longfellow's honeymoon."

"I think it's romantic. When I get married, I want to travel."

"And I'd rather be a comedian than a knight, but we can't all have what we want."

"Yes, just the King, I suppose."

"The more you have, the more you want."

Keesh sighed. "I want a life of peace."

"I'd settle for breakfast. Do you think the kitchen servants are up yet?"

"I should hope so."

***

"We really ought to do this more often."

"Oh, shut up, Robin."

"What? We hardly ever get to ride in formation anymore, and the scenery is quite lovely."

Dwain pulled a leftover breakfast roll out of a satchel and hurled it at the bold knight's head.

Sir Robin coloured. "Bernard," he ordered, "give me something to throw back at Sir Dwain."

"I'm sorry, sir, but I really should concentrate on steering. Horses are easier to control, or so I've heard."

"Stop complaining so much. Horses are for knights, and you're just a minstrel. You're lucky I let you ride a pig."

"But my feet drag on the ground."

"Put them in the stirrups."

"Then my knees are up by my ears."

Sir Robin sighed. "It's always something with you, isn't it?"

"I've decided to keep a travel journal," Keesh announced. "Every time we stop to rest the horses, I shall pluck some flower or leaf. This way we shall always remember our quest."

"No need to trouble ourselves," said the King. "Why, they will be composing all manner of heroic epics to commemorate our brave deeds. We shall go down in history for this."

"Yes, sire, but I like to give things a personal touch."

"Time for some travel music!" cried Robin. "Bernard!"

The minstrel, having given up trying to ride the pig and now waddling along with his feet either side of it, had his hands free so he could favour them with the following ballad entitled *King Arthur's Feast*:

"King Arthur's men are very fine,
And likewise is the way they dine.
Pasties of veal with sweet wine,
The best that cometh from the vine.

"A rich meal before them is spread,
With cheese and pie and mounds of bread.
Baker and cook stand nearby.
The h'r of eating now is nigh.

"Knights sit along the wooden board.
Each one of them is strong of sword:
Lancelot, Tristram, and Kay,
And Keith, Gawaine, all blithe and gay.

"The first course soon is passed full 'round.
All food is served both fresh and sound.
Tarts are there and suckling pig,

Sweetmeats and apples green and big.

"Then suddenly King Arthur shouts.
To him now all men turn about.
Heavy a frown on his face –
Such makes the hearts of all knights race.

"'Where is my salad?!' cries the King.
All corners of the hall do ring.
'Fetch me the cook, haul him here!'
They rise to do his will with fear.

"The cook is brought before Arthur.
His body trembles much sharper,
Paling his face with his fear,
Aware what he is soon to hear.

"'I want a salad,' the King moans,
'Why have you no green herbs here grown?'
'Majesty . . . ' the cook's voice broke.
He is afraid that he will choke.

"In darts the kitchen maid full fast.
She runs into the hall aghast.
'Here is your salad, oh King.
There be no need for a hanging.'

"King Arthur merry is again,
And also are his fellow men,
Laughing and feasting with might,
So glad all is now sooth and right."

"Who is this King Arthur person?" Xander asked.

Bernard shrugged. "I just made him up."

"What a ridiculous name. And those knights you listed – who would ever name a child Keith?"

"I never would," said Keesh. "But isn't that story basically what happened at our feast last week, when the cook forgot to send up the rutabaga stroganoff, and – "

Dwain decided to change the subject. "How long until we get there, majesty?"

"Get where?"

"The central post office."

"Oh, that. Not until we have forged across mighty rivers, navigated through impenetrable forests, and cheated death over mountainous terrain."

Dwain sighed. "You have no idea where it is, do you?"

"I figured we'd have some perilous, spinetingling adventures for a few years, and bump into it eventually."

"Or we could stop and ask for directions."

"Kings don't ask for directions. People need to have confidence in our infallibility as leaders."

"But a lowly knight could ask for directions."

"Don't be silly. He must demand! never acknowledging he is inferior in any way."

"Fine."

"Longfellow may do it. He knows how to handle these sorts of things."

***

The peasant recoiled in fright from the towering black warhorse: its foaming jaws, hot breath, and eyes twisted back in its skull. The beast reared and stamped. Sweat spilled down its flanks.

What caused a thrill of pure fear to jolt through the peasant – even to his fingers and toes – and made his organs shrivel and tremble, was the warrior mounted on this brute. He was over six feet tall, and controlled his beast with a single hand. The other grasped the hilt of a long blade strapped to his side. The tensed muscles of his face drew his skin tight against the bone. Worst of all were his eyes, filled half with hate, half indifference.

"You, peasant, where is the central post office?"

"Back that way, sir. It's by the King's castle, along with all the other important government services."

"Blast it!"

"Did you not know that, sir?" The peasant peeked up at Longfellow through his eyelashes.

"Of course, you bloody nit. I was only testing you. Now get back to work." Sir Guy dug his heels into the stallion's sides and away they charged.

***

"Do we really have to ride all the way back?" Robin asked, hearing the news. "I think I'm getting hemorrhoids."

Dwain recoiled. "Ugh. Thanks for sharing."

"We must return with all speed," proclaimed the King. "Our duty is a sacred one, and vitally important to ensure the continuation of the human race."

"Which duty was that, again?"

"We could take the ferry," Gene suggested. "'Twould be a more direct route."

Keesh frowned. "I thought the only ferry went to Avalon."

"They want to expand. There are more pilgrimages to Londinium."

Dwain shrugged. "Sounds alright to me. Where do we catch this ferry?"

"Right over there." Gene pointed.

A boat was sailing gently towards shore. Onboard stood an unmoving captain, but no crew.

"Creepy," Dwain observed.

"I heard they're controlled by radios," Bernard murmured, lest the sound of his voice should break the spell. "Or possibly hypnosis."

"Come, men. We must continue with our quest. Let us board the ferry."

"Shotgun!" Dwain called.

It was a smooth, relaxing ride back to Londinium. The only sounds were the warm wind filling the sails, and Sir Robin the Bold heaving his breakfast over the gunwale.

✳✳✳

The ferry couldn't take them quite all the way to Londinium, however. Instead it sank.

Fortunately their horses, and Bernard's pig, could swim.

Once ashore, Robin sat fanning his legs with his hands. "Bernard, my greaves are soaked. Blow them dry before they rust."

The young minstrel sank slowly to his knees as though through quicksand.

"This is intolerable!" cried Xander as their mounts waded in. "Britons already can't hold faith in their postal service, and now public transportation is nosediving!"

"To be fair," said Dwain, "the ferry sinking wasn't the captain's fault."

"You're saying this country's safety inspectors are also incompetent?"

"No, rather I'm saying that our national security could be

better."

"But we're our national security," said Gene. "We didn't plunge a hole in the ferry, even if that captain deserved it, saying we were over the weight limit. We're in prime physical condition – and so are our horses and armour, though maybe not Bernard's pig – he doesn't know what he's talking about."

Keesh looked around. "Did anyone remember to save the captain from drowning, by the way?"

"Don't you remember," Dwain said, "after we repelled the barbarians, when we were trying to implement measures to keep the kingdom secure . . . and one of those measures was installing spikes in the rivers leading into Londinium, to scuttle any ships that might try to invade?"

Longfellow shrugged. "At least it's working."

"And his majesty insisted the spikes be installed at night, and kept strictly secret."

Xander frowned. "For the sake of national security."

"Exactly."

"Are you suggesting that a country's problems stem from faults in its leadership?"

"I'm suggesting they can do."

Robin frowned. "But we're out here travelling in an enormous circle because the King had a vision in his sleep – how can you find any fault with that?"

"Well, you would think that the location of a government institution would be known to the head of government, and that decisions would be based on facts and the needs of the people rather than impulse and circular reasoning that – "

Xander's brow blackened, and the veins stabbing through his eyeballs swelled red with blood, glaring at Dwain.

"You know," Dwain swallowed several times, feeling as though his stomach had turned to moths trying to flutter up his throat, "talking doesn't solve anything. Let's get moving. I'm pretty sure Londinium's that way. Last one there's a rotten egg." He urged his horse into a canter.

***

"At last." Xander's cheeks shimmered with tears, dismounting outside Britain's central post office. "After all we've endured, our quest is nearly complete."

Dwain nodded. "We should get home before dinner if all goes well. All in all, this hasn't been the worst quest we've ever attempted."

The King drew his massive sword, knelt down, and uttered a prayer of thanksgiving and hope of victory. The others joined him in the amen. Then they all drew their swords and strode into the post office. Bernard remained outside with their mounts, whistling as he maneuvered to keep from getting crushed between the horses or tripped up by the pig.

"Service!" cried the King. "I demand service!"

The clerk behind the counter peered over at them. "I'm sorry, sir," he said at last, "but you're going to have to wait in line like everybody else."

Xander eyed the occupants of said line with keenest distaste. There were shepherds caked in mud, blacksmiths with ashen fingernails, and fullers with urine-soaked feet. And even all of these gave the tanners a wide berth.

"Kings don't wait in lines."

Longfellow sneered. "Neither do knights."

"Robin, tell Bernard to come in and wait."

"So this stench can rub off on my minstrel? I have to take him home with me, you know. He's rather grown to expect it."

"Any suggestions, then?"

Gene shrugged. "Well, we could hack everyone ahead of us in line to tiny bits."

Something almost like a smile flitted across Guy Longfellow's face and, for a moment, his eyes held an ounce of admiration. It was a look that said, "This is why I married you."

"But I just had my sword polished," Keesh whined. "It cost a mint, but look how shiny."

"You know, sire," Dwain ventured, "I bet, if you told them you were the King, they'd help us right away."

Xander nodded. "Yes. There is always that. Gene, we'll call yours plan B."

In the event, plan A was a rousing success. They were escorted into the office of the head letter carrier.

"How can I help you today, your majesty?"

"Your immediate resignation will make a good start."

The man was taken aback. "Your majesty?"

"This post office is a disgrace. All letters arrive woefully late. Your inaction detrimentally impacts two million people. Why, hardly anyone attended the wedding of my best knight and my secret weapon – all because the invitations weren't delivered in time."

Longfellow blinked. "Um, what?"

"Don't worry, you'll have your revenge." Xander gave him an encouraging slap on the back. "Boil him in a cauldron, break his limbs and weave him through a wagon wheel – whatever you like."

"That's what this has all been about?" Gene asked.

"Yes – justice!"

"Sire," Sir Guy actually winced, "we never mailed any invitations."

"What was that?"

"Well, we don't really enjoy anyone's company. Neither of us is what you'd tend to call 'friendship material.' Besides, everyone seems afraid of us, and we really rather prefer it that way."

Xander bit his nether lip. "I see."

"But what about my issues of *Stone Cottage Digest?*" Keesh asked.

The King took courage and turned back to the grand pooh-bah of the post office. "Indeed."

The man shrugged. "I'm sorry, sir knight, but I don't believe there is a magazine by that name."

Keesh took a moment to mull over this new information. "Come to think of it, that subscription sales boy did seem a tad shifty. He laughed altogether too maniacally when I gave him the money for my five hundred introductory issues."

"But," Xander stammered, "Bernard's bank statement?"

Sir Robin laughed. "The cute little bugger certainly hasn't enough to open a bank account. I should know – I'm the one who's supposed to be paying him. Though I would like to know why my sweepstakes letter hasn't arrived."

The head letter carrier shrugged again. "It's the sixth century. We're not even supposed to have a post office yet. Or knights. Or a united kingdom with only one man ruling over it."

"Someone obviously hasn't read Geoffrey of Monmouth." Dwain grinned.

Xander held his head in his hands. "How could this have gone so terribly wrong? I had a vision."

"Looks like Robin's the one who has visions." Dwain's grin grew still wider. "He dreamt he was going to be seasick and then he was."

"That's right!" The King's face was aglow. "Sir Robin, you are now my chief councillor. Tell what you have seen in your sleep every night, and that will dictate what we do during the day."

Dwain's grin dissolved instantly. "Your majesty – "

"Well," Robin considered, "I did have a dream that the rest of you were feeding me chocolates."

"I am not – "

"Except Sir Dwain. He was massaging my feet with exotic lotions."

Xander made for the doorway. "Come, my men. We obviously have much work ahead of us."

Guy and Gene had already slipped out of the room ahead of them.

Dwain exchanged a mortified glance with Keesh. "You understand now why I prefer to be a mere comedian?"

"If I don't, I soon will."

"I should take Bernard with me, spare him this."

Keesh shrugged. "At least your hands will smell nice."

"Should we feign disease or insanity?"

"Perhaps death this time."

Dwain trudged out of the post office and mounted his horse. "And so ends the glorious journey of King Xander and his Knights of the Roundish Table. Henceforth and forever to be known as the Quest for the Slowly Mail."

La Morted Xander

Then it was that King Xander, accompanied by the noble members of his Council of the Boot – and Sir Robin – went aquesting across the wildlands of Britain, there not being anything good on TV that week. Thus, they entered the bramble forests that grew amongst the misty hills of . . . oh gosh, how do you pronounce that? Anyway, they were riding through the trees when –

The horses reared, flinging their heads. Like fish in the bottom of a boat.

"Whoa!"

"Steady."

"Stupid horse – only people walk on two feet!"

Xander, being King, was the first able to calm his mount, through the sheer force of his regality, which only took about a quarter of an hour. "What was that noise that spooked them? It sounded as though the heavens themselves were crashing to earth, whilst dynamiting a drumset."

"Oh, excuse me."

Everyone glanced backwards.

Mervin the Magician sat amidst a patch of ferns, patting his belly. "Too much haddock soft drink at lunch."

"Galloping wombats, where did you come from?"

"The park, I think." Mervin's fingers tangled in his beard. "How did I get here?"

"That's what I'm asking you!"

By now Gene and the knights had settled their horses.

"Well, let's see. I had forty-seven haddock soft drinks, an eel pie, blood pudding, and this revolting thing called a banana for lunch. Then I felt all bloaty, so I went for a walk in the park. But the grass was all prickly and made my feet sore, so I sat down on a bench, and all this lovely scenery kept going by – ”

“That's not a bench,” said Dwain, “that's a sheep.”

“Oh! Well, it's all lovely and cushiony anyway. I did find it odd that my bench kept nibbling the grass – proper benches aren't supposed to do that sort of thing, you know. Rest easy, because I don't feel bloaty anymore.”

The King rubbed his palm along his forehead. “You silly old man, go back home before you make butterflies dart out of our ears every time we use the loo again.”

Sir Robin gave a shiver. “That was tickly.”

“I rather enjoyed it,” said Keesh.

Bernard's arms crossed. “You didn't have the runs.”

“BAA-AA-AA!” Mervin's bench darted into the forest, vanishing in the thistles that lined the road.

Xander sighed. “We'll have to fetch him back.”

“But how?” cried Sir Robin. “Finding a sheep in the woods is like looking for chalk in an art supply store!”

Dwain squinted. “Are you suggesting we ask a forester to point us towards the sheep aisle?”

“I've got it!” Keesh tried to pound his hand with his fist and missed. “We'll entice the animal with a pomegranate. No sheep can resist the alluring fragrance of a freshly picked pomegranate.”

“That,” said the King, “is the most ridiculous thing I have ever heard.”

Gene rolled her eyes. “I'll fetch Mervin. Wait here.” She plunged her mount into the brush.

Guy Longfellow rode after her.

The forest seemed made of lead, rather than leaves. Light came through only in cracks.

"Mervin!" Gene squinted about. "Mervin!"

Her horse brought her to a clearing and halted. Branches crisscrossed, preventing her continuing through the other side.

The horse reared again. To stay on, Gene threw herself forwards on its neck.

"Excuse me." Mervin shuffled into the clearing, patting his belly.

Gene forced her mount back to all fours. "You idiot!"

Mervin hung back, looking stung. "When I trained you, it wasn't to use that sort of language."

Gene sighed. "Sorry, Uncle. Where is your sheep?"

"My bench, you mean? Bolted into the forest. Comfortable thing, but terribly flighty."

"Here, ride with me." Gene offered her hand.

Mervin walked towards her.

Longfellow had lost sight of his wife amongst the trunks and darkness. He steered right upon hearing her shout, splashing into a clearing to find – a pony.

Or, what had once been a pony and was now a whacking great warhorse, mounted by a knight a head taller than any man Sir Guy of Longfellow had ever seen. Each inch of this knight was shrouded in armour painted a sickly, slithering green. And he was hacking at Gene.

She was on foot, backed against a thicket, sword up to ward off the Green Knight's hail of blows, unable to impart any herself.

Mervin lay pinned by the Green Knight's squire perched atop his chest. The old man was striking at him with a stalk of heather.

Guy spurred towards the Green Knight, whipping his sword about his head like a lasso.

The Green Knight saw and hesitated. Gene maneuvered her blade and struck under his sword arm, slicing through the mail. The knight dropped his arm, and nearly his weapon.

"My lord!" The squire had stuffed Mervin in a sack, fastening it about the old man's ankles, so only his flapping feet showed.

The Green Knight dropped his uninjured shoulder and barrelled into Gene. Not anticipating this form of attack, she tumbled sideways off her horse.

Guy roared, bashing indiscriminately, causing no more damage to the Green Knight than a few bruises and a clatter.

Gene yelled, "*Stop*!"

Longfellow roared, but let his horse turn through a circle as the Green Knight galloped into the woods.

"You *bastard*! They're gone!"

Longfellow glanced aside and saw the squire had vanished with his load. "We'll find them."

Gene shoved to her feet. "You can't find anything in this *bloody forest*!" She flailed at the nearest branches with her sword.

Sliding from his saddle, Guy made to grasp her shoulders.

She spun on him. "You stupid fool! You could have saved him!"

"Your *life* was in danger."

"I can fend for myself – I am the King's secret weapon against the barbarian hordes – and yet you ride after me and coddle me."

"You are my wife. Mervin is the most powerful magician in Europe."

"And yet he needs an army of servants just to schedule a haircut. You drooling, moronic dolt!"

Longfellow snorted and turned his back, remounting.

Xander and the others entered the clearing.

"What happened?" asked Dwain. "We heard some kind of heavy metal jam session and came to join the moshing."

"I prefer line dancing," said Keesh.

"A knight in green armour has taken Mervin." Gene hauled into her saddle. "We must find him."

Sir Robin burst into the clearing. "I've done it, everyone. Look, I've found the potato."

"We were *looking* for my uncle Mervin," growled Gene.

"Wow, I found a potato and I wasn't even looking for one. I'm talented."

Xander frowned. "How was my mentor kidnapped from under the noses of my two finest warriors?"

"But I and my nose were with you, sire," said Robin. "Oh – oohh."

"The knight wore green armour?" Bernard asked.

Sir Robin hissed at him. "What have I told you about interrupting when goody-goodies are about to get yelled at?"

Bernard let his head flop to one side. "Don't ruin your fun, or you'll make me go back to riding a pig, instead of this lovely orseh."

"That's right. I swear, Bernard, it looks so like a horse you're putting on airs, thinking minstrels are as good as knights."

"I only thought the Green Knight might live in that green castle over there."

Dwain turned to look. Battlements showed just above the trees. "Couldn't have spotted that from a pig. So what's the ploy? Flaming bag of dung on the drawbridge? Travelling turnip salesmen? Trojan wombat?"

"Full frontal assault," Guy growled.

Gene scoffed. "Are you mad? Think if you bash the palisade enough with your mace you'll bore a hole through it?"

"I don't see why we can't just ask nicely," said Keesh.

"Hear, hear," said Robin. "The worst the Green Knight can do is say 'no.'"

Guy of Longfellow nudged his horse abreast of Sir Robin's and barked into his face. "No, the worst the Green Knight can do is pour acid in your eye sockets, julienne your manhood without ever severing it from your body, and haul your intestines out through your ear to string up Mervin whilst playing outdated singles by Soul Decision."

"Eeep!"

Bernard and Keesh had to steady themselves in their saddles, and even Gene's face blanched slightly at the thought.

"Come now, Longfellow," said the King. "Attempting to frighten Sir Robin is like spitting in the ocean to render it wet. There's no point. You will hang back with Gene whilst the rest of us call upon the Green Knight's hospitality. He does not know that we ride together, and so shall grant us entry."

The castle of the Green Knight resembled a treehouse rather more than a fortress. Branches were leaned against the palisade to disguise it, and even these were painted green. The doorbell, also green, took a good two hours to find – fortunately, Keesh de Lattice's horse located and licked it.

A busty woman with long, black braids and a green dress came and peered at them through the portcullis. "Good day, gentlemen. Who are you and why are you calling?"

The King showed a smile. "Good morrow, fair lady. I am King Xander, and this is my Council of the Boot. We come seeking meat and wine. Might your lord be at home?"

"Indeed he is." The lady smiled back, twisting her torso as though attempting to hypnotize them. "Come in by all means, and bring those two cowering in the forest as well."

Xander looked haughty, because he felt determined not to look sheepish, signalling to Gene and Guy.

So the seven of them rode into the bailey, the keep in its centre and all the other buildings painted green like the outer walls.

"I've never known a castle with grass *everywhere*," said Sir

Dwain. "Usually it's worn away by foot traffic."

The lady grinned. "Astroturf. Follow me, please."

They did, up a set of green wooden stairs, to the second floor of the green keep, where they entered a green great hall.

Dwain glanced about. "And I expected it to be pink."

"*No*," said the lady. "Allow me to offer you each a cup of ale."

"How very St. Patrick's Day of you."

A servant liveried in green appeared with a green tray of green cups.

Bernard blinked. "This is starting to affect mine eyes."

"But it's a lovely hall," said Keesh. "Larger than the King's in Londinium, even."

Xander cleared his throat. "You carry courtesy too far, de Lattice. This paltry place is hardly half the size of my grand, lordly, regnal hall. But you must find it cozy, my lady . . . ?"

"Lady Beryl Green."

"Because your elder sisters had already been named Jade, Olive, and Emerald?"

"Sir Dwain, be courteous to our lady host."

"Sage," murmured Gene.

"Myrtle," said Guy.

Robin laughed. "Heather."

"That's violet."

"Violet isn't green."

"I *know*!"

"Is everyone else seeing green ale?" asked Bernard.

"Lady Beryl," Xander said, "we would have an audience with your lord."

She gave a quizzical little smile. "Regarding the return of your magician? No fretting. It shan't take long."

"Yes," a man entered the great hall, "it shall." He wore a robe of green velvet that flowed like a wind-rippled meadow. Not a hair speckled his pate, and he stood at least a head shorter than any of them.

"My lord." Lady Beryl curtsied.

"No," said Longfellow. "The man we fought sat a good deal taller."

"His armour was taller," said Gene. "Look how he carries his right arm – it's wounded. Where I struck him."

The Green Knight inclined his head. "E'en so, good maid."

"Lady," Guy snapped.

"Ah."

"Why," interrupted Xander, "have you apprehended my magician? He was clearly labelled; you couldn't have mistaken him for your own."

"No," answered the Green Knight, "but when I saw him riding that sheep through my forest, I saw opportunity."

"All forests belong to the crown."

"Inanimate objects have no rights of ownership. I saw my chance, and lured your magician's sheep to me with a pomegranate the cook had packed in my lunch. The getaway was nearly clean, too." He eyed Gene. "But I can see it was all for nothing."

Lady Beryl made a step forwards. "Is he proving difficult?"

"No, impossible." The Green Knight glared at Xander. "Your magician is less adept at sorcery than my wife's soiled stockings."

"Really?" And Xander mumbled, "I find him rather *too* adept."

"If you find him useless, then give him back." Gene made to draw her sword.

"I shall return him," the Green Knight whisked a cup from a tray proffered him, "once you accomplish the task I thought meet for him."

"Is it anything to do with singing or playing the lute?" asked Sir

Robin. "Because my minstrel can do those things." He indicated Bernard, who was blinking rapidly with his hand close before his eyes.

"Erm . . . no. No, there is a meddlesome beast ranging through my forests. – "

"'*My*'?"

" – It frightens off the deer, urinates in my lady's herb garden, and roots out truffles, merely to smash them beneath its feet."

Guy scoffed. "You sought a magician for *this*? A knight should hunt as well as he fights."

"Besides," said Keesh, "could you not have simply asked our aid?"

The Green Knight stared at Keesh. "Anyway . . . I have ever proved a worthy hunter, slaying boar, wolf, tiger, and ocelot. Yet of this Questing Beast I have striven to glimpse merely a hair. The whole of Britain praises King Xander and his Council of the Boot. Surely, you will all make short work of the Questing Beast, then welcome to your magician and your way."

Dwain smacked his hands together. "Lovely. Free room and board."

The Green Knight flinched. "If there is one thing I cannot abide, it is presumption. You only, sir knight, must earn your keep. I shall give you all I get whilst out hunting, but you must give me all you get whilst in my home."

"I foresee a complete absence of complications in agreeing to such a proposal."

"But what if you find a lucky penny?" asked Keesh. "You wouldn't get to keep it."

"But you'd always have the memory." Lady Beryl winked at Dwain.

Xander's already lofty carriage raised itself another three inches.

150

"We accept your proposal, Green Knight, yet do not expect us to spend more than one night beneath your verdant roof."

"It even *smells* green," said Bernard. "Can anyone else smell that?"

***

"I am so *hungry*." Dwain practically doubled up in his saddle.

"Really?" said Guy. "Because you haven't bloody mentioned it for two minutes. I thought you had begun to – and do take the suggestion – eat your own lips."

"Brekky was delish, wasn't it?" asked Keesh. "I'd always felt curious over green eggs and ham."

"I should rather eat grass," Longfellow grumbled.

"For supper," Dwain said, "you may have to."

"SHUT UP!" Gene stood and swivelled in her stirrups, giving the uncomfortable impression that her head had twisted backwards. "The sooner you blasted oafs concentrate, the sooner we slay this ridiculous beast, and the sooner we have Mervin back."

"We've been at this for *hours*," whined Robin.

"We could split up to cover more ground," Bernard suggested.

"And become inextricably lost, unable to find one another in these horrible woods whilst the Questing Beast picks us off one by one? Boredom seems acceptable."

"We could signal one another. Every half hour, I could play three B flats upon this bell if all is well. Should I spot something unwell, I could immediately play three A sharps."

"So," said Guy, "unless we have perfect pitch, our only clue as to a threat would be the timing of your bells?"

Dwain shook his head. "Not even if we have perfect pitch: B flat and A sharp are the same note."

Bernard sighed. "It is a *bell*, gentlemen. It can play only the one note."

Xander snorted. "It should have proved simple. We are Britain's premier fighting force, and hunting is essentially fighting, except the prey is most often furrier."

"And you get to eat it," Dwain moaned.

"Too bad the Questing Beast isn't a sheep," said Keesh, "or we could simply lure it with a pomegranate."

"I could entice it with a song of ethereal beauty," Bernard said, "if this forest weren't so green." He shivered.

Dwain slapped his thigh. "Suppertime. Back to the castle."

"No!" Gene yelled.

Xander harrumphed. "I don't fancy the disgrace either, but soon we shall lose the light, and then the hunt will prove even more unprofitable. Tomorrow we shall settle this business. Tonight we shall feast."

"On green beans and olive loaf?"

"Don't scoff, Longfellow." Dwain was salivating. "That sounds delicious."

In fact, Dwain was the first dressed for supper and down to the great hall. Only to be told by Lady Beryl that, "My lord has only just returned from his own hunt, and the meat is not yet through roasting in the kitchen." She tilted her head to one side. "You poor man. My husband is being inordinately harsh with you, and for so offhand a remark. Come, sit, allow me to distract you."

Dwain plopped onto the bench she indicated, straining to keep his whimpers inaudible as he stared down the trestle table, imagining it covered with cheeses, jellies, and the juicy carcasses of everything from deer to griffins to baby griffins, with their adorable little glazed eyes staring up at him.

Lady Beryl's hands kneaded his shoulders. "What you require is a nice, soothing massage. Such broad shoulders need more relaxation than most. You must have fought very bravely to gain such big knots."

Dwain softened under her touch. "What manner of beast did your husband slay?"

"He slew a brace of hares. Though I fear they will not prove enough to slake your appetites."

"Well, I only possess the one."

"Is that so? Truly, I doubt it." Lady Beryl's hands drifted down to Dwain's chest and squeezed his pecs.

He jumped, twisting to stare at her.

She winked and floated away.

Dwain tried to squint his eyes back into their sockets.

Two servants carried in an off-silver platter loaded with roasted hares. The smell nearly lifted Dwain off his feet.

The Green Knight entered, chatting with King Xander and followed by the Council of the Boot, Bernard hanging onto Sir Robin's coattails to prevent himself stumbling into a wall.

"Ah, Sir Dwain." The Green Knight waved at the platter. "You see what I have for you. What have you for me?"

"Hah." Dwain grinned, trying to gain ahold of himself. He walked behind the Green Knight, and began massaging his shoulders.

"Aaaah. That is very good. Very good. Your hands are like tiny ballerinas. Who in my household rendered you such treatment?"

"One meets so many people. I must say, though, that you are in quite good shape." Dwain's hands skidded and briefly clutched the Green Knight's pecs. "Do you workout?"

"No more than the next fellow. I declare, that was invigorating. Come everyone – to meat!"

Dwain dove for the platter of hares.

Sir Guy caught him and yanked him aside, hissing, "What in *blazes* was that?"

Dwain glared at him. "I'm, so, *hungry.*"

Longfellow rolled his eyes and went to sit by Gene, who ignored him. He glanced up and caught Lady Beryl's eye. She smiled at him and he nodded in return.

✳✳✳

The next day, Sir Dwain set out with Keesh de Lattice, Robin the Bold, and an increasingly incoherent Bernard. They would hunt the Questing Beast whilst the others remained at the castle to try and spy out the dungeon where Mervin languished imprisoned.

"Unbelievable," said Dwain. "We've spent the better part of the day here *again*, and haven't seen a sign of this beast, let alone the beast itself."

"I fancy teatime the better part of the day myself," said Keesh.

"This Green Knight is obviously loony. Perhaps there is no beast. This could all be one horrendous joke to him. And his wife – grabbing me in that fashion. Well, all is thoroughly quiet on the eastern front. Keesh, should we try north or south?"

"Oh, well – " Keesh looked one way, then the other, and set to giggling.

"What is it?" cried Bernard. "What's the joke? I can't see."

Dwain sighed. "Keesh, I thought you'd got over this problem. It isn't even that difficult of a decision – certainly not difficult enough to giggle over."

"Can't be – aha heeh – helped, old chap."

"Well, let's head north, then. May as well sort this business alphabetically. Say, where's Robin got to?"

Where Robin had got to was actually a very funny story, or would have been, had there been anything actually funny about it. He had fallen asleep and dropped his reins, allowing his horse an unheard-of freedom, with which it did not know what to do.

Consequently, it continued to follow Dwain and Keesh, but at a much slower pace than heretofore. It was only when the beast flicked its tail at a ticklish fly, which turned out to be the bold knight's tongue, that Sir Robin snorked and awoke, smacking his stinging lips.

And that was how he came to find himself staring into the cold, slitted eyes of the Questing Beast.

A shriek blasted from Robin like bullet from gun. Which proved all the more impressive, as guns had yet to be invented. Unlike a gunshot, the shriek proved as enduring as a boulder.

No one felt more surprised at this than Robin's horse, which bolted as quickly as any bullet mentioned previously. In an instant it had nearly caught up Dwain and Keesh.

Barely thinking, Dwain threw up his arm to halt the animal.

Robin's horse did not slow. It did not swerve. Instead it ducked, leaving Robin clotheslined and brushed off behind its rump. And it kept running. Sir Robin gasped on the ground, flat on his back, winded.

"If I were to hazard a guess," said Dwain, "really big bees?"

"I say," quoth Keesh, "that really is a fine animal once it gets moving."

"Beast," Robin panted.

"Now, now. No need for name-calling."

"Questing Beast."

"Ah." Dwain leaned down closer. "Now we're getting somewhere. So, what does it look like?"

"Serpent."

"Giant serpent, eh?"

Robin whipped his head side to side. "Serpent head and neck. Leopard body."

"Leopard body?"

Robin nodded so hard they expected to watch his head fly off. "Lion haunches. Hart feet. Seared in brain. Mommy!"

Dwain exchanged a glance with Keesh. "We may have to retire early this afternoon. Someone's fallen asleep riding again and had a nightmare. Robin, I really think you should prove better served by a less comfortable horse."

"Not a dream!"

"One with a leg shorter than the other three. More of a choppy go of it."

"It wasn't a dream!"

Bernard trapped his head between his hands. "Stop it! You're all starting to *sound* green."

***

"How could you possibly fail *again* to find trace of an animal as destructive as the Questing Beast?!"

Dwain clapped his palms tight together. "Longfellow, I told you, Robin was on the verge of a nervous breakdown after that nightmare. Do you think I *like* starving all day because we're staying here? Anyway, you didn't find Mervin."

"ENOUGH!" Gene sprang at Dwain, pinning his neck to the wall of the castle corridor with her forearm. "Yes, we failed. We failed him. Do you think you can do better?"

Dwain gurgled.

Longfellow laid a hand on her deltoid but she shrugged him off.

"Lady Gene of Arc." Lady Beryl floated around a curve to join them. "Please, is it not better to keep peace between comrades?" She smiled sweetly.

Gene sneered, releasing Dwain. "It is *your* husband who has imprisoned *my* uncle."

"My husband is a disagreeable man. Surely, there is no reason to tread after his example."

"I need release. Come."

Longfellow glared at Gene as though he would turn her bowels to ash. But he followed her through the door into their chamber.

Lady Beryl tilted her head to watch him walk. "Most handsome, is he not?"

"Perhaps." Dwain shrugged. "But I fancy myself the snappier dresser."

"Yet blonds – "

A cry came from the closed chamber, followed by a series of shouts and crashes, punctuated by heavy panting.

"Oh my." Lady Beryl's fingers played across her décolletage. "Oh my."

"Nothing to get excited over."

"You cold thing." Lady Beryl squeezed Dwain's behind. "That is the most exquisite music this lonely castle has ever heard."

***

"Roast pheasant. And what have you for me?" The Green Knight stood grinning, fists on his hips.

Dwain stared at the pheasant, juices rolling down its crisp yet tender flesh. "Have you considered how much people would admire your generosity of spirit should you call off this arrangement? News should spread wide and far – Bernard would compose a ballad about it."

The minstrel crouched in the corner, rocking on his heels, hissing, "Greeeeeeeen, greeeeeeeeeeeeeeeeeeeen."

"Ah." The Green Knight rubbed his hands together. "You must have happened upon something good. Come now, out with it."

"Ha!" Dwain clenched his teeth to keep himself silent.

The Green Knight followed him from the edges of his eyes.

"Well, down the hatch." Dwain's eyes bugged from their

sockets and he squeezed the Green Knight's backside, bracing for a blow.

Instead, the Green Knight burst out laughing. "Oh, you cad. My wife warned me you were a character."

Lady Beryl winked and puckered.

Dwain tried very hard to believe that she was looking at her husband.

"To meat!" The Green Knight advanced on his table.

Longfellow pulled Dwain aside, hissing, "Whatever strumpet you're having to do with, she'll get you killed."

"I know, I know." Dwain writhed in Guy's grasp, staring at the pheasant.

"Think, you bumpkin. The Green Knight kept Gene pinned and unable to strike. He'll pull out your intestines through your brains."

Xander dealt himself into the discussion. "Sir Dwain, if you are becoming friendly with members of the household, you might see what intelligence you can gather regarding the location of Mervin's cell."

"Whatever information I get, I'll have to pass on to the Green Knight, and this is already getting awkward, in case your vision is going the way of Bernard's."

"Sir Dwain." The King clapped a hand to the knight's far shoulder. "I am your sovereign lord. Speak to me again with such insolence, and I shall send you to bed without supper."

Dwain dropped to his knees, clutching Xander's hand and kissing his ring.

"I find subjects more pliant when hungry."

Something nearly akin to a ghost of an impression of a smile flitted past Longfellow's lips, and was gone.

✶✶✶

They met a fork in the passage, and Xander growled in frustration. Searching the castle grid by grid did not proceed well when said castle's layout failed to follow the pattern of anything like a grid.

"We can search both ways, majesty," Guy said.

"How?" Gene snapped. "Will you split yourself in two and prove yourself twice as inept?"

"Gene – "

"Likely you would give one half both eyes and the other none, hoping the latter half should find Mervin by kicking him."

"Gene – "

"Which would prove just as well, because you should give the half with both eyes no legs and so it would just lie there, glaring at the ceiling as you're glaring at me now, as though it would do any good to – "

"Gene! *I* am going right. You go left. And to blazes if you find him." Guy stalked off.

"Blind, useless simpleton!"

Xander started down the left-hand passage, Gene a half step behind at his side. "You know, not all men have a right to pride. I consider Sir Guy of Longfellow one of those who does."

"His pride has no bearing on finding Mervin."

"I am not angry at you for that. It is the Green Knight, and the Green Knight alone who deserves the blame."

"Let us try this door, majesty." Gene set her shoulder to it, meeting a green room with a table flanked by two benches, and a fireplace flanked by two bears, dyed green and dressed as Roman legionaries.

Xander poked his head in. "And I thought *our* interior decorator had been sampling wild mushrooms. Come, Gene, I see another door not much farther on."

"This asinine castle sprawls as vast as the woods themselves."
Gene slammed the door shut.

Xander hauled open the next, finding a green room with a table
flanked by two benches, and a fireplace flanked by two bears, dyed
green and dressed as Roman legionaries.

Meanwhile, Longfellow was flinging open doors with all the
subtlety of a gorilla on steroids.

SLAM! BAM! WHAM! FLAN!

"With such strength, sir knight, you will surely wrench all our
doors from their hinges."

Longfellow stopped and bowed. "My lady."

Lady Beryl sauntered forwards, wagging her heavily exposed
bosom. "You are looking for your magician?"

"Merely a lost contact."

She smiled. "Worry not, I shall keep your search to myself."

"Your ladyship is most gracious."

"My husband has grown cold." She sauntered still nearer. "Not
so with you, as I overheard yesterday."

"I am sorry to have disturbed you, my lady. My wife and I were
engaged in swordplay."

"Is that your name for it?" Lady Beryl's gaze trickled down
Guy's body.

"I can assure your ladyship that your husband is not 'cold,' for
he engaged my wife in swordplay not long before our arrival here."

Lady Beryl's face hardened and she raised an eyebrow. "You
would not refuse a lady's request?"

"I scarcely think so."

"Then," Lady Beryl pushed full against him, "rip this bodice
from my heaving breasts, take me in your muscular arms, and make
love to me."

Longfellow stared at her. "*No.*"

"My desire is such that, if you do not, I shall plunge a dagger into my still-beating heart."

"Good riddance." Sir Guy stepped around her and continued down the passage.

***

Dwain, Keesh, and Robin had also decided to split up for the sake of covering more ground. Actually, Dwain and Keesh decided to each split up for the sake of not listening to Robin whimper at the chance of meeting the Questing Beast again.

So Keesh was riding through the forest, humming the latest ditty by that fair Lady Gaga, when he happened upon a damsel in a silken silver dress. "Fine morning, good maid."

"Yes, it is."

"Out for a walk?"

"No, not really. As you can see, I'm tied to this stake."

"Oh."

"And surrounded by a ring of enchanted fire."

Keesh adjusted his visor to bar the sun from his eyes. "So you are. So you are." He shuddered. Now able to clearly examine the damsel's face, he saw sagging skin, gnarled lips, eyes perched with at least an inch's difference in latitude, and a nose that may well have been inside out. "Ah."

"You are a knight?"

"Um . . . yes . . . I think."

"Then you can rescue me."

"From what, good maid?"

"Stake. Fire."

"You mean you did not implement these precautions yourself?"

"Why would I?"

"To prevent yourself being attacked by the Questing Beast, or other hazards of the forest. Not much can wade through enchanted fire unscathed."

"Except a knight of pure virtue."

"Yes, of course there is that."

"Are you?"

"Sorry?"

"A knight of pure virtue?"

"Modesty prevents – "

"And you have experience rescuing damsels in distress?"

"Assuredly. Which is how I know that you are not in distress now, but rather would be should I extract you from your flaming safe haven."

"Sir knight – "

Keesh touched his visor. "Good day."

Meanwhiler, Robin was riding through the forest, with Bernard a subservient distance behind, saying, "You are most fortunate, not having to venture through these woods alone, else the Questing Beast should consume you at a single gulp and you should slip down its scaly throat as easily as a feather through a tunnel of ice. A knighted escort is just the ticket, you may feel assured."

"This is the greenest smelling mount I have ever ridden upon." Bernard prodded his fingers against his horse's neck.

"Have no fear at all. I shall protect you. With all the strength in my – dear sweet kittens, what is that sound?"

Bernard cocked his head as the noise rumbled not around, but through each thing in its path. "It's like thirty couple hounds questing. Or one very angry badger. Either way, it's quite green."

"It is the Beast – it hungers. Quickly, Bernard, do your porterhouse steak impression."

"The half pounder or the full?"

"The full . . . obviously. How is a monster so horrendous supposed to gather excitement over half of anything? Honestly,

Bernard. I mean really."

* * *

Longfellow eventually reached a dead end and had to do an about-face. The splintered remnants of doors sagged from single hinges like breadcrumbs.

Lady Beryl waited with fingers interlaced before her and eyes demurely cast down. "Sir Guy, if I might trouble you to give ear to an apology?"

Longfellow stopped, a soft sound grating from the back of his throat.

"Thank you. Please understand that I find my husband as vile as do you. If I were privy to the location of your magician, I would certainly tell you."

Longfellow inclined his head.

"Yet there remains one problem."

"My lady?"

"My breasts." She threw herself back against the wall. "They *long* to be touched."

"Turn around."

"If I feel not your touch, I fear the extremes to which I shall be driven. I may plunge a handful of toothpicks into each of mine eye sockets."

"Marvelous." Sir Guy resumed retracing his steps.

Xander and Gene had been awaiting him.

"At *last*." Gene rolled her eyes. "Did you find Mervin?"

"If I had I'd have brought him along, would I not?"

"Perhaps he was under lock and key and you'd forgotten how to bash things with your sword butt."

"Enough of marital strife!" snapped the King. "Enough of bickering, enough of gallivanting about, and enough of this blasted Green Knight! What sort of castle is this he lords over? Rooms of used Q-tips, dozens of identical chambers guarded by green bears until you begin to believe yourself mad, rooms of hedge mazes with grass on the floor and vines on the walls so you think you've wandered outside."

Guy shuddered, closing his eyes. "And he collects Teletubbies memorabilia."

"Truly?" asked Gene.

He regarded her with a pained expression.

"That's it!" Xander's voice pulsed through the passageways. "No more of this tomfoolery. I am requisitioning something that will deal with the Green Knight once and for all. Now, to the great hall! I'm famished."

***

"What have you for me tonight, Sir Dwain?"

The young knight grinned. "I found this acorn upon the ground."

The Green Knight took it betwixt thumb and pinkie. "Your other offerings were more . . . gratifying."

"But this is at last a material good, and everyone knows material goods are better than fleeting interpersonal interactions."

"One who has never cared for any interpersonal in particular might imagine so. I can assure you it is otherwise." The Green Knight's gaze strayed to his wife.

The hunting party entered the great hall.

Robin sighed, spotting an ancient chair with a back carved like the strings of a spider's web. "Excellent. After such a far walk from my horse to here, it is imperative I rest my tootsies."

"NOOOOOOOOOO!"

Everyone turned to look at the Green Knight, including Sir Robin, whose butt cheeks hung suspended just a pair of inches above the seat.

"Set not your rump upon that chair, sir knight, for to plant your hindquarters there is death to all, excepting the one who will slay the Beast of Questing."

Robin sprang away from the chair as off a diving board.

"*Now* you care?"

Everyone turned to look at Gene, except Dwain, who was eyeing a suckling pig as though it had offered him three wishes, plus a free jacuzzi – only pay separate shipping and handling.

"You do not wish to see us harmed *now*, but did you care for Mervin when you had him stolen away in a sack, struggling and terrified? He is only an old man. And he should not be alone in this lunatic asylum of a castle. He should be with family, who know that what he really needs is attention, strong tea, and a nice banana once in awhile. Where *is* he?"

"Kill the Questing Beast and I shall show you."

"E-*nough*! I challenge you to a joust. Lose and return my uncle."

"And, should I win, what could I possibly extract from you? Nothing. So why should I fight?"

"To prove you are no coward."

"By assaulting a lady?"

"I am the King's champion, and you suffered no such reservation at our first meeting, when you stole my blood."

The Green Knight's expression sharpened, but he forced a shrug. "Very well, my lady. Tonight I shall feast you, tomorrow I shall fight you. Have you anything more to ask?"

"Only a comfy spot to sit." Bernard plopped down.

"No, not, there!" cried the Green Knight. "That's the Questing Chair!"

"I thought it was that one."

"That's a portrait of my mother!"

"Oh. Terrible, all this green flooding the eyes."

"Should you not be dead?" asked Keesh.

"Just so!" Robin cried. "The Green Knight has lied."

"To prevent us sitting in his favourite chair?"

"It isn't even that comfortable." Bernard shifted.

"I was not lying," the Green Knight marvelled. "The boy must be he who will slay the beast. Young man, tonight you dine at my right hand."

"Fiddlesticks!" Robin exclaimed. "A mere minstrel kill a monstrous beast? Stand up, Bernard. I am the only one who has spied the beastly monster. The chair must be confused."

Keesh and Dwain scrambled to hold back Sir Robin, who raised a leg and tried – if nothing else – to stand on the chair.

Longfellow emitted something between a scoff and a snort, stepping over and jamming in his elbow below the bold knight's ribs.

Robin fell back on the floor, wheezing to regain his breath.

"For all the good you do, I should let you strike death into yourself."

"Or," said Dwain, "we could eat."

***

"Sire," said Dwain, squinting in the dawn, "what are you doing out in the forest?"

"What a wonderfully leading question to aid me in the exposition of my subplot. I am secretly constructing a secret weapon to doom the Green Knight and ensure our victory. Secretly."

"Rest assured, sire, I won't tell anyone, but what about them?" Dwain pointed to the four or five dozen of the Green Knight's servants swarming Xander's lakeside construction site.

"Ah, them. I required labourers to construct my weapon, but it's rather difficult to motivate this lot. Faster! Livelier! Efficienter!"

The King whapped one man's bottom with the flat of his sword.

"Perhaps because you're eliciting their participation in a project intended to destroy the man who's been clothing and sheltering them. Not to mention feeding them. You don't happen to have any bits of breakfast still about you?"

"No. I said work hardier!" Xander lashed out again. This time the blade snapped. "What bony servants."

"El Caliburo!" Dwain gasped. "Sire, this is disastrous!"

"Not necessarily." The King turned to the workmen and shouted, "Does anyone have any ghee?"

A scream pierced the forest, shaking the leaves from several trees, and causing the birds and squirrels nestled in them to drop to the ground, stunned.

Queen Amanita appeared from the underbrush.

"Mother!"

"You have a perfectly good sword with which to defend your kingdom, and here I find you breaking it on your inferiors' backsides in the middle of nowhere. Craftsmanship is on the wane nowadays, what with the barbarians hacking all the skilled labour – and every other sort of labour – into pieces too small to feed your goldfish. This is precisely why I've told you time and again, my boy, to get a warranty on everything."

"Yes . . . of course . . . . "

"Xander, *how* many times have we discussed warranties?"

"*None* that I can recall, Mother."

"Give me that." Queen Amanita snatched the sword, and then the blade when Dwain stooped to get it for her. "Warranty or not, I am taking this back to the manufacturer, and we are putting this right." With that, she marched into the lake, not slowing down when the water reached her knees, her waist, or when it closed over her crown.

Several moments passed.

"Lady of the Lake," Xander muttered.

"Of course." Dwain grinned politely. "Majesty, how long can the Queen Mother hold her breath?"

"I've never known her to hold anything for long . . . breath . . . tongue . . . temper – what are you lot standing about for? My sword may be in the shop, but don't think me averse to chucking rocks at dawdlers."

***

The dawn had more to look upon than a construction project. Gene had donned full plate armour – her wedding armour, in fact – to meet the Green Knight on his battlefield deep in the forest. He again wore his green armour that gave the appearance of nearly two extra feet in height.

Gene paraded her horse to one end of the field, and wheeled to face the Green Knight. "Brace yourself, brigand. Charge!" Her horse bolted with amazing speed that felt too slow, too slow, too slow.

The Green Knight seemed to gallop towards her so much faster, the dappled sun drawing his horse on –

He vanished against the forest backdrop. Gene nearly drew up, but heard him closing, closing – she had to level her lance and –

***

"Good day again, sweet maid." Keesh saluted. "I see you are enjoying a different quarter of the forest this morning."

The ill-favoured damsel in the silken silver gown turned her head. "Oh. You again."

"My companions and I are seeking the Questing Beast. Should Fortune favour us, you will not need the protection of your enchanted fire much longer."

"And the stake? Why would I bind myself to a stake?"

"I assume so that you would not burn from falling into the fire should the day's pleasant warmth lull you to sleep."

"*How* would I bind myself to a stake?"

Keesh lit up. "Do you practice sleight of hand? I do so enjoy magic. And we've mislaid our magician, you know."

The maid grinned, enough to make a gargoyle scamper for the hills. Fortunately, Keesh had his visor down, and only caught glimpses. "Would you care to assist me in my next trick?"

"Most certainly. Prey, what is it?"

"The Escaporama Alakazam. If you would simply dismount and walk to me through the fire . . . . "

"Oh, this is most exciting."

"Indeed. Now, cut the ropes about my wrists – carefully. . . . Good. Now carry me through the fire to your horse."

Keesh did so. "Does the trick happen now?"

"It just has. By rescuing me, sir knight, we two are now betrothed, and you must wed me before sunset this very night, or else turn as ugly as I." The maid kissed his helm, which rang with the scratching of her whiskers. "We shall prove most happy, don't you think?"

"Um . . . what?"

✳✳✳

"Perhaps one of us should go in after her," said Dwain.

Xander frowned. "To what end?"

"Of course. Better just to drag the lake for her corpse."

"Corpse? No. Mother can endure more than Beowulf."

"Who?"

"Don't keep up with contemporary barbarian literature, do you?"

"No, sire. I prefer to support our homegrown authors."

"Rather narrows your worldview, though. Besides, Gildas holds

169

the market nearly cornered, what with everyone else so busy being slaughtered."

"Yes, by barbarians. Are you certain the Queen is alright? It's nearly been an hour."

"Patience, Sir Dwain. Perhaps if I recite the Beowulf's family tree for you, 'twill urge the time past faster."

"No, I really don't think it would."

"Can hold his breath all day, Beowulf. Anyway, four children sprang from him in succession – I forget who 'him' is – Heorogar, prince of troops, and Hrothgar, and Halga the good; I heard that Sigeneow was Onela's Queen, consort of the war – Scylfing. . . . "

"Sire, *please.*"

✳✳✳

Longfellow kicked open the door to his left, to find a room with a stylish living room set. He cursed, kicking open the door to his right. The same stylish living room set, on the ceiling. The next door and the same set, this time on the back wall. Longfellow bellowed an oath that would have bowled over a herd of cattle. The next door revealed an empty room – full of doors on the walls, floor, and ceiling. Longfellow screamed.

Only to hear himself matched from behind.

Spinning, he saw Gene, tearing down the passage in a green gown that hugged her body over all the curves her armour hid. Green lace concealed the better part of her chest, which had blanched bright white with rage.

"*A dress!*" she shouted. "He knocked me unconscious and shoved me in a dress! I'll pull off his fingers, squash his toes till they split, and see that he eats his own bloody ears!"

Guy grabbed Gene's shoulders, smashing her back against the wall, and pinning her there with his body full-length against her. He glared at her, panting, a growl growing in his throat. Then he clutched her neck, devouring her lips.

He fell backwards, slamming his hindquarters on the stone floor, blood surging from his mouth.

"How can you?!" Tears poked Gene's eyes like the stingers of so many scorpions. More embarrassed than angry, she fled before he could see.

***

"I should like to see *you* kill the Questing Beast, Bernard, when it is *I* who have discovered its trail."

"Forgive me, sir, but these look like deer tracks we're following."

"Have I not said the Questing Beast walks on the feet of a hart? Besides, Bernard, aren't your eyes still under the weather from all this green?"

"Of course, master. If you say these are the Questing Beast's tracks, then clearly they must be."

"Yes. Now, you make a noise like a freshly picked pomegranate and lure it out."

"I don't think that will – "

"Bernard, need we remember which of us is the knight, and which the minstrel?"

"Yes, sir. – No, sir."

"Then why aren't you making the noise?"

"I am – only at a frequency specially suited for a Questing Beast's ears."

"You should be performing for a snake's ears. It bears the head of a snake, you know. Oh, you don't, because *you've* never seen it."

"Yes, master."

"If you end up killing anything, it will be the wrong thing altogether, that's what it will be."

"As you say, master."

"Minstrels. They use you as their muse and get the idea they're some sort of puppet master. When here *you* are, feeding them, and clothing them, and tracking down Questing Beasts, until they're right in front of you napping under that tree, and all you want to do is scream and run away, but no, your minstrel's right there, and every time you wet yourself before a battle he sings about it, so you can't possibly show any self-preservative instinct without the outcome of thorough humiliation."

"Sir, I think my vision must be really worse than I thought. Under that tree I actually do see a beast with the feet of a hart, the haunches of a lion, the body of a leopard, and the neck and head of a serpent."

"Actually, it may be clearing up. I suspected fresh, forest air would prove a boon to your eyes, Bernard."

"Thank you, sir." The words rattled as the minstrel shook. "Will you slay the beast now?"

The Questing Beast stirred, as though it would wake, but instead rolled onto its back, legs curled in the air, batting occasionally.

Sir Robin drew his sword and leapt from his horse. "Poised to compose the most heroic ballad yet warbled?"

"Please, master, hurry!"

"HIII-YAH!"

Bernard shut his eyes and so did not see, but the war cry of Sir Robin the Bold was accompanied by a most mighty stroke. That Robin failed to see himself, having screwed his own eyes shut. Nevertheless, he proceeded valiantly, hacking and swinging and hi-yahhing quite thoroughly, until he deemed it safe to peek.

"You see, Bernard. *That* is how you kill a Questing Beast."

"Oh! It is even more hideous dead. That long tongue, protruding like that, the colour of a rotting, bloated corpse."

172

"Yes, yes. All within a day's work, of course. Set it on your orseh, so we can bring it to the Green Knight and show everyone how courageous *I* am."

"Right away, master. Will you help lift – "

"Bernard, you must do *some* work yourself, or else why do I keep you?"

"Yes, sir."

✻✻✻

" . . . His name was Wiglaf, Weohstan's son, a prince of the Scylfings, a peerless thane, Ælfhere's kinsmen. . . . "

"Majesty – please! This is worse than massaging the Green Knight."

✻✻✻

Having torn the green dress to confetti, torched the confetti to ashes, and coaxed pigeons to defecate quite profusely upon those ashes, Gene still felt hardly better. She thought about doing the same to some article Longfellow prized, yet all were metallic, from his collection of antique throwing nunchucks, to his Sunday morning slippers, to his toothbrush.

Gene donned her manliest harness of armour and walked down early to supper. All her life she had sought to appear in a certain light, even going so far as to use the masculine spelling of her name, and now her reputation had been obliterated in the eyes of the person whose opinion should have mattered most. Except she was finding out too late that he was just like the rest of them. Pig.

Gene found no respite for, a step outside her door, she could hear Longfellow's voice as he conversed with Lady Beryl.

"Come, my handsome knight," she was saying, "will you not even press my hand? Just once? Just for an instant? There could be nothing more innocent."

"Innocence is the surest road to guilt, my lady."

"Sir Guy, if you do not show me even this small courtesy, I shall shave my legs until the razor finds bone."

Longfellow stepped past her. "Exquisite."

Gene, unable to see him moving away from their hostess, burst cover, hurrying past the pair of them towards the great hall, glimpsing the graceful contours of Lady Beryl's exposed leg.

She heard Guy's spurs behind her, their hostess's rustling skirts behind him, and outpaced them both.

"Longfellow! Glorious day, hasn't it been?" Dwain swatted his shoulder and plunked into an alcove window seat.

Longfellow, having lost sight of Gene, stopped. "Perceptive as always."

"What? I mean, a poetry recitation from the King is quite a traumatizing ordeal, but at least I've managed to duck any – "

Lady Beryl appeared around the bend. "Sir Dwain! How serendipitously fortuitous. You can help demonstrate to Sir Guy just how much *fun* I can be."

"Wait, what – please, get off my lap – Longfellow – Longfellow, help!"

***

"What a joyous feast over which to preside!" declared the Green Knight. "The Questing Beast at last is slain, and we are to behold a wedding. Sir Keesh, as the groom you must choose: red wine or white?"

"I – um – ha – ahaha."

The Green Knight smiled politely. "Green it is. That's all that's in stock, in any case. Sir Dwain, there you are."

Dwain nodded. "Keesh, I see you've got hold of the Questing Beast. I owe you a Coke, it is real. But much uglier than Robin described.”

Keesh cleared his throat. “This is my intended. Apparently. That mangled thing on the giant platter is the Questing Beast.”

“Oh. Well, it’s rather cute in comparison then, isn’t it?”

“Lovely to meet you,” murmured the hideous damsel on Keesh’s arm.

“Now, Sir Dwain,” said the Green Knight, “it appears that this will be our last exchange. What have you for me tonight?”

“Tonight? Um . . . I heard a very long, boring poem today. Allow me to recite it for you, and if you should happen to doze off for the other thing I received today . . . . ”

“No, no. Just skip to the second thing, that’s fine.”

“But, sir knight, I am honour bound to bestow upon you all – ”

“Honour bound to me, and I forgive you the poem. Now, what is the second thing?”

“Should we not wait for the King?”

“No need.”

“You know . . . ” Dwain tried on a smile for size, “we’re leaving tomorrow, I think I’ll just wait for breakfast on the road. Fasting is good for the soul, they say.”

“Tonight we’re going all out. There’s an omelette station, and a sundae bar, and an entire turkey stuffed inside a pig inside an ostrich.”

Dwain’s chin trembled. “I’m fine.”

“And of course we shall roast the Questing Beast. Surely you don’t wish to be the only member of the Council of the Boot never to have tasted Questing Beast.”

Dwain drew a scorecard from inside his breastplate. “That would give me a bingo on consumed exotic animals. I should at last fulfill my quest to win a jet ski.”

“Excellent!”

Dwain glanced at Longfellow, who glared and shook his head. "It was ever my childhood dream to win a jet ski. Sir knight, if you could take a seat."

The Green Knight slapped himself down on a bench. "I can tell, from the way you've been stalling, that this is bound to be better than an acorn."

A few moments later, Bernard processed into the hall. "Announcing his magnificent boldness, Sir Robin, the slayer of – my eyes! MY EYES!"

Keesh, unable to take his gaze from the spectacle, asked, "The green, my fiancée, or the lap dance Sir Dwain is performing on the Green Knight?"

Bernard crumpled to the floor. "The latter! The latter!"

"I wish it could blind me, but somehow I cannot look away. Don't you find it so, Sir Guy?"

"No."

Sir Robin popped his head in. "Bernard, that was not a proper introduction. You promised to behave better. What is – oh, great gorging harrumpharumphs! Dwain – I can never eat cantaloupe again!"

"Still, it's strangely mesmerizing," said Keesh, "although I fully expect not to be able to sleep for days. Oh – argck-ck! Sir Guy, how can you stare at your boots at a time like this?"

"I caught the debut performance."

"In its way, it's hauntingly beautiful," said the hideous damsel. She poked Keesh. "We should do that tonight."

"*Excuse me?*"

Sir Robin's eyes filled with tears. "This is more emotionally scarring than battle."

With a final swirl of his hips, Dwain stood and executed an ostentatious bow.

The Green Knight burst with applause. "How wonderfully exotic! Wherever did you obtain such a lap dance, Sir Dwain?"

"Oh that's not – really, I don't – fancy you should – my, what big teeth you have."

"All . . . right . . . . Shall we begin the festivities? The fire's lit, the servants are bringing a giant spit – "

"Poetry," murmured Dwain, "so much poetry. Must cleanse self in fire – " He promptly fell on his face.

Gene rushed in.

Guy's head snapped up. "Where have you been?"

She ignored him. "You have your Questing Beast – where is my uncle?"

"Lady Gene. You needn't have changed for supper."

"You *bastard*! Where is he?"

"He is being brought here this very moment. Ahh, speak of the wizened old devil."

Mervin entered, escorted by two men-at-arms.

"Uncle!" Gene flew at him, wrapping him in an embrace and bounding off just as quickly.

"Oh, hello." Mervin smiled. "Tea time already?"

"No, Uncle, it's supper."

"Just as well. Can't work a teacup in these restraints." He raised his hands, which were connected by a finger trap. "Impossible to perform magic like this as well."

Gene forced her eyes not to roll, pushing Mervin's hands together so the finger trap bulged. She plucked it off.

"You've defeated the enchanted bonds!"

"Did they treat you well, Uncle?"

"Oh, quite well, yes. Bread and water like clockwork, cold drafts so I never felt overheated, hanged me upside down to work the kinks from my spine."

"They hanged you upside down?"

"And I thoroughly enjoyed it. Except that one night when I wet myself. Incontinence is a part of growing older, you know."

"That's nearly more disturbing than the lap dance," grumbled Longfellow.

Dwain pushed himself to his feet. "Then let's never speak of it again. Please."

"Or that grotesque young lady." Mervin pointed.

Keesh pivoted to shield his fiancée. "Not grotesque, aesthetically challenged."

Mervin waved a hand. "In any case, let's cut the giraffe and pour the wine."

"Isn't it supposed to be 'cut the rug'?" Dwain asked.

"The giraffe." Mervin motioned.

"You mean the Questing Beast?"

"*That's* what you call a Questing Beast? Small wonder my spells didn't work – "

"Because *you* cast them?"

" – since they were designed to ensnare an actual Questing Beast, not a *giraffe*."

"It is a Questing Beast." Robin stamped his foot. "And I killed it."

Mervin leaned towards the plattered beast, squinting. "No, my boy. What you've killed is a peaceful herbivore that spends its days nibbling leaves from the tops of trees. Not a monster of pure malevolence, intent upon the destruction of all virtue in this world and the apocalypse of all we hold dear, from simple laughter to bellybutton lint."

Longfellow ran a hand over his face. "God guard me from what I've married into."

"Does saying that help?" asked Keesh.

"If anything, it makes it worse. But then so does everything else." He glanced at Gene.

"But," said the Green Knight, "the Beast frightens off the deer, urinates in my lady's herb garden, and roots out truffles – "

"All innocent fun to a playful giraffe, so full of life." Mervin peered over the body. "Well – " He patted the head.

Which rose, opened its eyes, and blinked 'round the room.

"It's awake!" cried Sir Robin. "The undead monster thirsts for revenge – run for your lives!"

The Questing Beast unleashed a foot and a half long tongue, humming like a party blower whistle.

"Whilst that certainly is terrifying – " said Dwain, rolling his eyes " – I was promised Questing Beast. A giraffe won't win me that jet ski."

"But," said Keesh, "every time you straddled it, wouldn't you think of – "

"We – are – never speaking of that again, remember?"

Xander entered. "I'm late because I was just putting the finishing touches on something. Mervin, a pleasure to see you. Is that the Questing Beast? It was billed as being dead."

"It's a giraffe," said Mervin.

The beast licked him, grating its tongue along his cheek and removing half his beard.

"A particularly mischievous giraffe."

"Wonderful! Shall we eat it?"

"We need to be married first," piped up the hideous damsel, squeezing Keesh's arm.

"Who – urgh!" The King made a face upon catching sight of her.

"I can perform the ceremony," said the Green Knight.

"Legally?" Dwain asked.

"Were we on a ship, its captain could perform the ceremony. We are in a castle, thus I, its lord, can perform the ceremony."

"And *I* am *King*." Xander puffed his chest. "That trumps a lord."

"Does either of you know a *priest?*" Dwain asked.

"No time," said the Green Knight. "Dearly beloved, we gather here to join – "

"Sir Keesh de Lattice," Xander interrupted, "do you take this maid as your wife?"

Keesh giggled. "She says I must, so – "

"And do you . . . . "

"Pam," supplied the damsel.

The Green Knight swooped in. "Do you Pam take Sir Keesh as your husband?"

"I do."

"And does anyone here object?"

The entire room, including Sir Keesh and the Questing Beast, raised their arms.

"Overruled," Xander bellowed. "By the power vested in me by El Caliburo when I pulled it from – "

"Man and wife!" cried the Green Knight.

"And wife – jinx!"

Pam the hideous damsel, now Lady de Lattice, hurled her arms about Keesh's neck and planted a big, wet one that promptly made him faint dead away.

"This is without doubt," said Dwain, "the most romantically awkward adventure we've had to endure. Now, there's no Questing Beast. Is there at least a real sundae bar?"

✳✳✳

Sir Keesh awoke to find himself laid out upon a most sumptuous bed. The next moment he was nearly bounced off it.

"Hello, *lover.*"

Keesh braced himself and turned his eyes. Upon the fairest faced, rosiest lipped, goldenest haired maiden he had ever seen. "Oh, hello. And you are?"

She tossed her head, causing her hair to whirl in a wonderous shower. "Lady Pam de Lattice. Catchy, huh?"

"Um . . . yes . . . ."

"You're confused?"

"Perpetually."

"Oh, my darling knight." She caressed his face. "Like that ring of fire you pulled me from, I, too, am enchanted. But you, as my husband, can choose. Half the time I am hideous, the other half beautiful. Will you have me this way at night, when we share the marriage bed, or during the day, when all can see that I am your wife?"

"You wish *me* to decide?"

"*You* must."

Keesh giggled.

"This is a very serious matter."

"Oh yes, I know. Bwe-ha."

"Keesh! Do you think I like the sneers of everyone who sees me on your arm during the day? And yet, at night, knowing it disgusts you to touch me – "

"We could do nooners."

"Keesh!"

"Let's see, during winter the nights are longer, so you would spend more time being revolting – I mean repulsive – I mean unsightly – but summers would prove more pleasant – I mean agreeable – I mean . . . oh, why did I read that thesaurus?"

"*Really?*"

"Hee hee. Please, dearest Pam, I cannot choose. Do whatever you think is fit and I shall abide by it."

"Really?"

Keesh booped her nose. "You should have whatever you like, sweetheart."

Lady Pam beamed. "Then I choose to be beautiful *all* the time."

"Was that an option? I would have chosen that one."

"I was testing you, darling. And you've passed." She kissed him.

A thrill spilt through Keesh and he looked quite smug.

Lady Pam cocked an eyebrow. "By the way, does this dress make my butt look big?"

"I'd say it's more likely a trick of the shadows that's doing it."

"Ooo!" She bounded off the bed in a huff.

"Oh dear. I think I may need more of Longfellow's advice."

* * *

After a sleepless night, Gene was out of bed early, heading to the stables to urge the ostlers to make ready the horses. When she ran into a gorgeous blonde waif.

"Good morning," smiled the waif.

Gene nodded.

"Don't recognize me, do you? Lady Pam – Keesh's wife?"

Gene looked her up and down, nodding again.

"He's so gallant. I really am the luckiest bride."

"As I recall," said Gene, "he was not very eager last night, when you were unconscionably horrendous to look upon."

"Yes, but he loves me now."

"And you feel glad about that? Being married to a man who shows you love only due to what you look like?"

Lady Pam shrugged. "Emotions are transitory. I can keep myself beautiful forever and Keesh will always love me. Basing a marriage on feelings – that isn't stable enough for my tastes. Now, I want to arrange breakfast in bed for my bridegroom." She skipped off down the passage.

Gene sneered, stood a moment, and strode back to her bedroom.

Longfellow was just finishing dressing.

She paced up to him. "Will you press my hand?"

He glanced at her and grasped it to his chest. "What is wrong with you?"

Gene hesitated, forcing herself to stare him full in the face. "Do you love me?"

He looked at her as though she'd gone mad. "Of course I love you, you bloody idiot."

"Why?"

"Because," he dropped her hand, "you are the only one who understands me."

"No, I don't. I thought I did. I thought you didn't care what I looked like, but then you plaster yourself to me the first time you see me in a dress."

"It wasn't the dress, exactly."

"Then what?"

Guy's lips softened, almost as though they were preparing to smile. "I'd never seen you so *angry*."

"Oh."

"Perhaps you do not understand me as well as I thought."

Gene's gaze hardened and she shoved him. "Oh yes I do. You are callous and a brute. There is no one more cruel or savage, no one more sadistic or bestial, no one more carnal – "

Longfellow grabbed her, kissing her with such a gnashing of teeth he nearly tore the lips from her face.

"I very, very much love you."

"Get in my bed, woman, and show me."

Gene jabbed his kidney. "Don't you call me that."

Longfellow showed his teeth and pushed her down.

"I don't appreciate 'bloody idiot' either."

He snatched her leg, wrapping it behind his waist.

✳✳✳

Lady Beryl and the Green Knight came outside the castle walls to bid their guests adieu. Everyone was mounted, including Mervin, who sat astride the Questing Beast, which, unused to carrying a rider, shivered every so often in a way that caused the magician to chortle at being tickled.

"Farewell, friends," cried the Green Knight, "and be not hesitant to seek my hospitality again in future."

"'Hospitality'?" Xander spat. "You kidnapped my magician and held us all to ransom him, as it turns out for a beast residing mainly in your imagination! I should have you quartered for treason!"

"I have not betrayed my country in trying to safeguard my own land."

"It is *not* your own land. You hold it as a favour from me. I *am your King*!"

"You are *a* King. I am not in a position to deny that at present."

Xander flushed a most becoming shade of puce and bellowed. "That's it! Men, fire the cowapult!"

"Cowapult?" Dwain echoed.

The Green Knight pointed to something that had emerged above the trees, sailing towards them. "I say, what is that?"

Lady Beryl squinted. "I believe it's a cow, my lord."

"Rather smallish for a cow."

"Well, it is growing."

"Also rather too fuzzy."

"Did you forget your contacts this morning, darling?"

"Ah. I suppose it is large enough to be a cow."

The beast crashed with an irate bellow, and the crunch of each of its massive bones shattering.

Xander sighed and shouted, "A little to the left."

Lady Beryl turned to go inside. "I'll fetch some servants to clean this up."

"Sire," said Dwain, "I thought we had put the whole cowapult issue to bed."

"Because it has a range of over one hundred Brythonic metres, but we would have had to haul it into Saxon territory, and their metres are much shorter than ours. But, as you can see, we *are* on my land, as the cowapult is launching at full capacity."

The Green Knight raised an eyebrow. "It proves we are on Brythonic land, and I *am* Brythonic."

Violet polka dots began blazing through the puce. "You deny your King, and will face his wrath! Men, fire two!"

Nothing happened.

Dwain glanced over his shoulder. "It's a bird, it's a plane, it's – nope. No cows, majesty."

A voice came from the woods. "We've done reloading now."

"Oh, for goodness – " Xander ground his teeth into his tongue and gulped blood. "*Fire* two!"

What happened next was difficult to say. Indeed, some later asserted that the cow flew exceptionally quickly, whilst others insisted exceptionally slowly. And no one proved able to assert quite how, but they could all assert that the cow sailed directly onto the Green Knight's head, smashing him into a mush of gooey bits. Said cow, now a leathery sack of jagged bone shards and mush itself, then bounced off the Green former Knight, and onto King Xander, bashing him flat.

Keesh wretched.

Robin turned pale white and fainted face-first into his horse's mane.

Gene and Guy looked as though they would have liked to do both, but ended doing neither.

A scream shook the clearing.

Queen Amanita stepped into view, carrying the King's sword. "Here. These lake ladies are such divas. It cost a good deal of tongue-lashing, but she finally repaired the thing for free, and signed a ten-year warrantee. I've only just surfaced."

"You've been under that long – " Dwain gaped. "And you're not even damp!"

"Queens can't be damp. And they appreciate being *bowed* to."

Everyone scrambled to dismount, and bent towards her.

"That's better. Now, where is my son, so I no longer have to lug this stubby thing?"

"Your majesty." Longfellow stepped forwards, looking like a man who has only just felt the garrotte at his throat. "The King is dead."

Amanita cocked her head. "I know I cannot have misheard you. You must have misspoken."

"It's true." Gene's voice slithered like sand.

"Well." The Queen stared at her son's sword a moment, then shoved it towards Gene. "You take this and – how did he die?"

"A cow, majesty," said Dwain.

"You knights must learn elocution."

"Really, a cow." He pointed.

The mound of flesh had begun to leak blood over the greensward.

"If it killed the King, it must be executed."

"Execute the dead cow?"

"I *have* been schooled in elocution. Hanged, drawn, and quartered."

"And the men that launched it?" asked Longfellow.

"Them, too, of course."

Longfellow stalked off, Gene behind him.

"Of course," Amanita murmured, her eyes gone blank. She jolted. "Whose land is this? The Green Knight? Execute him, too. Accessory to regicide."

"He's there." Dwain pointed to the more compact, spilling mound.

"Do it anyway."

Lady Beryl emerged from the castle, followed by servants.

Amanita pointed. "And her. And that one, and that one, and those two, and especially that short one there, and . . . . " Her finger swept with her gaze.

Bernard dodged.

" . . . that." She indicated the Questing Beast.

Dwain recited, "'Thus made their mourning the men of Geatland, / for their hero's passing his hearth-companions: / quoth that of all the Kings of earth, / of men he was mildest and most beloved, / to his kin the kindest, keenest for praise.'"

"Sir Dwain," said the Queen, "that is terrible poetry. You will not deliver the eulogy."

"Yes, majesty."

"'No, majesty.'"

"No, majesty."

"Better. Now come, we have much to arrange. And begin with the giraffe. I swear, it's pulling faces at me."

A. E. CHANDLER

Chrétien's *Yvain*: Abridged for People with Tight Schedules

Adapted directly from Chrétien de Troyes' *Knight with the Lion* c. 1177

Our story begins, as many often do, in Wales on the feast of Pentecost. It was there that King Arthur, against all decorum, retreated to Queen Guinevere's chamber after dinner for some horseplay, tuckering himself out so that he fell asleep. The Queen, being younger and more resilient, was not yet tired and so went in search of something to quell her boredom. Thus she found Sir Calogrenant just outside her door conversing with Dodinel, Sagremor, Kay, Gawain, and Yvain. Who apparently often stood right there whilst she entertained the King, as no one seemed to find this the slightest bit odd. The Queen, wearing her stealthy ninja slippers, got right into their midst before any of them noticed – except Calogrenant, who jumped up straight away. Kay, feeling embarrassed, and irked at being so, rattled off something to the effect of, "You think you're such hot stuff and we're not? Well, blow it out your ear."

Calogrenant replied, "Fine. Then I'm not telling you the end of my story."

"Lady," said Kay, "make him tell!"

"Calogrenant," spake the Queen, "ignore Sir Poopy Pants over here and finish your story, please."

"If you say so, my lady. Seven years ago I was out being errant and manly, when I stopped at this house that had great eats and the lord's daughter was a real looker. She had these great – "

188

"Skip ahead."

"Right. So the next morning I set out, finding some wild bulls guarded by an ugly rustic lout. He hadn't bathed in so long that he looked black. And certainly, as he appeared unkempt and evil, I asked to make sure before killing him. The rustic told me that if I wanted to see something awesome I should take the left-hand path. Because down that path was deadly peril that no one had yet survived.

"So I turned left, reaching a spring and scooping out some water, as the ugly rustic had counselled me, and pouring the water on this emerald atop a pile of rubies. That made a storm erupt, just as he'd said, with snow and rain and hail. And lightning – which was when I realized I was encased in metal and this probably hadn't been a smashing idea. All these birds and animals were fleeing for their lives – it was unbounded chaos.

"But somehow I survived. Then this knight rode into the clearing shouting, 'You idiot! Why do people keep doing this?! I live just over there, and now my house is flooded, my crops are ruined, and half my vassals have been electrocuted – what is *wrong* with you?!' Then he beat the crap out of me. But he was a big guy – like, really big – like, huge. So there was really no way I could have won, you know, he was so large. Anyway, it's still embarrassing. Which is why I waited seven years to tell anyone, and probably shouldn't have opened my big yap now."

"Cousin Calogrenant," cried Yvain, "no offence, but you are a complete moron. I am totally going to avenge your shame. Which no one has known about these past seven years, or would have known about if you hadn't just told us."

Kay scoffed. "Like you could avenge anything, wuss."

Then Arthur woke up and sought out the Queen, also not finding it off-putting that everyone had apparently been listening outside the door as he got lucky. Guinevere repeated Calogrenant's entire story, word for word, whilst everyone who had just heard it shifted about twiddling their thumbs and trying not to look bored.

"By the soul of my father," said Arthur, "and his son – which is me – and my mother, and my fourth cousin twice removed, and my uncle the mailman – whom I mysteriously resemble – we shall all go to this spring of which you speak and have a lovely camping trip with marshmallows, and s'mores, and scary stories. Woman, get packing!"

But Yvain did not like the sound of this plan. For if all the Round Table knights came along, one of them would be bound to call dibs on the knight who had beaten up his cousin, and then he would never get the opportunity to avenge properly. Plus, he really hated going places with groups, listening to a bunch of people asking the local guides stupid questions, waiting in interminably long lines for the facilities, and getting strangers' elbows in his snapshots. So he started out alone, knowing it would take the court a fortnight to pack up all of their cosmetics and collectible tent stakes.

Yvain spent the night at the castle of the lord with the foxy daughter, marvelled at the wild bulls, and made the left by the unkempt rustic, knowing full well that, if he did exactly what Calogrenant had done, then the end result would naturally be completely different. He even poured the spring water on the emerald and caused another storm.

When it was over, a large knight galloped up to him and cried, "What is the matter with you people? Can't any of you read the sign I posted?! *Don't* cause any storms. The insurance company just sent over the settlement cheque for the last tempest on Tuesday! I'm going to have to fill out all that paperwork again! I *hate* paperwork!"

The knight charged Yvain, and Yvain charged him right back, smashing the knight's head so his brains ran out all over his nice,

190

clean armour.

But this did not kill him, for some reason – possibly because he had never formally studied anatomy – and he rode back to his castle.

Yvain panicked, knowing that if he didn't show a dead body, or at least an ear or a toe or something, Kay would say he had made up the battle and the victory. So Yvain chased the knight into his castle. The drawbridge, however, was booby trapped. Yvain's horse tripped a spring, getting itself sliced in half and Yvain stuck inside with a bunch of grief-stricken people desperate to avenge their dying lord by eradicating his murderer.

As luck would have it, Yvain was at that moment approached by a girl with glasses and a ponytail, who said, "You probably don't remember me, but I came to King Arthur's court once and you were the only knight who would say two words to me. In fact, I think your exact words were, 'Two words.' In any case, here's a ring that will turn you invisible. Sit on this couch and don't move."

Meanwhile, the knight who owned the castle had died. And everyone, seeing the front half of Yvain's horse and knowing he was trapped in the castle, tramped around looking for him, stabbing into every corner and beating every piece of furniture. Except for the couch where the girl with glasses and a ponytail had placed Yvain, possibly because it was an ancient family heirloom that would be forfeited to the next inheritor in line if ever beaten, or possibly because of a gross case of plot manipulation.

In the midst of all these grief-crazed, would-be murderers, Yvain spotted a lady. She was screaming and swooning, clawing her face and tearing her hair, ripping her dress and crying so hard she could barely breathe.

'She must be the new widow,' Yvain thought to himself. 'What a looker.'

Eventually, everyone took a break from searching for their

lord's murderer to bury his corpse, which sincerely upset Yvain, who still needed some body part to prove to Kay and the court how awesome he was. It wasn't like the knight *needed* his body parts now anyway. Yet from a window, as Yvain watched the funeral procession march out, he couldn't help but wish that the widow would stop crying and ripping her hair, because she'd look much prettier if she smiled. She'd be a total fox, in fact. But no, she kept wailing about how there was only one man for her, and how he was so much better than everyone else was or ever could be, and generally being an unmitigated downer.

The girl with glasses and a ponytail, wanting to see Yvain happy and knowing herself so irreparably ugly that he would never be interested in her, decided to fix him up with her lady. She broached the subject a few days later in the new widow's chamber.

"My lady Laudine," she said, "you know King Arthur is coming soon to camp out and make s'mores, and who will defend us from such a travesty now that your lord is dead? And you're right that he was awesome and everything, but isn't the guy who won a fight against him by definition even awesomer? You should totally marry that guy – it's a definite trade up."

Whereupon the lady cried and yelled and kicked out the girl with glasses and a ponytail, who mumbled, "Fine, since you're going to be a total girl about it. But if you'd just think logically about the situation, you'd see that you're being silly. I mean, your husband's been dead a week – get over it already."

Laudine did think about the situation, realizing that Yvain had killed her husband because her husband was trying to kill him (for ruining his property values yet again), and not because he was trying to hurt her feelings. So, if Yvain didn't mean to hurt her feelings by killing her husband, then she didn't have any right to have hurt feelings, and should in fact marry him as soon as possible. She called back the girl with glasses and a ponytail and ordered her to, "Fetch Yvain here straight away. I have decided I am in love with him, despite never having interacted with him in any form. I cannot wait a day longer to see him – I want him – now, now, now!"

The girl with glasses and a ponytail went to her room, where she had kept Yvain hidden for a week, sneaking him table scraps and anchovies. She brought him to meet her lady. But thought it would be funnier if Yvain still believed that Laudine wanted him dead.

So he fell to his knees upon seeing the lady, pleading, "It's not my fault! I didn't mean to! He was coming straight at me and my lance slipped – honest! By the way, I'm in love with you."

"Then we shall marry." Laudine rose and marched off to meet her council.

When they heard that King Arthur was coming for a camp out, they practically begged the lady to marry Yvain, saying, "Lady Laudine, we must have a knight to defend us. All we have right now is a lady, and they're absolutely worthless. This guy isn't so bad – he's the son of a King, after all. And our old lord's dead, so who cares about him anymore?"

A horde of clergymen rushed in and the wedding happened then and there.

Meanwhile, King Arthur and his court had turned left at the unkempt rustic and reached the spring.

Kay laughed. "Here we are ready for some good, old-fashioned avenging and Yvain's disappeared. He boasts when he's drunk – that's his problem. Utter coward."

The King, eager to see rain, poured a whole buttload of water from the spring upon the emerald. A storm exploded and soon Yvain appeared on horseback to defend his new land. Unfortunately, without a nametag, no one recognized him.

"Dibs!" cried Kay.

"So it is called; so it shall be," spake the King.

"Whoo-hoo!" Kay charged forwards and was promptly clotheslined.

Yvain graciously did not whomp him repeatedly whilst he was down, prompting the court's praise. Instead, he handed Kay's horse to the King. "I believe this belongs to you, sire."

"And who are you, oh masked stranger?"

"It's me, Yvain. Can't you recognize my voice, at least? Though I suppose it is rather echoey in this helmet. Hellooooooo. Want to come back to my new place for some snacks? I just got married and boy is my new wife a tiger. To pass the time on our journey, allow me to tell you all about it."

Thus King Arthur and his court followed Sir Yvain to his new home, where the inhabitants were so ecstatic at not being slaughtered that they broke out the kettledrums and partied. Laudine gave the King a vigorous hug, and Gawain got it on with the girl with glasses and a ponytail, whose name turned out to be Lunete. In fact the entire evening, with ninety ladies supplied inside the castle, was shaping up to be quite the orgy with some extremely heavy petting and drinking going on. After staying a week, it was time for the court to move on, but Yvain was reluctant to depart, seeing as he'd just wed and this was his new home.

"Don't be one of those wussy married guys," said Gawain. "Women like it when you desert them for long periods of time to have hot, sweaty fights with other men. And beasts. And tree stumps, if they deserve it. Why, I totally love what's-her-face, but that isn't stopping me from going out there and sowing my head-bashing oats. Come on and be manly with me."

So Yvain went to his wife and said, "My lady, Gawain double dared me to do the tournament circuit. Can I go?"

"Of course, darling," she said, "but if you're not back in a year's time I'll hate you forever and never forgive you."

"But I could get sick, or lost, or be thrown in prison and not make it back on time even though it wouldn't be my fault."

"Fine. If you get sick or thrown in prison – or die – I won't hold it against you. Here's a magic ring that will keep you safe as long as you think about how much you love me. Now have fun. And I'll try not to read anything into the fact that we've been married a week and now you want to leave me for a year or more."

Yvain cried on parting from his love, and Laudine cried, too. So much so that Arthur told her to go back inside because her womanly emotions were unsettling his masculine non-emotions.

Gawain wouldn't let Yvain out of his sight. They kept going to tournaments together, changing armour together, spending every second together, because it's bros before hoes and always will be.

Time passed, and suddenly Yvain had a thought: it had been TWO years since he'd left his wife, and now she wouldn't take him back. So he burst out crying because he loved her so much that he couldn't live without her.

As coincidence would have it, that's when Lunete showed up at court, saying, "Hello, your majesty. Hello, Gawain. Hello to all the brave and bold knights – except Yvain. I just wanted to announce to everyone – except Yvain – that my lady is heartbroken, and no longer considers herself married to the slug who hasn't shown his face in two years. Also, she would like her ring back." She stepped forwards and snatched the ring off Yvain's finger. "Goodbye now, everyone – except Yvain."

Yvain felt so devastated that he slunk away, ripped off his clothes, and ran naked into the woods. To survive, he snatched a boy's bow and arrows, killing deer and devouring them raw. But, other than being able to hunt with abnormal acuity, he was basically catatonic with despair.

The knights, who had thought maybe Yvain just needed a moment alone to get over the implosion of his marriage, now went out searching but could not find him.

It was, of all people, a hermit who at last found Yvain and, perceiving him to be running around naked, expertly deduced that he probably wasn't quite right in the head. So the hermit went inside his hut but left some bread outside. Yvain ate the bread, even though it was hard, vile stuff, and thoroughly enjoyed it. He really was quite mad, eating peasant food. Utterly out of his senses, he still somehow managed to kill a deer every day and bring it to the hermit's hut to be cooked, and the hermit sold the furs, getting some money for once in his life.

Then one day Yvain was sleeping in the woods when two damsels and their mistress passed by. Seeing a naked man, one damsel naturally leapt from her horse and ran over to ogle him. She examined him closely for some clue to his identity, finally getting around to his face and noticing a glaringly obvious scar that identified him as Yvain.

Running back to her mistress, the damsel reported, "My lady, it's Sir Yvain, who would be totes helpful in fighting that evil count who keeps attacking you. Except . . . I think maybe he's a bit batty. I mean, it's a little strange, sleeping naked on the ground in the middle of the woods."

"Not a problem. Here, take this magical ointment and rub a little on him – just on his temples, since that's where the madness is. And here's a mantle to cover him up. We'll wait here and stare in every direction but that one so we won't be able to see if you're actually doing as you're told. There's a good girl."

The damsel hurried back and started massaging the ointment on Yvain's temples – and then on the rest of him all the way down to his ankles, because she REALLY wanted him to get better. She left the mantle on the ground beside him, deciding it would be less embarrassing for Yvain if he put it on himself – and she cared so much about his personal dignity – then hid behind a tree to watch him sleep.

Finally Yvain awoke, being apparently one of the soundest sleepers in the world, and noticed – his madness clearing – that he was naked. 'Oh how humiliating,' he thought, 'this is worse than that keg party where – no, not the time for that. Look, a brand new robe, just lying on the ground. What tremendous random luck. I do hope no one's seen me naked, though, especially with that misspelt tattoo.'

The damsel, mounting her horse, came riding by looking in every direction but Yvain's, pretending she hadn't seen him.

"Hey you!" Yvain cried.

The damsel looked left and behind and under her horse and inside her sleeve, but couldn't seem to find the source of the call.

"Over here. I appear to have had something odd befall me."

"Come into town with me, then," said the damsel, hucking the empty ointment box into a stream.

In town, the lady and her damsels took special care to bathe and shave Yvain. They even gave him a haircut, armour, and a horse, being exceedingly accommodating plot devices.

As pure chance would have it, an evil count rode into the town, plundering and lighting the things he didn't plunder on fire. Yvain, who had had a long rest and no exercise, was stronger than ever. He hacked up many of the count's men, at which the townspeople were duly impressed, admiring particularly Yvain's merciless technique and the amount of blood he proved able to splash all over his weapons.

"He's more vicious than Roland," they said. "We do hope he falls in love with our lady so he can rule over us."

Yvain's courtly massacre prompted the evil count to surrender and apologize, promising to rebuild everything that he'd smashed into a bazillion pieces and then torched.

The lady who had nursed Yvain was so grateful to him that she demanded to be his mistress – or possibly his wife – but he demurred and went away.

Went away to a deep wood where he found a lion and a serpent doing battle. Or rather, the serpent was breathing fire on the lion's bottom. Watching, Yvain decided to take the lion's part because serpents are evil and icky, so he hacked the serpent into tiny bits. Unfortunately, he also hacked off a piece of the lion's tail. The lion, however, was a very well-bred lion, and bowed his thanks for being saved. He followed after Yvain like a puppy, brutally slaughtering deer and waiting until Yvain ate his fill before rending the carcass in a feeding frenzy of his own, swallowing bones and all. He even "guarded" Yvain's horse as the knight slept.

About a week later, this singular pair found themselves at the magical spring that had started this whole mess, distressing Yvain so he fainted. As he collapsed, his sword managed to fall from its scabbard and pierce the armour at his neck. The lion, legitimately distressed, very dexterously drew out and positioned the sword against a fallen tree so that he could stab himself and die with his master. Whilst running at the sword point, the lion saw Yvain awake, and was able to abort self-destruction.

As Yvain moaned about the unfairness of life, who should appear but Lunete.

"What have you got to whine about?" she asked. "I'm the one who's about to be executed for treason. I fixed up my mistress with a deadbeat, and *she* thinks I did it on purpose. I was sentenced to trial by combat, and suffered from a momentary aneurysm, saying my champion could beat any three of hers – but I haven't got a champion."

"Wait a minute," Yvain said, "*I'm* that deadbeat. I'll champion you."

"But my mistress is so infuriated she'll kill you on sight."

"Well, I'll show up wearing my helmet so no one will know me. I kind of owe you for saving my life, anyway. I guess."

"The trial's tomorrow. Just show up on time or I'll die a horrific, excruciating death. Do you think you can handle that?"

"Horrific, excruciating, got it. I'm Mr. Punctuality, you know."

Yvain and his lion found a fortress and asked to spend the night, but the fortress was no pets allowed. Yvain ardently assured the people within that his lion was housebroken, and at length they relented.

Everyone fell over themselves to give Yvain anything for which he had a whim. Then the lord of the fortress told Yvain, "There's an evil mountain giant who's killed two of my sons and is holding the other four hostage, unless tomorrow I hand over my daughter – she's Gawain's niece, by the way – who the giant thought he'd like to marry, but now he thinks it would just be fun to let his many minions abuse her. If only someone could help."

"Wait a minute," Yvain said, "I'm a knight. I could fight him."

"What a wonderful idea," said the lord. "I wish I'd thought of it. Would you care for some more chocolate pillow mints? Or an upgrade to a deluxe suite for the night?"

"Why yes, thank you. I just hope your giant comes early, because I already have another fight scheduled for tomorrow."

The next day Yvain waited, and waited, and waited. And finally decided he'd better get moving, giant or no giant, when who should turn up but the giant. And the giant – walloped Yvain.

So the lion leapt in. He softened up the giant and Yvain finished him off. Everyone was grateful but Yvain said, "Sorry, must dash. I really am very late now, if not too late. Toodle pip. Tell Gawain I say hi."

Meanwhile, Lunette had been stripped to her shift and was about to be cast onto a flaming pyre. When Yvain finally showed up.

"*Buy a watch!*" Lunette cried, sweat streaming down her face.

"I'm here to fight for her innocence," Yvain told the three knights for the prosecution.

"Three to one, that's fair enough," said the knights, "but you can't bring a lion into the fight."

"Are you chicken? I've got to fight all of you, and I'm not afraid."

"Tell your lion to stay out of it, or we won't fight you. It wouldn't be fair."

"Oh, *alright.*"

The lion laid down, as it was told, and the three knights proceed to bash Yvain all at once. Rolling his eyes, the lion leapt in, exposing entrails and winning the fight despite getting wounded.

"Wow," said Yvain's wife, "Lunete, I guess you're free to go. But, sir knight, who are you?"

"Why, the Knight with the Lion, of course. Toodle pip."

Yvain found his way to a mansion that also so happened to be a full-service hospital, evidently, and got fixed up, now having been wailed on by three knights and a giant.

Meanwhile, at King Arthur's court, an inheritance struggle was coming to a head. A lord had died, leaving a share to each of his two daughters. But the older one didn't like the sound of this "share" business, so she didn't. She asked Gawain, Arthur's best knight, to be her champion, and he said yes even though she was a brat, because knights had to be courteous and do everything ladies requested of them, even possibly jumping off a bridge, though no one probably ever asked for that, unless they were particularly bored

200

one afternoon.

The younger sister went to the King and said, "You know my sister is a brat, but how am I supposed to get my share of the inheritance when there's no knight who can beat Gawain in a fight?"

Arthur shrugged. "There's always that Knight with the Lion of whose existence we conveniently learned just today."

"Very well. I shall ride out and find him."

And she did, following a bread crumb trail of glorious deeds until bumping into Lunete, who conveniently knew where Yvain had gone. Upon hearing the younger sister's request, Yvain agreed to help her.

The day was waning as they started back to Arthur's court. Reaching a town, they were told not to go inside. At which Yvain became indignant, having recently contracted oppositional defiant disorder.

An old woman told him, "It's for your own good."

"Maybe," he replied, "but I'll do whatever I feel like."

Even the porter said, "You so don't want to come in here."

But Yvain said, "Yes I do," and went in.

Then the porter locked them in and refused to let them out.

Yvain and the younger sister found a warehouse packed with three hundred maidens weaving silk and gold, captives of two devils forcing them to perform menial labour. So Yvain bravely wandered off, finding more hospitable people, and allowing these the privilege of putting him up for the night.

In the morning when Yvain wanted to go, his host said, "I wish you could, but I don't feel like letting you. Instead, battle the two strong devils and, if you don't die a nasty, greasy death, then you can marry my daughter and inherit all I have."

The devils came in carrying enormous clubs and growled, "Tell your lion not to interfere whilst we mash your brains in."

"That's so not going to happen," Yvain said.

"But we insist."

"Oh, *alright*."

Yvain shut up his lion in a room whilst the two devils wailed on him. Until the lion broke free and ripped a chunk out of the first devil. Whereupon both fiends surrendered.

"And now," said the host, "you can marry my daughter."

"How about I don't," Yvain said, "and you free those three hundred maidens."

"Then I won't open the door and let you out."

"But I'm on a quest to help this young woman here with her inheritance. Promise I'll come back and marry your daughter later – if I can."

"Oh, shove it. I'll just marry her to someone else. What do I care who she spends the rest of her life with?"

Yvain and the younger sister reached King Arthur's court, where they met the older sister and her champion, Gawain, who wore armour no one recognized because, hey – who doesn't love having a secret identity? So Yvain, who didn't know it was Gawain, and Gawain, who didn't know it was Yvain, started bashing the ever-living tar out of one another. Pretty soon each of their shields was in pieces, their armour torn, and their blood spilling out everywhere. Everyone said the King should stop the fight, as both knights were so honourable it would be a shame if one became less honourable by losing to the other, but the older sister wanted all the inheritance for herself, and the King said if that was what she wanted then the two knights would have to go on hacking pieces off one another until someone won – or died, whichever.

Yvain perceived that evening was coming on – or maybe everything was growing dark and he was seeing stars – and told his opponent, in a voice garbled by blood, that he didn't think it would shame either of them to call a truce for the night. "Besides, I'm not entirely sure my skull isn't caved in. You fight so awesome. By the way, what's your name?"

"No, you're awesome," said Gawain. "I think I'm going to faint any second now. My name's Gawain. Nice to meet you."

"Seriously? Bro, it's me, Yvain. I'd have totally surrendered if I'd known it was you – to heck with that younger sister and her rightful claim to her own inheritance. I forfeit."

"No way, BFF, I forfeit."

"No – you whacked the holy Hannah right out of me."

"No – I'm pretty sure I'm crippled for life."

So they hugged and kissed and kept insisting that the other had won.

Arthur and the spectating knights ran up. "That's not how you fight – what are you two doing?"

"My lord," said Gawain, "you won't believe it, but this guy asked me my name – which I never would have thought of doing – and it turns out he's Yvain. He wins – another few minutes and he totally would have killed me."

"No, you win."

"No, you win."

"No, you win."

After a few minutes, Arthur finally said, "Shut up already! You know what, why don't I just decide this legal matter myself, instead of having you try to decapitate one another? Never mind that if I'd just done that in the first place it would have saved us all a lot of time, trouble, and hospital bills. Older sister, I've known all along that you were in the wrong. So share with your younger sister. If you don't, I'll declare my nephew Gawain the loser."

Fortunately, the older sister didn't call his bluff. "Fine – if I *have* to."

"And now," said Arthur, "let us stalk off in a grand procession. Someone prop up Gawain and Yvain and peel off what's left of their armour."

Whilst this was happening, the lion ran in, prompting everyone with a strong survival instinct to run out.

"So you're the Knight with the Lion," said Gawain. "You totally saved my niece and nephews from that smelly giant."

Then they went to the hospital and Arthur sent for the best surgeon the royal treasury could afford. But Yvain was dying – dying of love for his spurned wife. He decided to go to the spring and whip up such a storm that she would have to take him back or be forever tortured by the wind and lightning. Because he loved her so much.

Yvain snuck off with his lion and started a storm that nearly crumpled his wife's castle and everything else on her lands, terrifying everyone so they cried out, "What genius decided to build our town here, anyway?!"

Lunete said to her lady, "It's too bad all your knights are cowards and won't go out in the rain to kill whoever's doing that. I bet the Knight with the Lion would, though, if he were here. Too bad his lady's pissed at him and he's all disturbed. Otherwise he'd be just the knight to help you out."

"Find him," said Lady Laudine, "and I'll do all I can to ease his mind."

"Swear on a relic?"

"Fine."

"Then I very courteously take you at your word. Now that you've sworn on a relic. Be right back." Lunete rode out and, passing the spring, saw it was Yvain who was trying to drown them all and destroy their livelihood. "Oh there you are. Your wife will take you back now."

"Really? I owe you one."

"No, that's alright. I am the ultimate facilitating character. I don't even mind that Gawain had his fun with me and ran off never to return. Come on, my lady's waiting."

When Yvain entered, unrecognizable in full armour, his wife said, "Hello, complete stranger. I'm willing to do anything to make you happy."

"As easily done as said," Lunete announced, "for this is Yvain, your husband."

"The bastard who killed my first husband, lied about loving me, broke his solemn promise, and abandoned me for two years? I'll get back together with him, but not because I want to – only because I don't intend to dishonour myself by breaking my word."

Yvain felt ecstatic at seeing things go so well. "Oh, happy day! You should know the only reason I forgot to come back is because I was barmy. I promise to behave from now on."

"Whatever. I made a promise and I'm keeping it."

And so Yvain was happy, and Lunete was happy for him, and he dismissed all his past troubles from his mind.

As far as I know, this is where the story ends. If anyone tells you differently, they're lying.

The Council of the Pineapple

Sir Dwain was in his bar slash club, counting out his money. Mervin, too, was in the club, munching bread all crumby. Bernard was out in front there, plucking on lute strings, when came a visitor, urgent news to bring.

The visitor had on a fine cloak of black velvet, and strode into the comedy club before Bernard could utter a greeting.

Mervin stood up when he saw this traveler, and a multitude of bread crumbs trickled down his long, white beard. "We're closed!" he barked. Then under his breath, "Rotten teenagers – who strolls around at two in the morning as if it were daylight? We're closed for goodness' sake."

"We're also barely breaking even," Dwain moped from a table across the room. "Are my jokes that bad? Is Bernard's singing? Are your magic tricks? Well, yes, they are, but still."

Every half hour Mervin performed the exact same tricks in the exact same order, claiming that continuity calmed the soul. However, if past experience was any indication, continuity was nothing if not an irritation.

"It's positively amazing how the barbarians can cram an entire country's worth of people into a single fortified city, and *still* each and every one of them manages to avoid this bar. On the bright side, at least we can't be robbed. What does the visitor want? A million pounds in small bills?"

"Actually, I've come to offer you all a job." The visitor removed her hood, and there was a blood curdling scream, though it was unclear from whom it came.

Queen Amanita stood before the old magician and the

floundering brown-haired comedian. She looked the very picture of a stout dowager, still wearing black to mourn the loss of her son. King Xander had died five years before, and ever since there had been a plague of disorder.

The Saxon invaders had conquered much of Britain. Unfortunately, they could not decide who would be King of them all, and so Britain had broken into smaller kingdoms warring against one another. If only King Xander had lived, he could have reunited the Council of the Boot, Britain's last defence, and driven out the barbarians permanently. He could also have solved world hunger, saved the rainforest, and established world peace. . . . After he had won back Britain, of course. Mustn't get carried away. First things first.

"A job?" Dwain asked. "What do you mean?"

The Queen snorted. "It's these rude barbarians. They keep quibbling amongst themselves and Britain suffers for it. Isn't anyone going to offer me a seat?"

"Of course, your grace." Dwain sprang up, still dazed, and hopped over to the Queen, pulling out a chair.

"I don't like that chair. I want another one."

Dwain swept his arm around the room. "Any chair your majesty wishes."

Queen Amanita glared around the room. The roof was about ready to cave in – Dwain, Mervin, and Bernard not being able to afford both wood *and* nails. The floor was mere dirt and, besides a bar and a stage at the far back, there was nothing but tipsy tables with rickety chairs to surround them. The only light flickered from two candles: one above where Dwain had been going over the finances, and another on a table nearby. "I'll stand. You should burn this place down and collect the insurance."

"I would, milady, except the barbarians won't let Britons buy insurance."

"And all we're allowed to eat is this awful stale bread." Mervin tugged at his beard, attempting to remove the crumbs.

"And we can only listen to music by the Spice Girls," Bernard came inside. "If I want to play anything I've written myself, I have to do it in a mini skirt and platform shoes. I never thought I'd see the day when minstrels were regarded as lower class."

The Queen gave Bernard a sideways look. "Do you wax your legs?"

"No, majesty, I shave them."

"Good lad. Now, I've come here to offer you all jobs, as I've said about ten times now. I can see you are no more enamoured with the barbarians' rule than are the rest of our people. Therefore, I propose we reunite the Council of the Boot and retake Britain by force."

Dwain hesitated. "But, your grace, Bernard and I are the only two members of the council left in Britain."

"Don't forget Sir Robin the Bold," Bernard piped up.

Dwain rolled his eyes. "The man is an absolute chicken. Do you remember when he thought he would drown if he wore his armour in the rain? We couldn't get him to fight for a month. He kept babbling on and on about how a storm could come up at any moment."

"Perhaps he's found his courage in the time we've been apart."

"We'll find out soon," the Queen interjected. "I've asked him here, and he should arrive momentarily. We're going to assemble the whole council. Our people will then be inspired to band together around you, and fight for their country once more."

"But King Xander is dead." Dwain's guts lumped together with a deep sadness. "The council broke up because we had no one to follow blindly. Who will lead us?"

"Well I certainly can't," the Queen retorted. "I married a King but I've no royal blood myself and besides, it would make things far too easy and the plot would suffer for it. Gene of Arc will lead you."

Gene and Sir Guy of Longfellow had left Britain shortly after the King's untimely demise.

"But she's not of royal blood, either," Bernard objected.

"Of course she is – she's my daughter."

Shock made everyone freeze. Gene of Arc was utterly uncourtly. Mervin had trained her in every form of combat possible, from Kung Fu to Klingon bat'leths.

A thought occurred to Dwain. "Wait a minute – how can Gene be your daughter when she's Mervin's niece?"

"Don't you know?" the Queen asked in blank surprise. "You old ruin, didn't you tell them?"

"No." Mervin blinked. "Yes? Wait, what?"

Bernard moved over to stand by Dwain. "Know what?"

"That Mervin is my brother. You clown, why didn't you tell them?"

Mervin thought a moment. "I'm sure I mentioned something about it."

"No you didn't!" Bernard shrieked.

"Oh but I'm sure I did."

"If you had we would remember." Dwain crossed his arms. "Imagine! All this time you've been doing magic shows and we never milked the royalty angle. You could have made us a fortune!"

"Or at least enough for a third lute string," Bernard mumbled.

"It doesn't matter!" the Queen boomed. "Mervin, as Xander's maternal uncle, was appointed royal mentor, teaching my son everything there is to know about being a King – when to behead someone as opposed to having them burned at the stake, and all that. When my husband King Uber died, Xander ascended, and Mervin became Gene's mentor."

"Correct me if I'm wrong, but this seems like something we should have known before now," Dwain said.

"I'm sure I told you." Mervin was deep in thought, attempting to recall the ever-fading details of his life without success. "I really didn't say anything?"

"*No.*"

"Not even in passing?"

Just then another cloaked figure came through the doorframe and threw back its hood.

There stood Sir Robin the Bold in all his glory. He had let his wavy auburn hair grow long and thick. His beard had also grown long and curls in it had emerged. He took a wide stance, parting his cloak to reveal the field of azure adorned with three golden crosses on his puffed-out chest. With fists on hips he let out a deep, hearty laugh.

Dwain's eyes bugged out. "Does anyone else feel extremely frightened by this? What happened to the scrawny wuss we used to know?"

"A thing of the past, my friend." Robin clapped a hand firmly on Dwain's shoulder and laughed again. "It's amazing what self-esteem and some steroids can do."

Dwain struggled under Robin's hefty mitt. "Don't you think perhaps what you perceive to be self-esteem is reliance on a drug?"

"Bernard! my trusty minstrel." Robin swung his other massive paw, catching the dark-haired lad on the shoulder. "I see you've become a man in these five years, but is your music just as fair?"

Bernard leaned closer with a grateful smile. "It's an honour to see you again, master, but it worries me that you're taking steroids."

Robin gave a hearty chortle. "You have nothing to fear, lad. They haven't killed me yet, which is why I'm still alive."

Mervin, a lost look in his eyes, approached the burly knight. "I at least told you, didn't I?"

Robin laughed again. "Whatever you're talking about, I'm sure you did."

The magician took on a feebly triumphant air. "I knew I did. That ought to show who's senile and who's not." He stuck out his tongue at Dwain and Bernard.

"You terrible old sod!" Robin cried. "I'll wring your neck dry of all blood for that!"

Bernard and Dwain dove out of the way whilst Mervin's eyes grew wide with dread at the hulking warrior bearing down on him.

"Sir Robin, control yourself!" Queen Amanita shouted.

The bold knight quivered with rage, yet restrained himself.

"Now then, it's time we got to the shore, for our ship is about to come in. Mervin, I think it best you stay behind."

The magician nodded and scuttled off behind the bar. Meanwhile, the Queen and her three council members adjourned to the seashore under the cover of darkness.

***

It had been a long boat ride to Britain for two of the three remaining members of the council. Gene and Sir Guy of Longfellow had been under constant duress from Sir Keesh de Lattice to view repeatedly the snapshots of his fifteen children.

"Five sets of triplets in four years. Amazing, isn't it?" Keesh would ask again and again. Though still quite young, his hair was greying. "I can hardly remember all their names, sometimes," he chuckled. Then the wallet would come out, the snapshots would be unfurled, and the list would be recited. "Ethelwerd, and Elfgiva, and Ethelhilda, and Edhilda. Isn't it cute how they all have Saxon names? Edburh, and Ethelbald, and Ethelwulf, and Ethelbert, oh bless him . . . . "

Longfellow would roll his eyes, long since having given up feigning interest. The first time he had been privy to the progeny recitation, Keesh had finished by remarking, "I do hope my wife can handle them all. I shall write to check up on her once we're done with all this business. Shouldn't imagine it will take long. Had to sneak out in the middle of the night. Didn't want to wake anyone. The screaming, you know."

Longfellow had nodded. "So you just left a note?"

"Heavens no," Keesh twittered. "I thought I was just going ice fishing. Then this boat sailed by, so I hopped aboard. I assumed I'd be back in time for breakfast."

"Won't your family worry?"

Keesh had shaken his head. "Nights in the Yukon get longer this time of year. They're probably not even up yet."

After that, Longfellow had decided it was best not to talk to Keesh.

When the three passengers came to port, there was quite a welcome awaiting them. As soon as their feet again caressed their homeland, Sir Robin was upon them sobbing gratefully and with all his might. He grasped Longfellow to his chest, weeping all over him. For his part, Sir Guy caused his eyes to grow wide in surprised outrage, and struggled in vain against the bold man's grip.

Robin let go as he caught sight of Gene yet, before he could lament over her, Longfellow stepped between them and allowed himself to be joyously mourned once more.

"Break it up now, really." Queen Amanita stepped forwards to separate Robin from a now deflated Sir Guy. Then she turned to Longfellow herself, smiling as she only did when he was near. "And how is my favorite knight? I think Sir Robin has taken care of the matter of greetings. Any children yet?"

"Not as such." Longfellow was still indignant from being

manhandled.

"Well soon, I hope. What have you been up to?"

"Robbing convenience stores and the like. Not very rewarding."

Amanita turned to Gene. "Have you told him why we're all here?"

Gene nodded. "I have."

"No you haven't," Longfellow countered, "and I'd bloody well appreciate knowing what's going on."

Dwain snorted from in back of the welcoming party. "Apparently we're going to drive out the barbarians so your wife can rule Britain."

Longfellow snorted back. "That's ridiculous. She hasn't got royal blood."

The Queen stared at Gene. "Didn't you tell him?"

Gene frowned. "I thought I did."

Longfellow frowned too. "Tell me what?"

"That she's the Queen's daughter, and King Xander's sister." It greatly satisfied Dwain to drop this bombshell on someone. It took some edge off learning of it himself.

Longfellow turned to his wife, voice carefully under control. "You're the next in line for the throne?!"

"I'm sure I told you." Gene looked puzzled.

"She told me," Keesh spoke up. "Sir Guy, are you quite sure you didn't know?"

After a moment Longfellow started cursing loudly, and the Queen cursed him right back. Then Gene joined in, and Sir Robin had another mood swing and decided to participate. Keesh went over to Dwain and Bernard, excited at having two new people to view his snapshots.

At long last the hubbub stopped when Queen Amanita slapped Sir Longfellow on the back and cried, "Not only are you my favourite knight, but you're my favourite son-in-law, too."

***

"Should I be calling you 'your majesty' now?"

Everyone was spending what was left of the night at the comedy club. They were in their rooms fast asleep, except for Gene and Guy, who were arguing. It had been a long and inconvenient walk back to the city where the Britons were forced to live. There had been long portages over hill and dale, a near fatality when skirting past an active volcano, and a dangerous trek straight up and then straight down when climbing over the wall surrounding the Britons' city, all the time avoiding being detected by barbarian sentries posted in exciting and various spiral patterns, awake or not. All this, combined with the equally long and taxing sea journey, and being reunited with their long-lost friends, had put both Gene and Guy in incurably sour moods.

"For the thousandth time – I thought I told you."

"*When?*"

"At Mervin's house, when I joined the council."

Longfellow slapped the side of his head with the heel of his hand. "Oh, of course. So when you said, and I quote, 'Yeah, yeah, when do we fight?' what I was supposed to have divined from that was, 'I'm the King's sister and therefore the heir apparent'!"

"Are you sure that's what I said? 'Yeah, yeah, when do we fight?' It sounds a bit callous."

"Yes, well, that's what I liked about you."

Gene snapped, "I should have known we wouldn't get on when I found out my mother liked you." Then, seeing the look on Guy's face, she changed the subject. "Have you noticed something odd about Sir Robin?"

Longfellow sighed. They wouldn't solve this in one night,

anyway. "I'm not blind. Nor am I deaf, remember? His face is ruddy and chubby, his shoulders must have doubled in size, and he's got quite a large belly now."

"He seems to be having mood swings."

"Well he did mention something about steroids."

"You remember what your precious friends tell you, but not your own wife."

"Blast it! You never told me, woman, it's as simple as that!"

***

The comedy club did not have the best beds to pass the night on. Britons were allowed beds made of wooden boards with no mattresses, and only blankets made of the itchiest possible wool. Insulation was also confiscated, and so the club itself was more of the same greying wood as the beds.

Dwain couldn't sleep because he was too busy worrying about finances, and Longfellow couldn't sleep because he was too busy thinking about a number of things. He approached the bar where Dwain was leaning with his eyes closed.

"This is quite the dump you've got here."

With an effort, Dwain moved his head to look at Guy. "Isn't it, though?"

"Get many customers?"

"Not really. We can only serve stale bread now, and it's not exactly flying off the shelves. But we've got a nice little division of labour: I do the comedian thing, Mervin puts on magic shows, and Bernard sings."

"How is that working out?"

"Let's put it this way: the only thing our crowd wants to hear are Polish jokes, they'll boo you off the stage if they think you're misrepresenting the Spice Girls by playing an instrument, and last week Mervin lit his beard on fire whilst trying to pull a quarter out of someone's ear."

"Sorry to hear it."

"Don't be." Dwain stretched. "The beard thing brought in more business than we'd normally see in a year. I just wish I could come up with some kind of act people would laugh at that doesn't involve insulting Polish people."

"Do you have any reservations about insulting Canadians?"

"Maybe blonds . . . . "

Longfellow snorted. "Do and I'll jam a microphone up your nose."

"See, now *you* could be a comedian."

"Britain and its people need their leader, I suppose."

"Yes, we really do."

By now the others were up. No one had gotten overmuch sleep, and they were ready to make whoever was available pay for it. Everyone gathered 'round the bar for stale bread and Evian water. During this repast, Bernard provided ambiance in the form of a new ballad he had been tinkering with:

"Earth Song

"To sea go the fish,
To sky go the birds,
To land go the beasts,
To court go the lords,
With them the ladies.
To you is where I go.

"Fish have water,
Birds have clouds,
Beasts have grassy plains,

Lords have court,
Ladies have lords.
I have thee by my side.

"Fish crave worms,
Birds crave fish,
And so do the beasts of the shore.
Lords crave court,
Ladies crave lords.
I crave thee by my side.

"Fish have fins,
Birds have wings,
Beasts have legs, all four.
Lords have arms,
As do ladies.
I have thee by my side.

"Fish have water,
Birds have clouds.
I have thee by my side."

"Excellent," proclaimed Robin. "It isn't often you hear a love song that can pull off talking about worms. And it's true: fish do crave worms, whilst lords do have arms. At least most of them seem to. Bravo, Bernard."

The minstrel blushed, summoning nerve to ask the question that had been wiggling away at the back of his mind since the night before. "I still don't understand," he spoke up warily, "why the Council of the Boot broke apart when Britain needed us most."

Dwain leaned forwards onto the bar. "I'll field this one. We broke up because Britain had been saved. The barbarian chieftain and his pet dragon were both slain, our nation at last had peace – besides, it's not like we don't have lives outside of saving the nation from certain doom – you know that. At any rate, the King dying was a great personal tragedy to us who knew him. We parted from each other distraught. If we hadn't, then Britain would never have been conquered, and there couldn't have been this epic reunion tale."

"Oh. Well then that makes perfect sense."

There was silence once more, everyone making what attempt they could at keeping down breakfast.

"So, your grace," Dwain said, "what happens now?"

Queen Amanita motioned with her hand, her mouth full of bread. "This is Gene's council now. That is up to her."

"Well," Gene felt unused to speaking to more than one person at a time, "I don't suppose our people will rally around us without some incentive, so Mervin – would you mind whipping us up a dragon, or some such mascot?"

"Not a problem. A griffin will suffice, do you think?" Mervin reached up to remove his hat. After a few intense moments a fluffy white rabbit was removed, along with forty-seven rolls of duct tape, a rhubarb plant, and a 2002 Volkswagen Beetle. "Now stand back, everyone." Mervin set the rabbit on the bar top, and took a step backwards himself. "It's hard to say just how large this thing will get. Abraka- *ow*!"

Mervin had been waving his arm to perform the spell when he hit himself in the forehead.

"Well." Dwain stepped forwards again to get a better look. "The rabbit's not any bigger, but at least now it's purple."

Bernard nodded encouragingly. "And instead of ears it's got a third set of legs. That's rather frightening."

Mervin considered a moment. "I suppose you're right. Is it up to

218

snuff, your majesty?"

Gene realized she was being spoken to. "Can you do any better?"

Just then the rabbit took a hop and let fly a horizontal mass of flame from its mouth.

Mervin frowned. "However did it manage that?"

"Doesn't matter." Gene shook her head. "The creature is fine as is. What else must be dealt with?"

Sir Guy of Longfellow spoke for the first time. "We should swear you our allegiance."

"Do we actually need to swear?" asked Keesh.

Guy rolled his eyes and mumbled, "I know I've got a couple choice words saved up."

"Could I make a suggestion?" asked Robin giddily. Gene sighed. "Go on."

Robin scrambled to place a hand over his heart and recited, "I salute you, Gene, the Queen of this here country. To you I pledge my love and loyalty."

Dwain considered. "That's actually not too bad."

Robin twittered at the compliment and bent at the knees, half crouching, before again standing to his full height. "It just came to me – just now. You're such a doll for saying that, Dwain. You're not just humouring me, are you?"

"Uh, no."

"You're such a doll!"

Gene interceded. "Is that it? Are we ready to go kick some Teutonic butt?"

"We must rename the council," Queen Amanita grumped. "My son was never very good at naming things. This is your council now, Gene, so you must come up with something better."

Gene sighed. "Couldn't we just leave it be? Who on earth will care what we call ourselves?"

"You know," Dwain jumped in, "whenever I look back on that first time we all met Gene, one thing always comes to mind: pineapples."

Queen Amanita turned on him. "Young man, are you suggesting that my daughter inspire her downtrodden subjects to mount a rebellion against dismal odds, when the only tools at her command are a rabbit with confused pigmentation, and a group of slavering morons who call themselves the Council of the *Pineapple*? Is that how you want this courageous last stand to go down in history?"

"Somehow, it doesn't sound as promising when you say it, your grace."

"The Council of the Pineapple it is." Gene grabbed her sword and scabbard off a table and strode for the door. "Let's just get to the fun part."

The Queen and the magician watched as Gene and her council trooped off into the new day, Bernard behind the rest and holding the purple rabbit at arm's length.

✳✳✳

Every one of the Britons – approximately two million people – had been conveniently rounded up and placed in a single walled city by the Saxons. Now all the people gathered together before a soapbox awaiting Gene, who was to tell them why they had all gathered together before a soapbox awaiting her to tell them why they had all gathered together. She and her knights had donned full armour, exempting their helmets, and Gene had set aside her own coat of arms for her brother's red and gold.

The council stood behind the wall before which the soapbox was set, preparing to appear and, hopefully, rouse their people to fight back against injustice. Bernard still regarded the purple rabbit warily. Upon the journey there the miniature beast had already turned two sheep, a cornfield, and a riding mower to ash.

Gene peered around the corner at the assembled crowd. "There are far too many people. I'm supposed to be the Ultimate Warrior, why must I make speeches?"

Longfellow rolled his eyes. "Because, darling, you're the Queen of Britain."

Dwain elbowed him, murmuring, "This is new for her, too. Don't be a jerk."

Longfellow gazed murderously back at his comrade-in-arms, amending through clenched teeth, "You'll do fine."

"Does anybody got milk?" Sir Robin was doubled over clutching his stomach.

"What's wrong with you?"

"Oh nothing. I just get this *intense pain* a few hours after I eat anything."

"That sounds rather like an ulcer." Dwain frowned, but Robin only waved his hand.

"No, nothing of the kind. It's simply an *intense pain*. Then there's the bloating, and the vomiting up blood, but it's nothing I can't manage. A nice glass of milk usually sets things to rights. I know we're only supposed to have bottled water – which the barbarians consider to be worse than tap water – but back at my castle I've hidden a wonderful milking cow that – "

"Quiet, you idiot!" Longfellow hissed. "Don't you remember that, when the King died, we all took a solemn oath to never again use *that word?*"

"You mean 'milking'?"

"No!"

"Oh, of course – you mean '*cow.*'"

Everyone's hands flew either to their ears or Robin's throat, remembering that fateful day five years ago when Xander had realized his dream of a stealth cowapult, hurling cud chewers to crush all enemies. And, unfortunately, the King himself.

Gene steeled her jaw. "We shall fight for my brother's memory, if for nothing else."

She stepped out from the cover of a rather large garbage pile beside the wall, and onto the soapbox. Robin and Keesh emerged to stand to her left, Longfellow and Dwain to her right. Gene spoke in a booming voice, not unlike her mother's: "My people, our King is dead, killed under most noble circumstances."

"A cow fell on his head," shouted a shepherd in the crowd.

Gene puffed. "I am aware of that."

"How is that noble?"

"It just is."

A soot-stained blacksmith called out, "As opposed to having a pig dropped on his head? At least the King died kosher."

"*Shut up*! The point is he departed to heaven whilst realizing a weapon for the defence of this country, and your persons. As the King's sister, it is my right to succeed him as ruler of Britain."

"How do we know you're the King's sister?"

The shepherd cried, "We'll get her DNA tested."

"We'll need the King's for comparison."

"Let's dig him up, then," said a clay-spattered potter. "Who's got a shovel?"

"I got a spade!"

"Oh, that won't work!"

Everyone began speaking at once.

Gene felt her neck grow hot. "We are *not* digging up the King!"

Someone shouted, "Who made you Queen of the world?"

"Not the world – Britain. I am the King's sister and, in the absence of any children had by him, it is my right to succeed."

"I dunno." The shepherd squinted at her. "I thought we were a culture of sexist brigands who only accepted male leaders."

The blacksmith shook his head. "No, we're Celts. We prefer male leaders, but have no qualms against females taking the job."

"Really? When did that happen?"

Dwain sighed to himself. "Where's the crowd's legal spokesperson when you need them?" He smirked, murmuring, "Probably caught in traffic."

Gene felt quite cross now. "This will take all day if you lot keep flapping on! I've gathered you to form an army that will march against our barbarian oppressors and win."

"Ooo!" The shepherd winced. "I'm afraid we're too busy."

"Doing what?"

"Cowering in fear. What makes you think we'll win?"

Gene straightened. "Our undying spirit. What makes you so sure we'll lose?"

"We don't have any spirit."

The blacksmith grinned. "We don't even have spirits."

This was quite enough for Longfellow, who stepped out and grasped the shepherd's jaw, lifting him onto the tips of his toes. "Do you hear your Queen addressing her people?"

The culprit dangled helplessly.

"Is what you have to say more important? Perhaps *you* defeated the barbarians before, and have a plan for doing so again? No? And your accomplice here?"

The blacksmith shook his head vehemently, looking a fair bit shorter than he had moments before.

"Then *listen*." Longfellow tossed the shepherd, as if he were unwanted rubbish, and resumed his place.

Gene surveyed the crowd. "It is time you learned of our trump card. Bernard, bring him out."

The minstrel emerged from behind the wall, holding the purple rabbit at arm's length. People began crying out.

"What is it?"

"Dunderhead – 'tis a colossal caterpillar."

"It's a rabbit," Gene said.

"A rabbit? Everyone knows rabbits are white or brown."

"Or black," said the potter. "Black rabbits are best – wouldn't you agree, Fergus?"

"Oh, yes, quite – you can't even tell if you've spilled somewhat on one."

"What? No, not habits – rabbits! What sort of rabbit's purple with three sets of legs?"

"This one." Gene hoped the Saxons would be taken just as off-guard. "Mervin the Magician conjured this up himself."

"It's a freak of nature."

A lass shrieked. "Don't look it in the eye – you'll turn into a mime."

"It's an illusion – something to do with mirrors."

Gene sought control. "I assure you, it's real."

"So what can it do?"

The rabbit let fly a flame, igniting the wall behind the council in crackling heat and light.

Gene smiled. "It can kick those barbarians' butts back to the days of the Roman Empire. Will you join us?"

A woman stepped forwards. She looked as if she was used to a fair amount of respect from her peers. She shrugged. "Not like we've got anything better to do – it's been a slow week."

"So you'll fight?" Gene pressed.

"On one condition: we get to name the rabbit."

"Very well, go ahead."

"Nigel!"

"Virgil!"

"Lolly!"

"Maurice!"

Gene sighed. "Maurice it is. Now you'll fight?"

"That we will," the woman replied. "To the death."

"To the death," the Britons repeated. "We fight for Queen, country – and Maurice!"

Dwain smirked to himself. "Close enough. If we stick close to the rabbit, this just might work."

So the Britons marched to Londinium with a wonderful confidence that they would be, one and all, mangled or dead before the day was through.

"Are we there yet?" Keesh asked.

"Blast all this sunlight." Sir Robin squinted, keeping pace with the Council of the Pineapple at the head of the makeshift army. "It gets my vision all blurred. I don't even want to think about the size my ankles will swell to with all this walking."

"Good," snapped Guy. "Don't talk about it, either."

"Robin," said Dwain, "why don't you ease off the steroids? You're causing yourself an awful lot of pain."

"But you thought I was a wuss before."

"You still are."

Robin flushed, his face already so red it was hard to tell. "I don't look like one. Besides, we're all going to die soon, so what's the point of quitting? Chopped, hacked, decapitated, butchered – "

"Shut up!" Longfellow barked. "You're as bad as that rabble back there."

"And if the barbarians don't get me, high blood pressure will," Robin retorted.

Keesh spoke up. "I say, are we there yet?"

"We would be if those blighter barbarians would let us ride horses," said Robin. "Riding a porcupine just isn't as impressive. I'm glad we decided to walk today. Even this plodding about like commoners is more dignified than the alternative. Keesh, you must feel thankful that, in the Yukon, you can ride a horse whenever you please."

"Well, they do tend to freeze rather solid."

Gene snorted, quickening her pace. What had Xander seen in these idiots that he had made them Knights of the Roundish Table? Robin the Bold was an insecure fool, Dwain of Eboracum was more court jester than warrior, Bernard was a mere minstrel, Keesh de Lattice was as mindless as a person could be, and Guy of Longfellow – without a fight to join in, he was the most irritating man on the planet – restless and pigheaded. Exactly like herself. She was already stuck living with herself; why had she deigned to espouse a duplicate? These ruminations spoiled her pleasure at once again having a cause to battle for.

Turrets spiked Londinium's high walls. As the Britons approached, they saw no signs of life above. The city gate was locked, and the drawbridge drawn up.

"We'll *never* get in!" wailed Robin. "I knew it! Now we'll all be slaves forever with no hope of salvation."

Dwain lifted an eyebrow. "Since when are we slaves?"

"I don't know. This is just all so *depressing*!" The bold knight wept.

"Can I throw him in the moat now?" Longfellow's eyes were closed as he frowned, rubbing the join between nose and forehead.

Dwain glanced at Gene to see if she was paying attention, then said, "Be my guest."

Longfellow's eyes popped open. "Good." He grasped Robin's shoulders, preparing to heave.

226

"Stop that!" Gene stared up at Londinium's battlements. Something wasn't right. The Saxons would not seemingly abandon the capital.

"What on earth are you waiting for, child?"

There was a scream of terror as Queen Amanita pushed her way through to the front of the Britons.

"Mother, what are you doing here?"

"I came to see how you're getting on."

"You're checking up on me!"

"I am not."

"You checked up on Xander relentlessly, and now you're doing it to me."

"I worry more about you since your brother was killed."

"You're worried Maurice will crush me to death?"

"Who's Maurice?"

"The rabbit."

"I'm hardly worried about that confounded thing."

"You should be – I might step on it, and cave in its skull."

A cry went up. "How dare you threaten our beloved Maurice?! We shall avenge him!"

The two Queens and the Council of the Pineapple stepped back in surprise as their own army advanced upon them.

"Wait!"

All looks were routed to a trembling Sir Keesh.

He forced a smile. "Would anyone like to see snapshots of my kids?"

A war cry rose, the Britons charging forwards. At the same moment the Saxons sprang up on the battlements, hurling javelins into the mob. The attacking Britons fell back. Well, not fell back so much as fled in terror as fast as their feet could carry them.

A cheer blasted from the barbarians.

The Council of the Pineapple slowly raised their heads. They had not run with the rest of their people but crouched, attempting to become invisible. Now they straightened back up, looking around and wondering that they had not been killed. Everyone was so preoccupied checking themselves from top to bottom for any injury, that no one noticed the look of wonder on Gene's face that Longfellow had shielded her from the javelins with his body. Neither did they notice the javelin embedded six inches deep in Sir Robin's side.

Until he did, of course, and proceeded to scream and swoon.

Bernard dropped the purple rabbit. He knelt to support Robin's head, tears spiking from his eyes.

"Is it mortal?" Keesh breathed.

Robin's eyelids flickered. "This deep it could hardly prove otherwise. So I'll die in battle after all – fancy that."

All the action was over, and not a single blow had been struck for their side, but no one bothered mentioning this.

"Bury me in the summertime, if you please." The bold knight shuddered. "On a chilly morning when the sun appears glassy, and no bird dares utter its song. Lay me face down in my grave so I can't see the dirt thrown over me.

"Use a trowel to dig my grave. I always wanted to give gardening a go, but never got 'round to it. Write that on my tombstone: 'Wanted to give gardening a go.' Then maybe when people read that it will give new meaning to their lives.

"I feel myself growing faint. Please, Bernard, take out the javelin before I pass on. I won't die with it in me. I trust you. Even if I cry out in pain, don't stop till it's out. Oh, why did they have to be armour-piercing javelins? That's so inconsiderate."

Bernard nodded, tears blurring his vision. Dwain, feeling the sting of conscience for so many past words, knelt down and took up the minstrel's post, his own eyes growing red.

Bernard planted his feet. At a minute nod from Robin, which seemed all the bold knight could manage, the minstrel began to pull.

Tears streamed down Bernard's face as his master cringed and writhed, grunting in agony.

Gene and Longfellow stood shoulder to shoulder, whilst Keesh clapped a hand to his mouth and Amanita pursed her lips.

The javelin wrenched free and Bernard collapsed to the ground in total exhaustion.

Keesh squinted at the six inches of javelin that had been embedded in Sir Robin the Bold. "What's that red stuff there – it can't be blood."

Bernard wiped away his tears to better see. "It looks like an enormous wad of hair." He squinted. "There's not a drop of blood in it."

"There's no pain now. I can feel myself slipping peacefully away . . . . " Robin spread his arms, as if he would fly.

"You idiot." Dwain stood, sending Robin's head to the ground.

"Ow – hey!"

"I'll bet it didn't even nick your skin." Dwain threw Robin's arm in his face, unstrapping the cuirass encircling the bold knight's midsection. Removing this, Dwain lifted the tunic underneath to see. "Foaming turnips!" He recoiled, and so did everyone else.

"That's disturbing." Gene clenched her fists.

Keesh spasmed. "I think I'm going to be sick!"

A growth of thick red hair curled over Sir Robin's body as far as the eye could see. Except where a mammoth clump had been ripped out by the javelin.

"Finally some good has come of your stupid steroids," Guy observed. "You'd have gotten a nice gash if not for all that bloody hair."

"It appears you're right." Robin examined himself. "All's well that ends well, I suppose."

Queen Amanita nodded. "Yes, yes. So much for a climactic last stand in battle. Now it's time we resign ourselves to Saxon rule until the whole trouble with the Vikings. Afterwards, the Battle of Hastings will take place, and that will be it for successful conquests of Britain."

Longfellow picked up Maurice, who had been enjoying a nearby cluster of taller grass, by the "ears." "And what's to become of this rubbish rapscallion?"

The Queen waved a hand. "Just toss it somewhere. You don't want plague fleas, do you?"

He hurled the purple rabbit so it sailed over Londinium's battlements.

Everyone turned to leave, when a gargantuan column of flame shot up to the sky. The drawbridge fell open, jolting the earth. Saxons went streaking towards the coast, screaming and tripping over tulips in their haste. The Council of the Pineapple watched as the last man disappeared over the crest of a hill, Maurice giving vehement purple rabbit chase.

Keesh gaped. "What just happened?"

"I think we won our country back." Gene frowned.

"But that wasn't supposed to happen, was it? I mean, as far as historical accuracy goes."

The beginnings of a grin lit Dwain's face. "Well gang, it would appear we have just irrevocably decimated history, and unleashed a six-legged fire-breathing purple rabbit on the world. Any bright ideas?"

Robin hesitated. "Does anyone think the little beast might be tetchy because he has extra feet instead of ears, and ends up continuously startled by people he can't hear approaching him?"

230

"Hm," Dwain said. "Any *other* bright ideas?"

Longfellow grunted. "I could use a belt. Anyone else?"

There arose a chorus of agreement as they trooped into the abandoned city to jimmy the lock on the barbarian chieftain's liquor cabinet.

***

<u>Important Notice</u>: Walk, do not run, to your nearest library and check out any and all books pertaining to British history. This is not, by any stretch of the imagination, a weak attempt to trick you into learning something. Seriously, check the books – have they been rewritten? Did the Britons end up winning? How bungled *is* the space-time continuum? To avoid any negative (or positive) effects of this sudden breech of historical fact, construct yourself a hat made entirely of Saran Wrap. (Tin foil is *so* cliché. Besides, all tests conclude that the only results are messing up your hair and making you look daft.) Once again, check out all British history books from your local library. Sure, they're thick and hardcover, but remember that your struggle to carry them out to your car is nothing compared to the struggle of the Britons; they didn't *have* cars to carry their library books out to. Truly a noble, read-worthy people.

The Vulcan Cycle

The man entered the throne room awash in purplish garments. Authority powered his stride, and yet seemed sapped by some hidden ailment. He advanced to the dais as though he would storm it.

Even as Guy Longfellow moved to intercept, the man halted and bowed. "Your majesty."

Gene, seated in the throne, rolled her eyes. "Arise. State your business."

The man's face turned a shade nearer his robes as he swayed to his feet. "Your majesty."

"You said that."

"My humble greetings to you, your consort, and all your gathered knights and courtiers."

Dwain looked up from his game of pinochle with Keesh, Bernard, and Robin in one corner of the enormous and otherwise empty great hall. "Humble greetings right back at you."

"Get *on* with it," Gene groaned.

The man suppressed a glimmer of confusion. "Your majesty."

"Oh for heaven's sake."

"Whilst your Council of the Pineapple has surely wrought a miracle by wresting back our noble Britain from the Saxons' clutches, the governing of our fair land must necessitate the addition of further knights to your most noble court."

Gene grunted. "My brother called all Britain's knights when first he formed his Council of the Boot. These four are the only ones left unslain."

"Pardon, oh Queen, but your illustrious brother called the *best* knights."

Dwain frowned at his cards. "Then why is Robin here?"

"More knights than these still populate our isle, and I can inform your majesty of their whereabouts."

"And you are . . . ?" asked Longfellow.

"Forgive me. I am the Phisher King and with this, my mystic crystal ball," he extracted it from his sleeve, "I can access all personal information of anyone in this kingdom."

Gene slung her chin in her hand. "That's a snow globe."

"Ah, it may appear so to the uninitiated, yet when it is upturned you will observe the orb grow cloudy, and then all you must do is ask the proper question, that you might gain what you seek."

Sir Guy perceived the glance from his wife and stepped forwards. "Our question being, would you prefer your eyeballs yanked from your skull, or pushed all the way back through your brain?"

"We already have an incompetent magician who performs useless spells," said Gene. "He's my uncle, so I'm not about to replace him. Leave now, and your eyeballs can stay where they are."

The Phisher King bustled back towards the exit, tripping over his flowing robes a half dozen times before reaching it.

Gene groaned again, louder. "Why does everyone think I need help running the kingdom?"

Guy murmured, "Apparently it's obvious."

"I can't think clearly, because you won't let me *fight*!"

"You're seven bloody months pregnant!"

Gene slammed down both hands on the arms of her throne. "I can fight!"

"If it makes you feel any better, majesty," Keesh twittered, "fighting isn't what Britain needs now anyway."

"He's right," said Dwain. "With the power vacuum left by the barbarians now we've sent them home with their tails between their legs, what Britain most needs is the restoration of a stable infrastructure, law and order, foreign and local trade relations, reliable currency, public works, stable employment, an end to religious persecution, a clear power structure – "

"Shut up! There is no power vacuum – I am Queen, as my brother was King before me, and our father before him – his father before him, his uncle before him, and his second cousin twice removed before him – unflinching continuity of leadership."

Keesh frowned, waggling his fingers in the air attempting to map out the family tree.

"When a county is lost, the best thing is to fight – bring everyone together for a cause. Singularity of purpose, perfect focus – there is nothing more relaxing than a fight."

Bernard snapped his cards onto the table. "Gin!"

Dwain lowered one eyelid to stare at him. "We're playing pinochle."

"I know, but I don't have pinochle. I have gin."

"I don't have gin." Robin pouted. "Dwain, do you have any threes?"

Dwain sighed. "Is it suppertime yet?"

"It is." Longfellow offered his hand to Gene.

Gene crossed her arms.

"What?"

"I'm so bored with this no fighting business. I won't eat unless first I see something wonderous."

Longfellow gritted his teeth. "The child – "

"Show. Me. A wonder."

"My minstrel is the most entertaining in all the land. *He* can show your majesty a wonder." Robin elbowed Bernard.

The minstrel stood. "Observe carefully, majesty." He held up both hands, and let leak a deep breath. Then Bernard slowly drew his hands apart. The stump of his thumb remained on his right hand, whilst its tip travelled with his left.

"Oh for heaven's sake." Gene rolled her eyes.

Dwain sprang up, shuffling. "Pick a card."

"*No.*"

Robin shrugged. "I have a rather wonderous-looking ingrown toenail."

"*No!*"

"Well." Keesh shuffled to his feet. "I suppose I may have the ticket, majesty." He produced a purse.

"If this is more pictures of your children – "

"No, majesty. My wife gifted me this purse. It is bottomless, and will provide for all my needs as long as I conceal the secret."

"What secret?"

"The secret of this purse."

"Which is?"

"A very secret one."

"Sir Keesh, I feel aggravated enough without catharsis, you need not build upon it. Sir Guy? A wonder?"

Guy Longfellow eyed his wife.

"Then supper will have to keep."

His face creased as his mind worked. Then, "A tournament." He hunched over her, leaning his hands on the throne's armrests. "A tournament, to which we invite all Britain's remaining knights. A chance to display your royal prestige, and handpick a court that can aid you in exercising authority. A chance for blood, steel, and brutal victory."

Gene's eyes resounded with light.

"However, as this wonder could not be organized and held before you starve to death, I urge your majesty to eat."

"And you promise to arrange the tournament?"

"I give you my word."

Gene grasped his forearm, and he hauled her to stand. "I do hope there are apples at supper. I have a craving for apples."

Longfellow grimaced, as the others pulled faces.

"Apples?" asked Keesh. "My own darling wife certainly craved some strange foods whilst swollen with our brood, but never anything as revolting as an apple."

"Indeed," said Longfellow. "Supper consists of much more sensible foods: haggis, peacock, and blood pudding." He scoffed, murmuring, "Apples."

Gene frowned as he slipped from her grip.

When she had first told him she suspected herself with child, Guy had shrugged off the possibility. When she had pressed her suspicions, he had stood frozen a moment, then said, "Fine." But, it certainly had not been fine.

They met Mervin in the not-so-great hall, where white-clothed trestle tables were set out for supper. Gene, followed by the others, held her hands over a bowl as a servant showered them with rosewater.

"What happened now?" Dwain plunked down on a bench next to Mervin. "You've another hole torn in your beard."

"The cook cut my midafternoon sandwich into a heart shape, yet there were still bits of crust on some edges."

"Well, then of course you lost your composure. I've never heard of a woman's uncle, rather than her husband, experiencing sympathy mood swings before."

Keesh was staring at Mervin's beard. "It's like a snowbank with a family of gophers living in it."

Mervin glowered, but addressed Gene. "The man-at-arms stationed in the tallest watchtower has been struck by lightning

236

again. We'll need a new fellow."

"We just got *that* one last week."

"Well he's no good to anyone now." Mervin gestured a servant to slice him a hunk of peacock. The bird, dressed as a knight with a spear, was riding a pig on a platter into the hall.

"I thought," said Dwain, "that peacock was too spicy for you."

Mervin shrugged. "I'm living backwards, remember? May as well eat the blasted thing when I've already had the heartburn. By the way, your majesty, you might want to give some thought to a system of calling the able-bodied populace to military service, should the barbarians mount a comeback invasion."

"I am Queen. The people will provide military service because I say so."

"Yeah," said Dwain, "the real world really doesn't work like that. It never has. King Xander knew that – "

"I am not my brother! I shall rule my own way!"

"Any changes to military service are best suited to after the tournament," Longfellow said, "once we know the number and abilities of the trained military."

"A tournament?" Mervin asked. "Who's coming?"

"Any knight – every knight – we must replenish our ranks to fend off a possible barbarian counterattack."

"I could send out invitations."

"Heralds will be fine."

"But nothing says bloodthirsty tournament like an engraved invitation."

"Yes, but we want the invitations actually sent, not all the guests turned into dental floss or baboons."

"You are *the* most ungrateful nephew-in-law – "

"Look, old man – "

Robin leaned towards Dwain. "How bad do you think it is?"

"The blood feud forming in front of us, or the food?"

"Bernard."

"*What's* wrong with Bernard?"

Robin sighed, as though Dwain were a simpleton. "Poor lad. When the Queen declined to view my wonder, he took it straight to heart. He'll never see me the same way again."

"As a bumbling coward whose idiocy rivals that of the Trojan who thought a nice wooden horse would really spruce up the place?"

"I was the boy's hero, his mentor, his sage, and now – now he looks on me with pity and regret."

"That's how everyone looks at you."

"I must win back the lad's respect, or else he will never again see me as a whole man."

"There's a joke there, but I'm going to let it go."

Longfellow and Mervin's argument drowned out the possibility of further conversation.

"*STOP IT*!" Gene slammed both fists on the table. "Stop it! Sir knight, apologize to the magician."

"You're joking."

"*Do* it."

Longfellow glanced down the table and about the room, at all of his fellow knights and the servants staring at him. "I said nothing unprovoked, majesty."

"I don't care. Tell him you're sorry."

"My Queen – "

"Sir Guy."

Longfellow licked his lips, now trying to angle his gaze as though he could not see anyone else in the room. "I apologize, Mervin, if you felt undue offense at anything I may have said in passion. It was not my intention to raise ill feeling in a member of my own family."

Mervin nodded, looking as satisfied as a cat having the base of its tail scratched.

Guy Longfellow slashed a glance at his wife, clenching his hands together.

***

Gene rolled herself into bed.

Longfellow still sat on its edge, dressed, with his back to her.

"Will you rub my feet? I've felt them throbbing all day."

"Get a servant to do it. God knows you've enough of them."

"You're my spouse. I want you to do it."

"I am also your chief knight, and tonight you humiliated me in front of every last one of my subordinates."

"I did no such thing. My uncle wanted an apology, and you gave him one."

"No one can lead without respect."

"You are still the best knight. They still respect you."

"*You* do not respect me. You do not respect anyone, which is why you cannot lead."

Gene's skin prickled hot. "You were behaving like an infant. I should have had you spanked, and sent to bed without supper."

Guy stood, striding for the door.

"Where are you going?"

"To find another room in which to pass the night. Before I commit high treason." The door slammed.

Gene shifted, feet still throbbing. Her mind wandered back to a play she and Guy had gone to see. A man in front of them had persisted in talking through the performance. After two threats, Guy had hacked off the man's head and given it to her as a pendant. It was her favourite necklace, until it rotted. He had been so sweet then, so attentive. Now he merely went through the motions.

***

"This looks hideous."

Mervin waved a dismissive hand at Longfellow. "Orange is the new blue."

"What if it's a girl?"

"Fluorescent orange is the new pink."

Longfellow screwed shut his eyes.

Gene looked around the nursery. The walls and ceiling had been painted, shag carpet laid down, mobiles hung – every bit of everything orange.

Mervin grinned. "Do you like the crib? It's carved to look like a tiger."

"It *looks* like the tiger is pouncing, about to devour any child laid in the crib." Longfellow rubbed his forehead.

"Then that child," Gene said, "will learn courage from a young age."

"If it doesn't opt for putting out its own eyes first."

"I've spent weeks perfecting this design – weeks!" Mervin wrenched a handful out from his beard. "Oh dear – not again."

They removed themselves to the passageway, to be confronted by Dwain, Keesh, and Robin.

"Your majesty." Dwain bowed. "A petitioner awaits you in the great hall: a noble damsel of immense beauty."

"Well, if she's got *immense* beauty, then I'd better hurry." Gene rolled her eyes and waddled off.

"This damsel really is a looker," Robin said. "Certainly our Queen is comely enough, but no great beauty."

Longfellow balked. "That's treason!"

"Treason?"

"Yes – the Queen must be the most beauteous woman in all the land, any land, moreover – "

"She isn't behind you anymore," Dwain said.

"Yes, she's really more of a six or a seven." Longfellow shrugged. "But the tens are inevitably such airheads."

"My old girlfriend was a nine." Mervin beamed. "I loved her so. We were inseparable. I taught her magic. Then she imprisoned me in a cave, and tried to overthrow the kingdom. She still writes."

"How lovely for you."

Keesh smiled. "Number rankings don't matter. I could never think any woman better-looking than my own, utterly adorable wife. She hasn't a single flaw in my opinion, other than the half dozen green, hairy warts on her backside, but I've grown almost entirely used to those."

The others exchanged glances.

Dwain swallowed a guffaw. "The half dozen what?"

"Oh. Oh dear." Keesh pulled out his purse and reached inside. He drew out a turkey baster. "Oh, I told the secret, I told the secret. No, no!"

"I thought your wife could make herself look however she wished."

"She can. Except for the half dozen green, hairy warts on her backside."

The others began to chuckle.

"I've told it again! Oh dear, oh dear." Keesh reached into the purse again, extracting a petunia. "Now what shall I live on?"

"There must be a way of repairing the magic," Dwain said, grinning so widely he could barely make himself understood.

Mervin whisked his wand from his sleeve. "I could give it a try."

"NO!" everyone shouted.

Keesh hugged the purse to his chest. "I could take it home for my wife to fix. But the Yukon is so far away."

Dwain nodded. "Plus, you snuck out in the middle of the night without telling her where you were going, and that was eight months ago."

"The only other way to fix it would be to perform a deed of unrivalled bravery and daring."

"Such as facing your wife after an eight-month unexplained absence."

"No you don't," said Robin. "*I'm* the only one who's going to be brave and daring. I'm setting out today on a quest that's destined to restore my minstrel's admiration of my butchness. Butchocity? Butchualism."

"Where is Bernard?"

"Packing. I've had him packing all night. We must be ready for any eventuality, you know."

"Bon voyage, then."

"And up yours." Robin processed away, nose in air.

✳✳✳

Dwain and Keesh proceeded to the great hall. By then, there was not one fair damsel before the Queen, but two. And both were bickering and screeching fit to drive a possum off its perch. Perch being one of the most delectable of fishes to the pallet of a possum.

"AaaaaAAAA*AAAA*!" Gene screamed, forcing everyone else into silence. "Enough! One more word, and I shall have everyone in this room beheaded!"

"But," Keesh peeped, "Dwain and I only just got here."

"Plus," said Dwain, casting Keesh a look, "beheading *every*one would include yourself, your majesty, which would be treason, and it would prove quite awkward if you were to commit treason against yourself."

"Fine. But *someone* must explain this disagreement in a way that does not prompt me to burn off their toenails."

"It is quite simple, your majesty," spake the younger of the two damsels. "Our father wished us to split his lands equally when he died, and he has died – choked on some trout whilst riding bareback across the blooming moors."

"I am the eldest," squawked the other damsel. "By rights, all of my father's land belongs to me."

"Fine, fine." Gene closed her eyes. "There is only one way to settle this."

"Consult the old man's will?" Dwain asked.

"Each damsel will choose her champion. These champions will do battle until the victor is decided. To the death, if necessary."

"Dibs on Sir Guy of Longfellow," said both sisters.

Gene frowned. "Sir Dwain, where is the royal consort?"

"Um, planning the upcoming tournament, I believe, majesty."

The older damsel rolled her eyes. "Fine. Then I'll take that one."

The younger nodded. "And I shall take the other, jittery-looking one."

Keesh looked to Dwain. "What's just happened?"

"The arrangement of a good, old-fashioned judicial combat." Gene strained to her feet. "To arms!"

✳✳✳

"Now Bernard, you just ride behind me and keep your mouth shut."

"Yes, master."

"That's talking."

"Sorry, master."

"Mouth shut, I said."

Bernard held up his index finger and thumb ringed in an A-OK sign. Robin nodded, and they rode out.

Bernard amused himself by singing "What's Love Got to Do

with It?" in his head as they journeyed along. Soon, though, he spotted trouble in the road ahead. 'My gosh,' he thought to himself, 'my master is off his guard and does not see what lies in the road before us. There is not one but . . . three! I must warn him!' "Master," Bernard called, "look ahead! In the road are three sheep, who will surely trip your horse if you do not shout to frighten them, for they do not bat a single eyelash at our approach."

Robin frowned. "What is this? You dare to disobey my command for silence? I shall forgive you this once, but try me again at your peril." Then Sir Robin the Bold filled his lungs, and shouted at the sheep on the highway. They ignored him completely. So he rode around them, trailed by Bernard.

They had not proceeded a league, and a minor league at that, when Bernard spotted this time five geese pecking for feed in the road, and again Robin seemed not to notice. 'Oh crap,' thought the minstrel. 'What am I to do? My master will surely punish me. Perhaps with hissing beetles up my nose, or more requests for songs by teen heartthrobs. Yet, if his horse throws him and breaks his neck, who will be my master then? Sir Dwain, I suppose, or Sir Keesh, or perhaps I shall be made a court minstrel, which would actually make quite the step up for my career, but, oh – ' "Master."

"What now?"

"I beg your pardon, but five geese stand ahead in the road. I fear they may spook your mount."

"This is the respect you have for me? To disobey even the simplest command? You are a poor servant, Bernard, and one I should be better rid of." Sir Robin shouted to the geese, who hissed back, spreading their wings and charging.

Thus, Sir Robing broke from the road, galloping away across a field with all speed, Bernard and the geese in hot pursuit.

***

Gene rubbed her hands together. "*This* is more like it."

Dwain and Keesh sat their mounts in the lists, awaiting the command to charge.

The damsels looked on from the royal dais, and Mervin was chomping down popcorn.

"Majesty," said Dwain, "there must surely be a better way of settling this. Eeny meeny miney mo, for instance. Or flipping a coin. Perhaps the damsels could thumb wrestle, or guess what number you're thinking of."

"Pictionary," said Keesh. "Nothing resolves interpersonal conflicts like Pictionary."

"CHARGE!" Gene shouted.

Dwain and Keesh's horses raced at one another. On the first shock, both knights' ashen lances smashed to splinters.

Dwain and Keesh barely kept their saddles. The horses, well-trained, wheeled about for a second pass.

"Draw your *swords*!" Gene called.

They did, giving half-hearted swings that both missed.

"Is this how knights honour their vows to ladies? Fight! Else honour and justice are dead!"

The damsels shouted fit to drown out overzealous hockey parents. Mervin choked on his popcorn and tore out another hunk of beard.

Dwain and Keesh hammered with their swords. Their shields cracked to pieces. Their mail hauberks rent to reveal as many gaps as the magician's beard. Using their sword pommels, the two knights pounded each other about the head and neck. Soon their nose guards were bent askew and cutting into their faces, their cheeks were swollen black and blue, and their brains were swimming about in their skulls like guppies.

This torrent of blows continued until both Dwain and Keesh felt so exhausted, and woozy from loss of blood, all that kept them upright were their horses. By this time Mervin had fallen asleep, and was snoring louder than the sword blows.

"Can we stop?" Dwain's voice emerged as a warble, what was left of his hauberk black with blood.

"Not until there is a winner!" Gene barked.

"Fine, then Keesh wins."

Keesh shook his head, disorienting his sense of balance, and nearly unseating himself. "No, you definitely win. I can feel myself bleeding even between my toes. There's a surgeon nearby, isn't there? Within shouting distance?"

They blacked out simultaneously.

Gene slumped back in her throne.

"Well?" asked the older damsel. "How much do we each inherit?"

"What do I care? That fight should at least have lasted to dinner."

"But the point was our inheritance."

"Then take up arms and fight each other. All of this peace and quiet – "

Here Mervin released a mighty snore.

" – is driving me mad."

✳✳✳

Having outrun the geese, a tapdancing badger, and a particularly grouchy ladybug, Sir Robin and Bernard were trotting alone again through the Brythonic countryside.

"We shall spend the night at the castle ahead."

"Am I again permitted to speak, master? Because, if so, I should like to point out that it is now only a smidge past noon."

Sir Robin bit his lip, and spurred his horse.

Surrounding the castle was a village. As knight and minstrel rode through, the inhabitants emerged from the huts to view the spectacle, there being nothing particularly engrossing on TV at that hour.

"Master," said Bernard, "why is everyone looking at us like that, and moaning, and wringing their hands?"

Sir Robin jerked his reins up to his face in an attempt to cower behind them, upsetting his horse. "Zombies!"

"We are not zombies." One of the villagers stepped forwards, inky circles pressed under his eyes. "We only mourn that yet another brave and handsome knight should fall prey to the cruel danger that lies ahead in yonder castle."

"Danger? Quite coincidentally I happen to be looking for danger. Up until now, in all the wrong places, it would seem. What sort of danger is it you harbour here?"

The villager shook his head. "It is too terrible to name."

"Then can I? I'm cracking good at naming things. Ooo – Maurice."

"Master," said Bernard, "that was the rabbit's name."

"Rabbit?"

"Yes, master, the purple one. With six legs. It breathed fire."

"Are you quite sure you're not describing a dream you had?"

The villager cleared his throat. "Our danger already has a name, sir knight. It is only that, once brave warriors such as yourself hear its name, they are so enticed to meet it that they cannot help but go forwards to their doom, and we never see any of them leave the castle alive."

"So there's a chance they could all be fine in there."

"We see their dismembered corpses tossed out over the wall."

"No need to worry for my master," said Bernard. "He can

withstand the temptation of meeting any danger, no matter its name."

The villager looked dubious, dropping his jaw and causing his face to appear even more gaunt. "Cross your heart you'll not face the danger if I reveal to you its name?"

Sir Robin raised his right hand. "Absoposilutely."

The villager heaved an arid sigh. "The danger is known throughout the land as: the Joy of the Court."

"That doesn't sound dangerous at all."

"I know. We're quite bad at names. We actually call our village Empty Field."

"In fact, it sounds delightful."

"My horse is named Cow, my cow is named Muskrat."

"I should quite like to experience the Joy of the Court for myself."

"But, sir knight, you promised."

"I had my fingers crossed."

"We call them toes here."

"Let us ride on, Bernard. To the Joy of the Court!"

"Hello." The villager waved after them.

Dark clouds banded together with unnatural rapidity as they entered through the castle's barbican.

∗∗∗

"You're late."

Longfellow gave his wife an overly grand bow. "My apologies."

"Where were you?" They had assembled in the not-so-great hall for supper, Gene already standing at the head table, one servant holding a bowl beneath her hands as another poured rosewater over them.

"Planning your tournament, majesty. I see Mervin is also late in coming."

"He's getting another man-at-arms. The one in the tallest watchtower was felled by lightning again. The servants couldn't find you. Not in the nursery, our bedchamber, your trophy room . . . ."

"Your castle boasts many rooms, majesty. Perhaps it should boast more servants."

"Perhaps you should stay where they can find you." Gene threw herself down into her seat. "In your trophy room, for instance."

Longfellow rolled his eyes, sitting along with the others. His trophy room was certainly an impressive enough venue from which to plan a royal tournament. It boasted such prizes as a giant's hand. Which the impertinent creature had snatched back and run off with, with the notion of sewing the thing back onto its bloody stump. Fortunately, Guy had come upon the giant whilst it was fishing some thread from a cupboard, cutting off its other hand and killing it. The collection also included a dragon's tongue mounted on a wall plaque. Unfortunately, due to its noxious fumes, no one could get anywhere near the thing. It had previously seen Guy passed out on his feet in a pond. Thankfully with his nose just above water.

Gene signed. "All afternoon I've endured a craving for mashed potatoes."

"With a sauce of fermented fish guts?" Longfellow asked, loading his own trencher.

"No, just with butter."

The knights along the board bridled.

Keesh shook his head. "What pregnancy does to the palette."

"You'll ruin our child, feeding it butter instead of garum," Guy said. "There's not a dish in the world unimproved by fermented fish guts."

Gene refused to look at him. "It is highly ungallant for a knight to address his lady so."

Longfellow bridled again. "I was not then addressing my lady, but my child's nursemaid."

"Sir knight." Gene's eyes blazed, her fingers digging into the board as though they would pierce it. "You owe me a penance."

"It seems you want one apology after another."

"You would prove incapable of meriting the delivery of any, if really you loved me."

"Drat, dropped my knife." Dwain elbowed Keesh. "Duck under the table with me, and let's find it."

"But your knife's right – "

"*Duck.*" Dwain and Keesh took cover.

"If I did not 'really love' you, don't you think I'd have strangled you before we'd been married a fortnight?"

"You haven't really loved me since Xander's death! You see me as an obligation. Even more of one now I'm like this." Gene gestured both hands over her swollen middle.

"You're hysterical."

"And you're frigid!" Gene struggled to get up.

Longfellow rose, taking her by the arm to her feet.

"I can't *stand* it when you help me!"

"You can't stand."

"If you *really* loved me you would do more than simply pace out the steps. You would – drink the water in which I've washed my hands."

Longfellow stared at her. Then reached for the greyed rosewater on the table. He upended the bowl, pouring the whole draught down his throat.

Gene glared back. "I am going to inspect the armoury."

"You inspected it just Tuesday."

"And I am inspecting it again!"

Dwain and Keesh peeked over the table's edge as Gene

thundered from the hall.

Guy watched after her a moment. Then he turned aside, doubling up and retching.

"Ah," Dwain climbed back onto the bench, "the joys of being in love."

Longfellow spat. "Brush the dust from your knees. Boy! Take the Queen her meal in the armoury. If she refuses to eat, tell it to me, and I shall come shove the food down her throat."

"I'm quite looking forwards to this."

Bernard stared up at the castle keep, painted pitch black. "Master, I really think we ought to turn back."

"Nonsense. The Joy of the Court awaits us."

"The castle is deserted. This is a place of death."

"Didn't you hear the villager? There is an entire court dwelling here somewhere. And they have joy."

"Master, please – "

"Bernard! We spent a time apart, and now you do not seem to remember just how incredibly great are my bravery and prowess. But fear not, now our road trip will remind you."

Bernard whimpered as they dismounted.

Sir Robin the Bold marched up the wooden steps to the keep's second storey. Cavalierly, he pushed aside the oaken door, stepping over the threshold with a flourish. "Helloo-oo."

The knight's only answer was his echo, and the scampering of tiny, muskrat-like feet.

Bernard hung back. "It is deserted. Let's leave. I believe I spotted an all-you-can-eat sauerkraut and curry smorgasbord back a ways."

"At this hour everyone must be at table in the great hall. Come, Bernard, a feast awaits."

A feast did indeed await in the great hall. Yet no one sat enjoying it. It mouldered on the tables, what parts had once been edible. The rest looked as though the servants had only just set it out. This included a dish that caused Bernard to jump upon finding it glaring straight at him. From the eerie depths of a lime green aspic coiled an entire eel, mouth wide to show its needle-sharp teeth, poised as though still swimming, about to shoot out and crunch the minstrel's face. Indeed, this particular aspic seemed to shudder under its own power.

"Master, can we leave now? There's no court, and there is certainly no joy."

"Pish. I spy joy aplenty." Sir Robin carved himself a piece of a livid purple aspic. "Ughk." He spat it out. "Huckleberry."

Bernard rolled his eyes. They landed on a bowl laced with greyish-burgundy strands. "This one looks like greasy, grimy gopher guts. Or maybe mutilated monkey meat."

"Aha. Look – dirty little birdies' feet. Bernard, you didn't forget your spoon, did you?"

"Um . . . yes. Yes I did."

"No matter. Here, I've brought my straw. Sample the gopherish substance. If it's good, let me know and I shall try some."

"Or we could take a nap. You've been riding so far and so gallantly, master. Does not a nap sound appealing?"

"But I'm not tired."

"You must be though, master, because I am. And besides, everything is spinning."

"It is not. It's just jiggling a bit."

"Please, master."

"Oh, alright, Bernard. But it's obvious who is the knight here, isn't it?"

✴✴✴

Gene stormed into the bedchamber. "The man-at-arms in the tallest watchtower has been struck by lightning. *Again.*"

Longfellow grunted. "Perhaps you should see about installing a lightning rod."

"Why, so the watchtower gets struck even more?"

He stood by the bed with his back to the wall. "This is your trouble. You think your councillors are to be ordered about, rather than sought advice from."

"*That* is my difficulty, is it?"

"A willful incapacity to take into account what others think, yes."

"I am Queen."

"It was present before your reign, and constitutes an even greater stumbling block now."

Gene either sat or fell on the bed. "You only say so because you do not love me anymore."

"I speak so that you will know what I think."

"You think you would have preferred to spare yourself the trouble of fathering children by me."

"I cannot convince you otherwise."

"You might." Gene twisted, trying to face him. "Downing dirtied rosewater makes a fine show of devotion, but it would rank as nothing next to what I would ask of you now."

Longfellow stepped into her eyeline.

"Tomorrow morning, when the daily parade of the dungeon's most pathetic criminals takes place, I want you to climb up in the cart with them, for all to see."

"Are you mad?"

"If you truly loved me, you would not hesitate, even for a moment."

Sir Guy regarded his wife. "Then make me King."

"What?"

"You have the power to do so. Proclaim me King, so that *I* can rule."

Gene sprang to her feet, to her full height. "You *dare* ask this of me?"

"You dare to order me into the cart. Sit down."

"No."

He gritted his teeth. "Do not ask for more than I can give. Gene, you, of all people, must show me respect. I am Britain's military leader – "

"No, *I* am Britain's military leader. As well as its political leader, its legislative leader, and every other kind of leader. I am your sovereign. I rule. I will be obeyed."

"What you ask me to do would damage your rule. You must see it is not weakness to accept help."

"As soon as I am cured of this," Gene gestured to her belly, "I mean to lead Britain into war against the Scotti over the western sea. Before then, I must know that your loyalty runs deeper than your skin."

"Why in blazes would you begin a war with the Scotti? We've only just rid ourselves of the Saxons."

"In war we knew where we stood; we're struggling now. I need to stand certain of your devotion. Ride in the cart tomorrow, or you may as well ride to the coast for a ship to carry you to a new country."

"I do not approve of your plan."

"How auspicious, then, that I do not seek your approval."

Longfellow stared towards the head of their bed, heaving a sigh that left his broad shoulders in ever so slight of a droop. "You are my sovereign, and you are bearing my child, so I shall remain. In

254

any bedchamber but this."

"Fortunate, as this is the only bedchamber in which, to a certainty, you are unwelcome."

***

"Master, are you sure we should be in this bedchamber?"

"Bernard, must you ask that of every room we enter? We have had our supper, and now it is time to sleep."

Bernard squinted at the bed, standing alone in the centre of a vast room lined with alcoves too ensconced in shadow to be bothered over showing whether anyone lurked within them. "Perhaps there is another, more cozy bedchamber in which to pass the night."

"'Cozy'? We are not in the business of cozy, Bernard. We are in the business of grandeur and glory. This provides the ideal setting for our well-earned, manful rest."

"'Manful'?"

"You may sleep on the floor at the bed's foot. Come, disrobe me."

Bernard cringed, so busy watching the shadows that he was, thankfully, able to ignore his master's pocked, naked flesh.

Sir Robin laid himself down, miffed that the minstrel had passed up the chance to note his physique.

Bernard crept low, propping himself on his elbow for a long time before finally settling down. A single candle lit the room. Not lit, really. It lent parts of the room a faint glow, one that made the walls shift and ooze, as though an enormous black serpent slipped slowly around the room. At last, exhausted, Bernard forced his eyes to shut.

He did not mean to drift off, but did almost without delay. And so he held no idea of how long it was before he bolted straight onto his feet at a horrendous CLASH!

"Bernard," Robin murmured, without opening his eyes, "stop

clashing and go to sleep."

Bernard stood frozen.

"I can feel you staring. Go to sleep." Sir Robin tried to roll into the middle of the bed, but was blocked by the flat of an enormous blade that had cleaved down through his mattress and lodged in the wood floor. "I've heard of quarrelling couples placing a sword between them in bed, but this seems somewhat like overkill." And he snorted softly back into sleep.

Bernard sank down again to the floor. The trap had been sprung with no harm to his master. There was no reason why they should not pass the night without having to worry over when the strike would come, now it was past.

Yet Bernard could not keep himself from vigilance. His eyes, at the least insistence from his ears, refused to shut for more than a few seconds at a stretch. As he stared into the darkness, his head against the rushes matting the floor, Bernard began imagining shapes to accompany the rustles he must also have been imagining. He sang to himself within his own mind, thinking to lull his nerves. A sweeping roar invaded the notes.

Bernard sat bolt upright.

The room rippled as it had not done before, and the blackness had receded, though not enough to reveal the alcoves' innards.

Bernard looked about, and found this was due to a flaming arrow lodged in the headboard, its orange mischief creeping slowly across the painted wood.

He yipped, leaping up, snatching the nearest vessel containing liquid – which happened to be a chamber pot – and heaved, draping the headboard, and incidentally a portion of the pillows, so that all but the thinnest flicker extinguished. Leaping up the bed, he patted this out of sight with his palm.

"BERNARD!" Sir Robin sat straight up, causing the minstrel to scramble whilst falling backwards. "Is this any way to behave in the presence of your master and lord?! Your lack of respect would appall the mangiest, flea-strewn dog that lolls about the garbage heaps!"

"There was a fire, master."

"It matters not whether there was a herd of hiccupping bison bringing the apocalypse. If you do not revere me, Bernard, we have nothing. And emptying a chamber pot over my head as I sleep shows nothing if not nonrespect."

"No, not non – master, I was endeavouring to protect you."

"Masters protect. Vassals serve."

"But – " Bernard pointed to the scorch marks on the headboard.

"Get *off,* Bernard."

The minstrel shrank back, off the foot of the bed.

Every sound reverberated in Bernard's chest, jostling his heart to beat faster. Hours dragged on, exhaustion weighted him down. His brain still would not allow him sleep. He opened his eyes and stared at the ceiling.

After a few minutes, Bernard thought he could discern something glinting up above. At first, his tired mind suggested that they might be stars. Yet, as he watched, they blinked.

Vicious cooing split the air.

"Master – " Yet, before Bernard could complete the word, the room was filled with warm squirts of pigeon excrement, in mouths, eyes, ears – and all was whitish blackness.

✳✳✳

Dwain wandered into Mervin's spell chamber, glancing about at the iridescent purple and green cobwebs. "Howdy-do. Have you seen Longfellow anywhere by chance? I've been tasked by the Queen with finding out how far he's progressed planning the tournament. Quite the joy, isn't it, when a wedded couple argues and reverts to behaving like teenagers? I've never seen two people more angrily married."

Mervin frowned, hunched over a bubbling concoction that sounded as though it were belching the alphabet. "After all that speeching, what question was it you wanted answered?"

Dwain smirked. "Come on, Mervin, what are you? Senile?"

"Senile?!" Mervin burst out, spilling half his cauldron's potion so it boiled through the floor. "Of course – I've been senile a bloody great long time. Have you any idea how old I am?"

"No." Dwain rolled his gaze about the room to avoid eye contact. "Well? Your age?"

"I've just *told* you I'm senile – are you in the same boat?" Mervin wrenched a handful from his beard.

"Eep. Look, just – have you seen Longfellow about today?"

"Let me think." Mervin leaned against his cauldron so it tilted, the other half of its potion dribbling another, though smaller, hole.

" . . . Mervin?"

"Hm? Drifted out to sea. What were we discussing?"

"I came in, asked if you'd seen Longfellow, you droned on about senility, I asked again – "

"Senile?!" Mervin tore loose another handful of beard. "Of course – have you any idea how old I am?"

"You live backwards so, younger than when I met you?"

"Yes." He glanced into his cauldron. "What did you want again?"

"Never mind." Dwain stalked out, spiralling up the nearest turret to the bed and guest chambers. Longfellow had to be laying his head somewhere at night, though it likely wasn't with the Queen.

Upon approximately the seventy-fourth try, Dwain found Longfellow in a chamber not whitewashed like the others, but painted a deep blood red, these walls covered with axes, swords, and maces, many modified with numerous spikes, and all carrying either a dried brown coating along an edge, or a tangle of matted hair.

Longfellow quickly shut the wardrobe, which he had been gazing into with an odd, faraway expression.

"I've been searching for you."

Guy grunted. "Yes. Well?"

"The Queen wishes to hear of your progress with the tournament." Dwain couldn't stop his eyes wandering to the closed wardrobe.

"All the invitations are sent, and rooms are being readied for our guests. The steward is procuring the necessary food. The Queen may occupy her mind with her own plans."

Dwain took a moment sizing up Guy of Longfellow. "This may be none of my concern, though the pair of you seem intent upon making it so, but – Keesh is off pulling ukuleles and bowling pins out of the purse his wife gave him to live on, when all he must do to fix it would be simply having a conversation with the woman he took as his life mate. Does that not seem somewhat foolish to you?"

Longfellow leaned against the wardrobe door, exhaling. "It is not a dilemma of communication, but of duty."

"The bit about the green, hairy warts I suppose was both, considering it was supposed to stay a secret."

"Not Keesh! As knights we are dutybound to uphold certain principles. Our honour depends upon it. We dedicate our brave deeds to ladies and, for love of those ladies, we are inspired to ever greater deeds. But how can we remain true knights when our loyalties are divided? How do we act when one vow seeks to tear us in two directions?"

"I don't think that's possible, one vow, two directions."

"It is." Guy closed his eyes. "I have dedicated my life to defending Britain."

"That's been going rather well, though, lately."

"I find myself longing to hear that bloodcurdling scream that preceded the Queen Mother."

"That's because you were her favourite."

"She could put all this to rights."

"Sometimes I think the reason the present Queen had her old mother entombed within three sarcophagi was to prevent her rising from the dead."

Guy smiled. "If she could rise from the dead, no tomb then could stay her."

"Hello? Hello?" Keesh popped in through the open door. "Oh, there you chaps are. I was on the outer wall, seeing if I couldn't coax something of value out of this preposterous purse . . . holy Gila monsters – who decorated this horrifying place? I could only feel at ease sleeping here if I laid down in full armour."

"And?" Dwain asked. "Any luck with the purse?"

"What? No, I was plucking out a pair of shoelaces when I spied an odd procession heading our way. You must see."

Longfellow straightened. "No one could have responded to the tournament invitation so swiftly."

They hurried out onto the crenellated wall, past the charred corpse of another lightning-fried man-at-arms fallen from the highest tower.

"Look!" Keesh pointed.

A mass of mounted huntsmen clad in green and red were riding towards them, each with a bloody hunk of dripping meat tied behind their saddles. Two horsemen galloped ahead of the rest, reaching the castle gate.

"Halloooo!"

Dwain frowned. "Robin? Bernard?"

Sir Robin grinned up at them. "Yes, lads, it is I, Sir Robin the

Bold of Estrangorre. My hunt has been a grand success."

"I thought you were questing for butchualism."

"I suspect that will prove successful come dinnertime," said Longfellow.

"I performed the butchery myself." Robin beamed. "In the courtliest possible fashion, as is the height of courtliness. Ishness. Nessism. Anyway, I've ordered the huntsmen to deliver the meat by riding with all the bits in their proper places so that everyone can observe by their formation just what precisely it is that I've manfully slaughtered."

Dwain cringed.

"Just be thankful you missed the puppet show he put on with the beast's kidneys," said Bernard.

"Hush now." Robin grinned. "Come, sirs knights, tell me what it is I've brought to fill our Queen's table this day."

Dwain squinted. "It's a . . . wombat?"

"*No.*"

"A badger?"

"No!"

"I really think it looks like an octopus," said Keesh.

Longfellow snorted. "More like a walrus."

"Fellows!" shouted Robin.

Dwain shrugged. "A feather duster?"

"That's enough. No more of your ridiculous guesses."

"It really does look like a feather duster," said Longfellow, and Keesh nodded.

"It's a deer!"

"No . . . no," said Dwain, "it really isn't."

"No dinner for anyone!"

"Fine. Keep your butchualism to yourself."

Keesh tilted his head. "I suppose, from this angle, it could almost be a zebra, but those aren't as common as octopi in this part of the world."

Robin's face had turned as bright as his hair.

"Don't fret, master," said Bernard. "It's the huntsmen you hired. They aren't nearly as professional at this high courtliness as one could wish."

Robin nodded. "Thank you, Bernard."

"Not at all, sir."

***

Gene sat at the high table, staring past the food set before her, watching Guy Longfellow from the corner of her eye. She rubbed her belly. This had all proved a dread mistake. Ever since he had learned she was heir to the throne there had existed a wall between them. When he had shielded her with his body from the Saxons' volley of javelins, she had thought it a glimmer of his old love. But no, it had been the duty of a knight to a monarch. After jimmying open the barbarian chieftain's liquor cabinet and getting drunk over their victory, the two of them had wound up in the royal chamber. Head spinning, Gene had dropped down on the bed. He had sat next to her and, thinking of how he had protected her with his own life, she had kissed him. He had let her, had undressed her, and for the first time their lovemaking had been tender.

Then, come morning, she had awakened and smiled at him. Longfellow had rolled to face the other way.

"Eat."

Now she looked fully at him.

"The child is hungry, even if you are not."

"I cannot eat this."

"Inside out liver in marrow sauce is suddenly not to your liking?"

"I have been craving dry toast."

Keesh's cheeks bulged, as though he would retch.

Longfellow winced. "I shall be glad when we can have done with this pregnancy business."

"And get on with the infant rearing business?" Gene asked.

Guy downed a swallow of wine.

"So that's what I did," Robin was murmuring to Dwain. "I told Bernard to remain silent, and pretended I did not see the dangers ahead. And, though I chastised and threatened him severely, he could not help but warn me."

"And why did you play this meanspirited mind game?"

"Because," Robin looked astonished, "it proves that Bernard loves me as his master."

"If you threatened me, I'd consider any misfortunes that befell you well-deserved."

Robin beamed. "That, precisely, is why Bernard is my minstrel, and you are not."

"Well, it certainly has nothing whatsoever to do with songwriting ability."

Gene continued to watch Longfellow under her lashes, even as her toast was brought. When she had informed him, after that night, that she was with child, he had merely said, "Ah . . . very well," without even looking at her. He had hardly looked at her since.

When the meal was over, he helped her to her feet.

"Sir Guy, I wish you to escort me to my bedchamber."

Dwain and Keesh did a poor job stopping their eyeballs from bulging.

Gene wrapped Longfellow's arm around hers to keep him from slipping away as they processed through the various adjoining rooms. "Where have you been sleeping?"

"It is of little consequence to you."

"You are my husband. Why do you wish there to be such distance between us?"

"May I speak as your husband? Or am I to answer as your subordinate?"

"You may answer as my husband."

"Then such distance exists because you plan to betray Britain."

"Betray? You would have us grow weak again in peace, as we did under the Romans? Unable to defend ourselves against the barbarians when the need came?"

He sneered. "I would have our land and people safe from unprovoked wars."

"This distance came before I ever revealed my plans to you. You resent me because I am Queen, and rule you."

"I resent that you refuse responsibility for even the slightest of your actions."

"I was born to royalty."

Longfellow's voice lowered. "I trusted you. Gene, I followed you blindly back to this country, only to learn from *Dwain* that you were King Xander's sister."

"I thought I *told* you."

"But you didn't. You betrayed me, and you have never sought to apologize. If you had trusted me then, even if you trusted me now, it could ensure the prosperity of our people. You would rather see them drown in useless fighting for your bloodlust."

"You are no true knight, but a coward."

"As a knight, I protect those under me. I serve those above me. Decide: are you my wife or my Queen?"

***

Mervin marched onto the tournament dais with a twinkle in his eye.

264

Dwain blinked. "What on earth is on your face?"

"My beard looked a shambles with all those holes I was tearing through it, so I bought this prosthetic one. It doesn't look fake, does it?"

Dwain was still staring. "I'm sorry. I didn't catch a word of that."

"Senile? Have you any idea how old I am?"

"What?"

"What? And deaf."

Gene ascended the dais on Longfellow's arm, to uproarious cheers from the onlookers. All of Londinium seemed gathered to absorb the spectacle. They crowded the bleachers surrounding the meadow of combat.

Bernard, the tournament's designated herald, stood on the dais edge, the feathers in his cap hanging long enough to hide half his face, so he was constantly spitting out tufts of them. "Hear ya, hear ya. The combatants from far and wide for today's contest are newcomers all."

Guy dashed a glance at Gene.

She refused to return it. "If I am not allowed to take part, neither are you."

"Welcome all to the Tournament of Vulcan," Bernard shouted, "Roman deity of fire and metalworking. Our first knight comes from Nowhereville in Middle Nowhere: Sir Mercifal."

The knight rode forwards, then clambered onto the dais. He pointed. "What's that?"

Longfellow rose to stand between the young man and Gene. "The royal throne."

"Oh. What's it for?"

"For *sitting*."

"Can I sit in it?"

"Only the monarch may occupy the throne."

"What's a monarch?"

"The ruler of Britain."

"What's Britain?"

"This island where we live."

"What's an island?"

"A land surrounded by water."

"Oh. What are those shiny things on your feet?"

"Sabatons."

"Can I wear them?"

Longfellow started for Mercifal's throat.

"Look!" Dwain waved his finger haphazardly. "Isn't that amazing!"

Sir Mercifal immediately leapt from the dais, catching up something from the ground near where Dwain had been pointing. "What *is* it?"

Dwain squinted. "A clump of moss."

"*Wow.*"

Bernard fumbled to find his voice. "Next, Sir Palahad."

The knight mounted the dais steps.

"Palahad?" Dwain echoed. "Why, we're blood brothers."

Sir Palahad clapped him on the shoulder. "Haven't seen you in ages, old boy."

"I've been meaning to write. Saving Britain and all. We should get together for a proper catch up. How are you?"

"I have leprosy."

"Well, catching up's been fun."

Palahad gave a dazed smile and wandered off, saluting Gene, who drew back, even behind Longfellow's shielding arm.

"So nice to see an old friend, isn't it?" asked Keesh.

"Sir Rogaine," Bernard called.

266

An elderly gentleman with a creepily full head of hair crossed the dais.

"Sir Grayharis."

An even more elderly man, with but a few tufts amidst his liver spots.

"Sir Agravateth."

Who did not cease noisily chewing his nails even when saluting the Queen.

"Sir Stareth."

Dwain, Keesh, and Robin balked as the unrelenting pair of eyeballs floated by, possibly with a man behind them.

"Sir Lordid."

A young knight with slicked black hair came to stand before Gene, one fist on his hip, glaring at her.

Longfellow spoke through gritted teeth. "Salute your Queen."

"Queen? I am Sir Lordid of Dover, son of Vorgana."

Keesh leaned closer. "Dover's still in Britain, you know."

"My mother Vorgana is the eldest daughter of King Uber."

"My father?" Gene echoed. "Impossible. He had only two children: Xander and myself."

"Not so. My grandmother was his second wife."

"He was still married to my mother when he died."

"He married your mother, divorced her, married my grandmother, then your mother once more, and she harangued him to death before he could divorce her again."

"You will not speak flippantly of my father! All know well that King Uber was an uber King."

"Ohhh."

Everyone looked at Mervin.

"That's right, the divorce, the other daughter – Gene, did I never tell you of that?"

Gene's lips appeared to be attempting to burrow back through her teeth, and Guy Longfellow looked vaguely gratified.

"I believe," said Lordid, "that you are sitting in my seat."

"Hey!" cried Sir Mercifal, "that cloud looks like a seahorse!"

"It doesn't matter," Gene growled.

"Neigh, little seahorse."

"I am King Uber's own child. You are merely his grandchild."

"Yes," said Sir Lordid, "but my mother was older than you. King Xander died without direct heirs, and so the throne should pass to the line of the secondborn child. First the worst, second the best, third the *nerd*."

Longfellow grasped Lordid by the throat. "You *dare* insult the Queen before her court – "

"I – am – royal – blood."

Longfellow released him.

"I shall win this tournament before the court, and before the citizens of Londinium. Then they will demand that I be crowned King!"

"But Sir Guy of Longfellow has won countless tournaments," said Keesh, "and no one has ever crowned him King."

Guy's tongue strained behind his top teeth, and he stepped back.

Dwain hissed at Bernard, "Hey, introduce the next knight already – the guy in the black armour with the blank shield – who's he?"

Bernard shuffled through his index cards. "I have no idea."

"Great. So glad we put you through heraldry night school."

"Also," Bernard cried, "the black knight, and a couple hundred other guys. Fight on!"

The field erupted, everyone hacking and flailing and slashing at everyone else.

Dozens of casualties were struck down in the first hour.

Amongst these were Sir Stareth, who ended up with two black eyes that swelled shut, rendering him blind and defenseless; Sir Agravateth, who was very unchivalrously kicked to death after repeatedly blowing his nose and willy-nilly tossing the tissues into other knights' laps; and Sir Grayharis, who fell asleep in the midst of a duel and tumbled off his horse.

After that, the fighting spilled into the bleachers, causing something of a stampede as the citizens of Londinium strove to flee in the face of blood-crusted iron and flailing hooves. This did little good because the tournament spilled into the very streets of Londinium, where it raged long after nightfall.

One particularly poignant incident occurred when a knight from Hereford, his leg broken, was dragged into the shelter of a tavern by a fellow knight who sat there hosting some of his companions to supper. He then proceeded, quite generously, to gift the injured knight to one of his companions, earning everyone's highest praise. Ransoms and harnesses were won and lost that day by the hundred.

Gene sat leaned forwards in her throne throughout, or as far forwards as she could get with her enormous belly.

Longfellow laid a hand on her wrist, which could well have been corded wood so tight was her grasp upon the throne's arms. "Majesty, it is past time you laid in bed."

Gene ignored him.

"Majesty, given your state of health – "

Gene threw up her arm, casting him off.

" – I must insist – "

"Go to your own bed if you feel so weak with fatigue. I have waited overlong for a spectacle such as this, and shall absorb every moment of it. A few weeks and I shall wield mine own sword again. Then let them churn against me, it will do them no good!"

Longfellow walked along the dais towards its end, an almost

pained look upon his face.

"So," said Dwain, "you thought her watching hundreds of knights hacking at one another for days on end would help distract her from fighting?"

Longfellow ceased walking and stared before him.

"The two of you really both have one-track minds, don't you?"

Longfellow still did not move.

Dwain paused. "Sir Mercifal's still in the tournament, can you believe it? He's been belly to the ground all this time, watching what he calls 'a perfect hoofprint' slowly seep full of blood. The other knights don't seem to have noticed that he's still in the running. Sir Lordid was bested. Not sure where he's got to, but that's a bolt dodged there, I suppose. Longfellow, you're really not alright, are you?"

"I don't think we could win another war."

"I don't think we won the previous one. It was some sort of fluke, really."

"I doubted I would have a child."

"Did you say would or should?"

"I no longer remember why I became a knight."

"Britain would not still be Britain without you. Knowing those vain barbarians, they would have renamed it after themselves: Angle-world, or Saxon-land, or some rubbish."

"It may not last long in any case."

Dwain watched Longfellow walk back to the castle, at a pace that would have put a hare to shame, though compared to Longfellow's usual stride he may as well have been trudging. He returned to the bedchamber with the red walls, opening the wardrobe.

There, on the back of the door, hung a plaid skirt stained with vomit, a wrinkled white blouse, and a torn navy sweater. On the wardrobe's bottom lay a pair of knee-high socks, beside Mary Janes with nails punched through their soles to make them cleats. The wardrobe's other contents – ballgowns and crenellated dresses – looked to have been shredded with a serrated blade. He remembered the sound of those cleats clattering across the floor, the smell of the sweat that wrinkled the blouse so it sealed to her body, the feel of the vomit as they toppled into it, the thrill when he rent that rip in her sweater. She had been his first love. Guy picked a blonde hair off the sweater and twirled it around his fingers, feeling it bite in. If she had stayed, and he hadn't been left to fall next in love with Gene, she would know what to do now, that hard-headed girl. She had freed him once. And he had locked himself into a different trap without her.

The council knights returned to the tournament field at dawn. The Queen remained in the same posture as when they had left, her eyes glued to the fighting as though they had not blinked in the past hour, nor would in the next. Mervin snored in the seat beside hers, and Bernard, crouched on a stool, fumbled about in his parchments.

"How goes it?" Dwain asked.

Bernard glanced up. "Oh, fine, fine. Sir Rogaine had a heart attack when he spied someone charging for him, so he's out now. Sir Lordid hasn't reared his head again, so there's a load off the old mind. Sir Mercifal seems to have wandered off, and no one knows where he is."

"Wandered off?!" Longfellow barked. "How could any worthy knight have *wandered* off from battle?"

"Well, apparently someone slipped a stick in the plume holder on his helmet, and tied a shiny spoon to dangle on its other end. He meandered off chasing the spoon."

"Why didn't anyone just knock his head off?!"

"I don't know, sir. Right now we seem to have an extra knight on the field, though, and I'm trying to figure out who he is."

"Where?"

"There, sir," Bernard pointed, "the one whose shield device looks identical to Sir Lordid's, except there's a red stripe through it and it's upside down."

Dwain nodded. "The one who looks like Sir Lordid wearing a black cardboard moustache?"

"Exactly. He says his name is Sir Dredmor and – wait – Sir Dredmor backward is Sir Mordred, and Mordred sounds like Lordid – he's Sir Lordid!"

"Another heraldic mystery solved."

Guy leapt from the dais onto the field. "Sir Lordid!"

The knight half turned. "Are you . . . speaking to me? My name is actually Sir Redmord."

"You mean Sir Dredmor?"

"Yes, something like that. I'm from Dover, I mean Canterbury, and – "

"You were defeated. Remove yourself from this field."

"Or what?" The knight laughed. "You'll shed royal blood?"

"Of course not." Sir Guy pulled a mace from in back of his armour.

"Oh. Oh dear. Oh – "

"Sir Palahad excelled all through the night," Bernard said. "None of the other knights cared to come near him with a ten-foot pole."

"They didn't think of using their spears?" Dwain asked.

"He really was doing quite well. Until his arm dropped off."

"Ewgh. I should send him a condolence card, or at least shout something comforting in his direction."

Lordid crashed to the ground, mouth open, twitching like a fish.

"Men-at-arms, have him dragged from the field and stripped of his armour." Longfellow remounted the dais.

"So that's twelve knights remaining in the – " Bernard glanced up, "eleven, ten – that black knight is quite something. He spent awhile reading magazines on the sidelines, letting the other knights think he wasn't actually in the tournament."

"On horseback, armed, in full plate? And they swallowed that?" Dwain scoffed.

Longfellow grinned, the way a wolf grins at its prey. "This black knight fights well."

Another opponent went flying, his horse scurrying off the field.

"Yes," said Bernard. "He's sustained several blows to the head – you can see how dented his helmet is – but none have seemed to phase him."

"He is the perfect warrior," Gene breathed. "His use to Britain will prove invaluable."

A knight crashed into the dais edge, back bending at a right angle.

"Yes," Dwain said, "now we just have to find an army for him to fight in. You know, one he hasn't already broken into tiny pieces."

"Our tournament champion."

"Actually, your majesty," said Bernard, "the black knight cannot be declared tournament champion until finding and defeating Sir Mercifal."

"Hello."

Keesh and Robin started.

Sir Mercifal walked around from behind the dais.

Dwain raised his eyebrows. "What happened to your spoon?"

"Yes, it was just the shiniest, dangliest spoon you ever did see, wasn't it? Wish I could find it, but there was this blue soap dish, the exact shade as – ”

The black knight plowed a forearm into Sir Mercifal's face, flipping him over backwards.

"The black knight wins!" Bernard cried.

"Come, sir knight," purred the Queen, "doff your helmet and pay homage. You have won a prized place in our court this day."

The black knight pulled at his helmet. It would not budge.

Dwain's eyebrows shirked higher. "What was that you said, Bernard, about impressive blows to the head?"

"Oh dear. Okay. Just a moment, sir knight. We can fix this." Bernard leapt from the dais.

A moment later he returned alongside the blacksmith, who brought his anvil mounted atop a wooden cart that he dragged like a wheelbarrow.

"Come here, sir knight, if you would, and we shall have you fixed up in a jiffy."

The black knight knelt beside the anvil, laying his head upon it. The blacksmith drew out a hammer, setting to work.

Mervin burst from his sleep with a yelp that was lost to the council's ears.

"Well, if we weren't worrying about brain damage before," Dwain called over the clatter of blows, "why do so now?"

"Precisely." Bernard grinned.

"I'd worry more over deafness," shouted Keesh.

The blacksmith stood back, proudly surveying his work.

"Now, sir knight," said Gene, "let us look upon the face of our champion, and hear finally his name."

The black knight stood, removing his helmet.

"Good God!" Guy shouted.

Dwain gaped. "Great horny toads."

"But – but – but – but – but – ” Keesh pointed, looking about helplessly.

Robin fainted, thunking his head on the dais, for even Bernard stood frozen to the spot.

Sir Mercifal sat up where he had been felled on the field. "Who is that?"

"I am Xander, son of King Uber the uber King." He nodded towards Gene. "And you are sitting on my throne."

Her fingers dug into its wooden arms.

Longfellow went to his knees. Dwain, Keesh, and Bernard fumbled, following suit.

"But what – how – ?" stammered Dwain.

Xander motioned. "My devoted magician."

"*Mervin?*"

The old man appeared quite puffed up beneath his prosthetic beard. "That's so. I've been endeavouring for years now, and have finally hit upon it: the cure for being crushed by a cow."

"Seriously," said Dwain, "Mervin?"

"Not only have I found the cure for being crushed by a cow," beamed the magician, "but also the cure for being crushed by a camel, though not yet the cure for being crushed by a harpsicord, or vice versa."

"How many people get crushed to death by a harpsicord, say, in a year?"

Mervin leapt up, balling his fists. "Do I look like a statistician to you?!"

Dwain balked. "I've never really thought about it."

"In any case," said Xander, "I'm grateful. I'm also rather tired from spending the last twenty-five hours fighting, and would appreciate having a sit. Gene?"

She darted glances at everyone staring at her.

"Gene?"

"No."

"No?"

"No. I have plans for this kingdom. You were ruler, and you died. It's my turn."

"Gene," hissed Longfellow, "he is your elder brother."

"Is he? He's only been alive two days."

Mervin hemmed. "Two and a half, more like."

"And you." Gene turned on him. "How could you do this to me? And without one word."

"He's your brother. I assumed you liked him better when his flesh wasn't rotting off his skull."

"Well, of course, but – I am leading Britain now. This is my council, and with it I intend to lead this country to glory again."

Robin came out from his swoon. "Your majesty, it's so good to see you. You've no idea how much we've missed you."

Xander smiled. "My loyal knights. Glad at heart am I to return to you all. Together, we shall enjoy an era of peace and prosperity unrivalled in the annals of our history. All Britons will know only safety and happiness from now on, for we shall put down all those who seek to destroy that peace."

The council whooped and cheered.

"Now, little sister, as you've grown big, allow me to help you in vacating the throne."

Gene's hands clenched around its arms.

A sword blocked Xander as he reached for the throne.

"Um . . . Sir Guy?" said Robin. "Your sword seems to have slipped out of its scabbard."

"No one touches the Queen."

Xander frowned. "What is the difficulty?"

"No one touches the Queen." Longfellow stared dead into Xander's eyes.

"As King, I order you to stand aside, sir knight, by the oath you swore."

"My oath to you terminated with your death, sir." Longfellow swallowed as though he wished to vomit. "It is now my oath to the Queen that must be honoured."

"But . . . Longfellow?" Dwain shrugged. "He's the King."

"Yes," said Keesh, "he is. I recall it quite vividly."

Longfellow groped a moment for breath to say, "Each man of us must follow his own conscience. Do as you see fit as men of honour. I must uphold the Queen."

"Remove yourself, Sir Guy," barked the King.

"I am sorry, sir, I cannot. Know well that I have command of Britain's men-at-arms."

"Those that haven't been fried by lightning keeping watch," Dwain murmured.

"Of course, some may decide to follow you. The people will certainly be divided. If you insist on the throne, sir, you will plunge Britain into civil war with herself."

Xander glared. "How can you commit such a treason?"

"I serve, and I protect. It is in your hands, sir, but my Queen does not vacate her throne."

Gene lifted her chin, staring down her nose at Xander.

"Come," he said, "all you who would follow me."

Dwain and Keesh rose from their knees, casting back glances at Longfellow as they followed their King down from the dais. Robin and Bernard followed along.

Xander huddled up with his remaining knights and amateur herald minstrel. "He's right about the men-at-arms, and the people. This is best kept as a quarrel amongst knights."

"So," said Dwain, "that's two of us, plus Robin, which comes out to one knight total, versus Longfellow – sire, we're in trouble.

Longfellow can best any of us in single combat."

Robin frowned. "But there are three of us."

"Yes, but the three of us, including you, evens out to one knight on our side."

Keesh looked about. "Where's Sir Mercifal?"

"I think he's off staring at a ketchup stain."

Xander pinched the apex of his nose. "You people haven't spent a great deal of time on personal development whilst I've been dead, have you?"

"I've learned heraldry," Bernard grumbled.

"I co-owned a comedy club," Dwain said.

"I was on steroids," said Robin, "but I'm not anymore."

"And I've fathered fifteen children." Keesh smiled. "Here, I can show you their pictures. Oops – plastic honey bear. That was my purse, not my wallet."

Xander gave a frustrated growl.

"I know. I really ought to see to getting that fixed."

Meanwhile, Mervin was saying to Gene, "I just don't understand it. You loved your brother. You were upset when he died – so much so that you abandoned your country – now you won't give it back to him?"

Gene motioned a karate chop at her belly. "I'm growing a bloody dynasty that will at last see Britain above the whims of her neighbours and – of all the times you've tried to enchant people back to life, why did it have to work *now*?"

"Should you ever be crushed to death by any large quadruped beginning with the letter C, you will certainly thank me *then*."

"Why? Will you have instigated my crushing whilst attempting a spell to make a door hinge stop squeaking?"

"You know very well that spell produces nothing heavier than a large horde of rattlesnakes."

278

Longfellow squeezed his eyes shut. "Would the pair of you *stop arguing*?!"

Mervin stared, wide-eyed. "Gracious, lad. We're only doing what family does."

"Then why can't you do what my family does, and ignore each other completely?"

"That's what your family does?" Gene asked.

"Yes, and whilst it's bloody well stomach-churning, it's better than what the two of you do."

"Look," said Mervin, "here comes that scraggly little minstrel with the hokey songs. I do hope he performs something with a good kazoo solo this time."

Bernard bowed. "Lady Gene, the King issues a challenge. He does not wish for war to invade this land, and so he proposes a battle of champions to decide Britain's fate."

Gene nodded. "Very well. Sir Guy?"

"I am ready, your majesty."

"Remember, this is a fight to the death."

"I know, your majesty. Bernard, whom must I fight?"

The minstrel swallowed. "King Xander of Britain."

Longfellow looked down the field to Dwain, Keesh, and Robin, who swayed about, unable to meet his eyes.

"He cannot fight for himself," Gene said. "He must designate a champion."

"The King has elected to champion himself, my lady." Bernard could not seem to bring his gaze up from the ground.

"What do you wish me to do?" Longfellow asked.

Gene sat a moment, dazed. Then her knuckles whitened on the throne arms.

Longfellow stepped forwards, helping her to rise.

She caught his hands in hers, staggering a step closer, away from the throne. "Fight well, sir knight."

Longfellow stared back at her, and at last he nodded. "Very well." He withdrew his hands, donning his gauntlets.

Gene rubbed her swollen belly. "You will win, as always."

"He cannot use his helmet. I shall not use mine."

"I love you."

"Let Mervin help you back into your seat." Longfellow dropped from the dais to the dirt.

"Majesty," hissed Dwain, "is this really what you want to do?"

Xander turned to face Longfellow approach. "Do not question me again."

"I can't watch." Robin laced his fingers over his eyes, still peeping through.

Keesh raised his eyebrows. "Why don't you put on your helmet and lower your visor?"

"Oh. Right."

Longfellow came to stand before the King. "Sir."

"Knight."

They saluted, drew their swords.

"The tournament must have tired you. Do you wish for quarter?"

"To the contrary, I feel better than I have for years past."

Longfellow's expression lightened. "No doubt."

"Begin."

Guy swung his sword down on the King's head. Xander knocked it off course, slashing at Longfellow's chest. Guy leapt back, off-balance. Xander charged, knocking him to the ground.

Longfellow rolled, flailing his sword in the King's face. Xander hung back a moment. Guy sprang to his feet.

Mervin tossed two spiked war hammers onto the field between them.

Gene whirled on him. "What are you doing?!"

"Those swords won't do much good against plate armour. If you want them to kill each other, they need something with more impact."

Gene shrieked in frustration, turning back to watch.

The two caught up the war hammers. Longfellow twisted his head aside to avoid Xander's spike, bringing his hammer down on the breastplate so the King felt all the air knocked from him.

Gene caught at Mervin's arm. "If they maim one another to death, can you resurrect them?"

The magician frowned. "Whyever would I have wasted my time working out a spell for that?"

Guy hacked his sword in the gorget around the King's neck, causing Xander to stagger sideways. He followed, seeking to knock Xander over. The King swung his war hammer, piercing the cuisse, causing Longfellow to cry out as blood flowed down his thigh.

Gene pressed a blanched hand over her mouth.

Xander tried to straighten. Longfellow cuffed the back of his skull with his sword pommel, sending the King staggering again.

Gene's hand sank to her stomach.

Guy swung his sword blade for the King's head, but Xander toppled over, causing him to miss.

Longfellow stepped closer, standing over him.

"Traitor!" hissed the King.

Longfellow hesitated.

Flipping his grip on his sword, Xander hooked Guy's ankle with the hilt, pulling him to the ground.

Longfellow shouted, landing on his injured leg.

The King rolled, regaining his feet.

Guy shoved to his knees, raising his war hammer.

Xander laid his sword blade against Guy's neck. "Yield."

Longfellow raised his eyes to meet the King's. "I yield me."

Gene lurched in her throne.

"Before you die, you were my best knight, I shall grant you a boon."

Guy cast away his weapons. "Sire, I ask only that you would oversee the upbringing of my child at court, that you would not allow my actions, nor his mother's, to mar how others treat him, so that he can grow to honour. Raise him as your own son or daughter, rather than mine."

Xander regarded him. "I shall grant your boon."

"Thank you. I submit to your justice, my King." Longfellow bowed his head.

Xander raised his sword. "God have mercy on you."

"Wait!" Gene was awkwardly crushing Mervin and Bernard as they tried to help her down from the dais. "Please, Xander!" She jostled over, clutching her belly under both arms. "Don't do this, brother, please."

"He has committed treason."

"He has been nothing but loyal. He has tried to have me see reason, through all my wrongheadedness. He has supported me in everything, even when he has opposed my plans. He has done all in his power to make me a ruler worthy of Britain, no matter how awfully I treated him. Please, this is all my fault. You cannot execute him."

"Stand back. I shall deal with you afterwards."

"No!" Gene stepped between the two of them. "Xander, he is my husband."

"Gene! Out of the way!"

"Kill me instead." She grasped his breastplate. "Please, kill me instead."

"You're with child," Longfellow yelled.

"Imprison me, then. Execute me after I've given birth. Only

282

spare him. Xander, please spare him. I cannot live with him gone." Gene sank to her knees.

Longfellow shouted in her ear, "*Go!*"

She cringed and stayed put.

"When my best knight," said Xander, "rises up and betrays me it is too grave to pass off. He has dishonoured himself and you. It is better that he die."

Longfellow looked up. "I am a knight, sire. I serve, and I protect. There was no one else willing to protect the woman I love. I would not for all the world change what I have done."

Gene turned, pressed his face between her hands, and her forehead to his, tears pulsing down her face.

"Get away, now!" Longfellow wrenched himself free from her.

Gene caught him again, kissing him.

"Sire." Dwain stepped forwards, followed by Keesh and a stumbling Sir Robin, who had accidentally put on his helmet sideways. "If you extended mercy to Longfellow, we would all feel grateful for it. His conscience has been in knots lately. 'Twould be a shame to damn him, just when he seems to have gotten it sorted."

"I shall not say that I shall pardon him," said Xander, "but I shall spare him at least. Gene, you and your husband are prisoners, forbidden to leave Castle Londinium until I decide how best to deal with you."

"Thank you." She dug her arms tight around Longfellow's neck and he tried to pry her off. "Thank you, brother."

***

Once his wound was dressed, Sir Guy of Longfellow hobbled to the blood red bedchamber. He opened one door to the wardrobe, leaning against the other. That plaid skirt, that wrinkled blouse, that torn sweater. She was out somewhere in the world, and now he was trapped here, where he would never see her. Because he had fallen in love with a woman who seemed never content.

Gene entered the chamber. "There you are."

Longfellow grunted.

"You should be lying down, have your feet up, something."

"I am fine." He slammed shut the wardrobe.

"Xander took back his bedchamber, saying we could just as well stay here."

"Together?"

Gene shrugged. "I suppose he thought it fitting, to send me to my old room to contemplate my deeds."

"'Old room'?"

She rubbed her stomach. "I'm craving low fat vanilla ice cream. Is that strange?"

"This can't be your old room."

"Of course it is." Gene walked over, opening the wardrobe. "My last school uniform is still here even."

"But the girl who wore these clothes was blonde."

"Yes, that was back when I bleached my hair. Like the warriors who frightened off Caesar from our shores."

"Your hair? . . . But – in the hall – on the table – "

"They never could launder Sir Robin's vomit out of that skirt."

"It was *you*?"

"Of course it was me. Who else would it have been?"

"But . . . why didn't you ever *tell* me?"

Gene shrugged. "I thought you knew."

Longfellow's eyes bugged from his head, and he sputtered. Then he seemed to settle somewhat. He stared Gene in the eye. "So, only twice I've fallen in love, and both times were with you." He leaned in to kiss her, but stopped. "What else do you think you've already told me?"

Gene smiled, draping her arms about his neck. "That I love you, that you are unbridledly handsome, and that you will prove a most worthy father to our triplets."

"*Triplets*?!"

"Relax; it's only twins."

"*Twins*?!"

***

"What's that?"

Xander glanced up. "A roofbeam."

"Oh. What's it for?"

He rubbed his forehead. "To keep the roof from falling down into the hall."

"Oh." Sir Mercifal rocked onto his toes, then back onto his heels. "Why?"

"Because if the roof fell in we would be flattened."

"So what?"

"So, then we would die."

"And?"

"And I can't remember why that would be a tragedy just now." Sir Mercifal pointed. "What's that?"

"A bench."

"*Wow.*" He wandered closer for a look.

"Bumpkin," Xander murmured.

Dwain and Keesh entered the hall, flanking an elderly lady with hair as long and pure white as her robe.

"Two months!" cried the King. "Two months of inane questions and unrelenting stares, and – who is this?"

As they came to a standstill, the lady shed her escort. "Sire, I have been known a long time as Blanche the beautiful maiden."

"Beautiful . . . maiden, right."

"I am here because that man," she pointed to Sir Mercifal, "was supposed to rescue me from the tower of a despicable troll. It has been years, and he never came."

Dwain raised his eyebrows. "Slipped his mind, did it?"

"The troll finally died of old age."

"I see," said the King.

"Then he rotted."

Keesh made a face.

"I used his ribs as climbing spikes to descend the side of the tower."

The King nodded. "How resourceful of you."

"And now that man," she shouted, pointing to Sir Mercifal, "owes me an explanation."

The knight's blank stare turned into something more perplexed. "*Oh.* Yes, I quite forgot."

"You *forgot?*"

"Yes, I was journeying to rescue you, but kept getting sidetracked. At one point I forgot the whole thing for two years together. I tried tying strings to my fingers, but they were such lovely colours, and the way they used to flutter in the wind – " Sir Mercifal pedalled his fingers before him, entranced by their motion.

"Sire, with your permission, this knight owes me several years of my life back. I would like him to come with me and begin by repairing my manor house, which has grown quite dilapidated during my imprisonment."

Xander motioned. "Be my guest and good riddance."

And with that, Blanche the now whitehaired maiden dragged Sir Mercifal from the hall by his nose.

"Ow-ow-ow. My voice sounds so absorbingly altered this way."

Xander raised an eyebrow at their exit. "Now we're short a knight."

"Perhaps something from my purse could help with that, your majesty." Keesh pulled out a book of matches. "Apparently not.

Though this does go splendidly with the kerosene lamp I extracted yesterday. And that carton of cigarettes."

"You don't smoke," said Dwain.

"No, but I am short of cash, and cigarettes are as good as currency on the inside."

"The inside of what?"

"You know, the big house."

"This castle is the biggest house in Britain, and none of *us* smoke, either."

Bernard ran in, emitting a high-pitched screech.

Mervin came chasing after him. "Bloody false advertiser! Think you can come in here dressed as a filthy pedlar and sell me some clump of dirt claiming it's the Philosopher's Stone?!"

"Wow," said Dwain, "that took awhile, didn't it?"

"Stop chasing my minstrel!" Robin snapped.

"Look what your minstrel's done." Mervin gestured to the prosthetic monstrosity curtaining his chin. "He's gotten me so worked up now I've ripped handfuls out of my beard again. Here I am a pensioner, and look at the expense this is causing me."

"True," said Dwain, "but it makes you look like Charlemagne."

"Really? You think so?"

"More to the point – or, a couple of points ago – your majesty, since you're short a knight, perhaps it's time to consider having Longfellow rejoin your council."

"Actually," Xander smiled like a cat, "I was considering doing a bit more than that. I thought I might make Gene an official member of the Council of the Boot in her own right. And since I've no plans to remarry and have children of my own, little Yander and Zandra I could designate as my heirs."

Dwain murmured, "Like *that* never backfires."

"Such wonderful baby names," Keesh sighed. "It really was for the best, sire, that part of Sir Guy and Lady Gene's punishment was to let you name their children. Imagine, wanting to name people John and Anne. All their friends would have made fun of them."

"Precisely." Xander beamed.

"Oh, that reminds me." Dwain left the hall, heading upstairs to the nursery, with its orange and fluorescent orange striped walls surrounding its sculpted tiger crib, the head of which Longfellow had cut off, weighted down with a mobile of orange-painted rocks, and thrown into the moat.

Guy and Gene stood bent over the foot of the crib.

"Here." Dwain handed Gene a half-sized baseball bat. "Keesh pulled it out of his purse yesterday, and I thought your twins might enjoy it."

"Oh, yes." Gene tried to wrap Zandra's small fingers around the bat.

"I meant in a few years. When they'll know better than to unwittingly clobber each other with it."

"Oh." Gene straightened, holding the bat. "Yes."

Dwain nodded, murmuring as he left the nursery, "Definitely. Nothing's going to backfire at all."

Gene stared at the bat. "We're going to make horrendous parents."

Longfellow grunted. "Very probably."

"I'll go put this somewhere for safekeeping." Gene kissed Guy's cheek and went to the doorway.

Longfellow lifted Yander out from the crib. "That's your mother." He kissed the small boy's head. "She's a six, but I wouldn't trade her for all the tens in the world."

Yander drooled.

"Stop that. And listen, I want to teach you and your sister some swordplay. Britain won't remain at peace forever, and you can trust me when I tell you there is no better life than that of a knight. None better at all."

INTRODUCTION

Welcome. I've placed this introduction at the end, so hopefully you've read the stories before coming here. Most introductions seem to absentmindedly assume that a reader is already familiar with the book they haven't read yet, explaining things the reader does not have context for, and causing confusion instead of banishing it; revealing spoilers it would have been more enjoyable to learn from the narrative itself; and delaying a reader from diving into a story they want to begin with ten, twenty, thirty – or more – pages of information they don't care about yet. It can be tricky to decide whether it would be better to read an introduction before or after the book itself. This one should certainly be read after and, for convenience's sake, has been placed appropriately at the end.

Knights of the Roundish Table was not written in order, appropriately enough. The first story was "The Council of the Boot," though chronologically it comes second. "The Council of the Boot" was intended as a one-off, and I had no inkling there would be any further stories about these characters. The idea to write a spoof of King Arthur and his knights seemed natural, as at the time I was working on my (not a spoof) historical novel *The Scarlet Forest: A Tale of Robin Hood*. Written as an assignment, "The Council of the Boot" was supposed to be between one and three pages long, but turned out to be a full-length short story complete with sheet music for Bernard's song. Also, the knights were originally dinosaurs. After the first draft, it seemed to make much more sense for them to be humans. And, now being humans, for Robin's character – a satire on Sir Brunor, aka the Good Knight Without Fear – to be an homage to that modern classic of Arthurian satires: *Monty Python and the*

Holy Grail. With Robin named after the infamous Monty Python character, Dwain was named after Gawain, Keesh after Keith (whose Wife of Bathesque betrothal story I first read in Howard Pyle), and Amanita after a poisonous mushroom. The seven (sometimes nine) characters had an enjoyable group dynamic to write, playing off one another, and working together as a team despite their differences. I don't have favourite characters, but usually I do have a character in each story who, though not the main character, strikes me as especially interesting, and in this case it was Longfellow, whose first name comes from the also foul-tempered Guy of Gisborne, Robin Hood's evil literary twin. "The Council of the Boot" originally concluded with an epilogue, providing closure on where the characters ended up. It has been cut here, since the other stories cover that timespan, but for anyone curious it is on my author website on the page for *Knights of the Roundish Table.* Dwain's throwaway line that Gene seems like Longfellow's type turned into an epilogue mention of them marrying, which turned into an unintended relationship that came to be integral to the stories.

I had an idea of expanding "The Council of the Boot" into a novel, which didn't work out, but "The Council of the Pineapple" was a bit of a surprise. It was written as a sequel to "The Council of the Boot" and, once again, I thought there weren't going to be further stories. "Pineapple" picked up awhile after the epilogue for "Boot," and was named after my favourite part of "The Council of the Boot": the pineapple sketch, where Dwain and Mervin the Magician argue over, yes, a pineapple. Robin's steroid addiction was particularly interesting to research. In this story, I learned that Gene was actually Xander's younger sister. (See? Spoilers. Introductions just can't help themselves.) I remember writing at least some of "Pineapple" at a friend's house while a group watched the movie *A Knight's Tale* which, at the time, I told them I considered an affront to medieval culture and the people who lived it. Maybe it isn't. I still haven't seen the movie. I have seen *Braveheart*, but that is a whole other, very long discussion.

"The Quest for the Slowly Mail" was written partially during a family road trip out to Vancouver Island. Titled after the Quest for the Holy Grail, "Quest" later gained the ballad of King Arthur's feast, as sung by Bernard. The ballad was originally an early part of *The Scarlet Forest: A Tale of Robin Hood*, but was obviously too silly to remain in a serious historical novel. The idea of writing a novel based on Xander and his knights didn't get off the ground for the same reason: too much silliness, and it didn't work in the context of a historical novel about war and invasion. If there was going to be a novel about the Council, it would have to be a serious one, no matter how much I loved the humourous back and forth between the characters. That novel is in the works.

"The Knights of the Roundish Table" was written fourth, as a prequel. Again I thought it was going to be the final story, and so poured in a spoof of every Arthurian character I could, including Sir Glancelot, mentioned in "The Council of the Boot" as having been killed by the Saxons' dragon. It was fun to feature Mervin as more of a main character, living backwards like Merlin in T. H. White's *The Once and Future King*.

"La Morted Xander" is named after Thomas Malory's *Le Morte Darthur*, about the death of King Arthur. The "Boot" epilogue had set out how Xander would die. "Morted" is mostly a spoof of the Gawain Poet's *Sir Gawain and the Green Knight*, with the Questing Beast thrown in, as well as Chaucer's The Wife of Bath's Tale in the subplot of Keesh's new wife. Basically, a lot of enduring medieval literature went into this one. It's an odd balance, having a bunch of Brythonic heroes from around the turn of the sixth century gallivanting about in a twelfth century English setting demonstrating medieval French values. They shouldn't be wearing plate armour. They would never have heard of courtly love. But there are dragons and a Questing Beast, and enchanters running roughshod, so wild historical anachronisms of more than half a millennium seem to be the least of the characters' worries.

"The Vulcan Cycle" is named after the Vulgate Cycle, an early thirteenth century version of the Lancelot-Grail stories. All of the bits leftover from the rest of the series came together, such as Robin and Bernard's subplot à la Chrétien de Troyes's classic *Erec and Enide*, and Mervin's stress-induced beard pulling mimicking Charlemagne in *The Song of Roland*. I had so much fun – if that's the right word – writing about Longfellow's turmoil. Gene is ruling as Queen. She is his lady, both in the feudal sense and in the courtly love, or *fin amor*, sense. Though a wonderfully angry person, Longfellow actually follows the knightly code of *fin'amor* pretty close to the letter. He's still grumpy, but he acts as an almost perfect knight, even when Gene leans into terrible leadership decisions, and pits Longfellow against his former King. When Longfellow drinks the fouled rosewater Gene washed in, this is something knights were apparently asked to do by their lady loves, and it must have been disgusting. In the medieval tales, Gawain comes quite close to being a perfect knight, and Lancelot fails miserably – notably when he momentarily hesitates to leap into the back of the notorious-cart-of-utter-disgrace simply because his lady love asks it. The conflict over the Queen having to be the most beautiful woman is a major one in the medieval romance of *Sir Launfal*. Upon completing "The Vulcan Cycle," for the first time I felt poised to continue the series. Which I figured probably meant it was finally done.

Fortunately, that was not the case. Though no more medieval romances popped out as being particularly tempting to spoof, I found a book of Celtic myths in my grandparents' log-house. Most of the incidents in "The Knights with the Goat" come from Welsh myths, though a couple features are from Irish ones. It seemed like time to have some fun with the original culture from which King Arthur sprang. I started writing "Goat" during another family road trip out to Vancouver Island, adding in descriptions of the mountainous landscape along the way, the Rocky Mountains looking more dramatic than the Welsh hills-with-some-rocks-on-them that the characters trekked through. Placing a story at this spot on the timeline made sense, as it had been a jump from Dwain's suggesting to Longfellow that Gene might be his type to marriage. It was also a chance to contrast Xander's example of good kingship, despite somewhat of a tendency towards ridiculous decisions, with Gene's impetuous nature that later leads her into decisively bad queenship.

The abridged version of Chrétien de Troyes's (yes, him again) *The Knight with the Lion* has little to do with any of this. This was the first of the five brilliant Arthurian works of Chrétien's that I read, and I laughed the whole way through. It's absolutely hilarious. A lot of people will probably argue that it's not supposed to be. Still, abridging it to highlight the humour was something obvious to me that I had to do. *The Knight of the Cart* is better written, and *The Story of the Grail* holds up a worthier example of knighthood, but *The Knight with the Lion* is indisputably the funniest of these hugely important and enjoyable works of medieval literature.

So, for anyone keeping track, chronologically for the characters the stories go "Roundish," "Boot," "Goat," "Quest," "Morted," "Pineapple," "Vulcan." Meanwhile, they were written in the order of "Boot," "Pineapple," "Quest," "Roundish," "Morted," "Vulcan," "Goat." Medieval history and literature offer rich grounds for stories. They provide insight into cultures populated by people who worked hard, reflected deeply on the world around them, and

294

enjoyed a good belly laugh. These individuals' ideas, values, and feelings live on through their stories, and are a joy to retell and re-experience. Thank you for reading this introduction. I hope that you enjoyed the book.

MORE BY A. E. CHANDLER

The Scarlet Forest: A Tale of Robin Hood
(historical novel)

Questionable Quizzes series
(humour quiz books)

Into the World: 62 Devotions to Edify & Inspire
(daily devotional)

You can find more bonus material on A. E. Chandler's author website. There, you can also gain free access to the original second chapter from *The Scarlet Forest: A Tale of Robin Hood* by signing up for the *Outlaws of England* e-newsletter, which comes out every six weeks.

aechandler.wixsite.com/author
amazon.com/author/aechandler
goodreads.com/aechandler

Please consider leaving a review on Amazon, Indigo, Goodreads, or elsewhere.

EXCERPT FROM *QUESTIONABLE QUIZZES*, BY A. E. CHANDLER

~ Do You Know Anything About English History? ~

1. What is the most important event in England's history?
a) The Norman Conquest
b) Magna Carta
c) Monty Python
d) The discovery of tea

2. Before the Anglo-Saxons, what is now England was occupied by the:
a) Greeks
b) Scots
c) Welsh
d) Venezuelans

3. The Anglo-Saxon capital city was:
a) Canterbury
b) Winchester
c) Gotham City
d) Worcestershiresuresher

4. The only English king to be called "the Great" was:
a) Edward III
b) Henry V

c) Ethelwulf
d) Alfred

5. Which of the following invaded and took over England?
a) The Huns
b) The Visigoths
c) The Vikings
d) The Antlantians

6. Which of the following is not the nickname of a king of
England?
a) Rufus
b) Beauclerc
c) Harefoot
d) the Fierce

7. Which of the following was <u>not</u> a consequence of the
Norman Conquest:
a) More extensive international trade
b) Greater cultural and literary exchange
c) Massive innovations in secular and religious architecture
d) Cooties

8. The royal house of Plantagenet was named after a:
a) City
b) Horse
c) Flower
d) Flavour of chewing gum

9. The point of Magna Carta was to:
a) Limit the king's power with new laws

b) Reinforce the freedoms of the common people
c) Put into writing laws that balanced the king's power
primarily with regard to the nobility
d) Make it illegal to dress goats in pirate costumes

10. The first popular *English* literary figure was:
a) King Arthur
b) Robin Hood
c) The Wife of Bath
d) Rumpelstiltskin

Answers: 1. A 2. C 3. B 4. D 5. C 6. D 7. D 8. C 9. C 10. B
Robin Hood was the first English figure to have his legend
develop exclusively in the English language, while the older
King Arthur was Welsh and had a multilingual development.

For more humourous quizzes on English history, travel, work,
relationships, and life, check out *Questionable Quizzes* in paperback
or e-book.

EXCERPT FROM *THE SCARLET FOREST: A TALE OF ROBIN HOOD*, BY A. E. CHANDLER

CHAPTER ONE
"Oak"

Along the forest paths a fair youth strode for Nottingham Town. Sherwood kept special watch over this newcomer into its kingdom. The merry month of March had come in the night, and all was uncommonly blithe as the birds clamoured amidst the branches.

The youth stood tall and wore fine yet simple clothes. A red feather extended back from his cap, and a broadsword was girded at his side. He carried a stout longbow of English yew, and a linen bag slung from the back of his belt held a sheaf of arrows. The arrows' crests showed they belonged to the Earl of Huntington's second son.

The law banned the carrying of bows in the greenwood, lest someone should poach the King's deer. Yet Robert found he could think better when alone amidst the trees. No one could be seen upon the paths today, so he walked silently on to Nottingham. His thoughts cycled far away from the forest upon this most important day of his life.

Robert was journeying to a shooting match in Nottingham. He expected to win, for none could match his skill at archery, the closest competition being his friend Marian, the eldest of Baron Fitzwalter's five daughters.

At age seven, Robert had been sent away to serve the ladies of Baron Fitzwalter's household as a page, before his mother and her ladies could spoil him. Upon turning fourteen, he had become the baron's squire, receiving instruction in courtesy and combat, in the hope that at twenty-one he would show himself worthy of a knighthood. His elder brother, David, would inherit the title of Earl of Huntington, thus he was free of that charge.

Robert and Marian were the best of friends. Whenever the two had a moment free they would hunt, or shoot, or he would teach her what he knew of combat. They had dreamt that once Robert became a knight she would be his squire, and thus they would continue to have adventures together all their lives. Yet such a life could only be a fancy.

Six months before the day of this shooting match, Robert's long-ill father had passed into heaven. David was being schooled in France, and their elder sister Margaret was married to Squire Gamewell. Thus the youth, two months from being eighteen, had temporarily given up training as a knight to aid his grieving mother in governing the family's lands. Though she entreated him to continue his knightly training, Robert insisted upon caring for her until his elder brother could return.

One month ago his life had undergone yet another change, when Marian turned eighteen. Neither of them told a soul what had happened, yet today at the shooting match Robert was to meet with his mother as well as the Fitzwalters and Marian. Then they would reveal their secret.

Around the next bend a group of green-clad foresters lazed at food and drink, with kegs of fine October ale. When they saw the youth coming towards them, they called him back to the plane he walked with every manner of taunt they could muster in their drunken states. The slur of alcohol sounded stronger in some voices than in others.

"Ho, lads! See how the fledgling dresses!"

"Learn to crawl before thou dost walk, boy!"

"Art thou too ignorant not to bring thy bow to the greenwood, young hood?"

Being of an age when he considered himself a man, and his pride giving him a sour temper, Robert's anger beat hard against his chest. He had not expected to be ambushed yet kept his tongue, remembering the foresters were drunk and did not mean their insults.

A shout went up: "Let us take him to the Sheriff! To be punished for his crime!"

"Nay," quoth a forester with red hair. He seemed to lead the party. "Let us have sport with him first. Three marks thou canst not e'en pull that bow, little robin."

"There done!" cried Robert, finally losing his temper. He would gladly have all his limbs broken before he let a man breach his pride. "Name the mark."

Not thinking the arrow would fly so far, or perhaps not thinking at all, the lead forester stretched out his arm. "Seest thou that herd of the King's deer ten-score and more yards down the path, young hood? If thou canst fell one, all our coins to thee."

Robert pulled back his bowstring. The weight of it felt akin to lifting a man above his head. His anger was rampant and the foresters insisted upon insulting him even now, but his skill was such that this rated as no distraction. The string sang, sending forth the shaft. Struck even as he tried to leap away, the life of the herd's lead stag fled whilst his body could not.

The foresters stood so amazed they scarcely moved. They had truly not thought this lad would make the shot. The deer were for the King's pleasure alone, to be hunted and eaten at his will. No one else must kill, or even touch one of them.

"Your coins now, fellows. I have won them all."

At last the lead forester spake. "Dost thou know what thou hast done, boy? Thine eyes are forfeit, and it is our sworn duty to arrest thee."

Robert felt himself go cold, so he might start to shiver. "Do not speak of mine eyes. The new law says I must pay a fine to the King, and I shall pay it."

"Nay, but we like the old law." Another of the foresters crept towards Robert, his limbs rolling like those of a wolf stalking its prey. "And we shall take thine eyes before bringing thee to the Sheriff. It is good sport, and one we like to see."

Panic welled in Robert's breast. Almost without thought he nocked another arrow. "The next to move shall die!"

Fear pushed all else from the lad's head. In his anger, it had not occurred to him that he might be signing away his life in the stag's blood. A man with no eyes could never be a knight, nor could he be anything else. There was no place for a man without eyes. The bow felt rude in Robert's hands. It had always been a friend to him, and a link to his father. Now it felt alien to him, and he doubted his accuracy if forced to shoot.

The frozen foresters stood spread around him, as numerous as the shafts in the linen bag upon his belt. They watched, waiting for a good chance to spring forward and bind him. Without a sound, an arrow rose from the rear of the group. It flew high, arcing down towards Robert. This same moment the foresters parted, revealing the lead man as he who had shot.

For a blend of true history, new stories, and almost forgotten medieval legends written by a University of Nottingham archer and medievalist, check out the historical novel *The Scarlet Forest: A Tale of Robin Hood* in hardcover, paperback, e-book, or audiobook.

www.ingramcontent.com/pod-product-compliance
Lightning Source LLC
Chambersburg PA
CBHW030610170726
48283CB00002B/540